NEW YORK TIMES and USA TODAY Bestselling Author

LORA LEIGH

SAVAGE LEGACY

ELLORA'S CAVE
ROMANTICA PUBLISHING

What the critics are saying...

ॐ

"The talented pen of Lora Leigh returns to gift us with another glimpse into the world of sexy dominant warriors and the extraordinary women who fight by their side. [...] I won't tell you to enjoy because I know you will." ~ *A Romance Review*

"**Lora Leigh** does an excellent job of lulling the reader into a false sense of security before bringing out the big guns such as the sword fights and the alien encounters." ~ *Love Romances*

"As always with Lora Leigh's books, the sex is hotter than hot, and the two have a chemistry that burns up the pages. If you haven't read the rest of the series, you will definitely want to pick them up when you are through with this one." ~ *The Romance Studio*

An Ellora's Cave Romantica Publication

www.ellorascave.com

Savage Legacy

ISBN 9781419954665
ALL RIGHTS RESERVED.
Savage Legacy Copyright © 2004 Lora Leigh
Edited by Sue-Ellen Gower.
Cover art by Syneca.

This book printed in the U.S.A. by Jasmine–Jade Enterprises, LLC.

Electronic Book Publication September 2004
Trade paperback Publication June 2007

Also by Lora Leigh

ဢ

About the Author

ഇ

Lora Leigh is a wife and mother living in Kentucky. She dreams in bright, vivid images of the characters intent on taking over her writing life, and fights a constant battle to put them on the hard drive of her computer before they can disappear as fast as they appeared.

Lora's family and her writing life co-exist, if not in harmony, in relative peace with each other. An understanding husband is the key to late nights with difficult scenes and stubborn characters. His insights into human nature and the workings of the male psyche provide her hours of laughter, and innumerable romantic ideas that she works tirelessly to put into effect.

Lora welcomes comments from readers. You can find her website and email address on her author bio page at www.ellorascave.com.

Tell Us What You Think

We appreciate hearing reader opinions about our books. You can email us at Comments@EllorasCave.com.

SAVAGE LEGACY

ॐ

Dedication

꿈

Dedicated to Lady Gloria, for all you've done.
But most especially for all your friendship and support.
Thank You!

For Suz, for all your help when it looked like I would
never figure the plot out.

To those very special readers who go above and beyond
the call of duty.

And to Roxie! For the late night readings and for putting
up with me. You're the best!

To all of you, you have my deepest thanks.

Prologue

ဢ

"His legend will be retold as long as the Earth and its protective mother have breath to sustain life..." Her grandmother's voice entered her dreams and Ariel felt a small smile cross her lips. She had missed these dreams in the past years. Her grandmother had meant everything to her for the short time she had known her.

Laken Lamont had been half-French, with liquid dark eyes and long black hair. A delicate, fragile woman who looked like the pictures Ariel had of her mother. She had come to her during a time when Ariel knew, if it hadn't been for her grandmother's steadying influence, that she would have lost her mind.

"He is that Savage, but don't let his name fool you," she advised her granddaughter. *"He is merciless with his enemies, but he is patience and love itself for the one who holds his heart."*

"Who holds his heart, Grandmama?" she asked, staring up at the frail old woman as she held her snugly on her lap.

"The Mistress of the Wind holds his heart, Ariel." She had touched the crystal she had placed around Ariel's neck that first week she had lived in the sterile home Ariel's father had provided for them. *"The Mistress of the Wind holds his soul. In times of fear or of need, she only has to call out to him, to allow the crystal and the power that connects them, to do as it was meant to."*

"Am I the Mistress, Grandmama?" Ariel remembered how awed she had been. She carried the stone, she had thought. She would be the one to possess the Savage's heart.

"I don't know, Ariel." Sadness flickered in the old woman's eyes. *"The Mistress will know great danger. She will know great pain before her warrior arrives. She will have to be strong enough to*

13

look past her fears and past the horrors she will see to accept her warrior."

"*Tell me the story again, Grandmama.*" She had laid her head at her grandmother's breast, closing her eyes, wishing she had a warrior to protect her from the bleak darkness her father often confined her to. "*Tell me about him again.*"

"*There is a legend near forgotten by time, and hazy to even the oldest memory. A legend that has never been told by those who wield the pen, but lives in the hearts and souls of those who wield the sword. The Legend of the Savage Warrior.*

"*When the world was young, and man fought against man in battles of darkness, in forests heavy with magic and the power of the Earth, he rose as one of four. A warrior of strength and justice, one who held the power of the gods. He was as tall as the oak, as mighty as the mountain, and as strong as truth itself.*

"*To this warrior, whose heart and soul was most pure, the Earth Mother gifted to him, her most precious daughter. One scarred by betrayal, but one who knew the need for love, for the gentleness of this non-gentle warrior. And they were bound. During the darkest times of history, they clung to one another, each stronger than before, fighting the battle against an unspeakable, dark evil.*

"*But evil will have its due. And before Mother Earth could claim victory for her children, a horrible price was demanded by Fate and Destiny for the machinations of bringing together the son of the gods and a daughter of the Earth. So it was declared. As long as the Wind Mistress kept her eyes closed to the power, her ears dead to the Earth and her heart cold from her trials, so then would the Savage roam. Lost, unaided but by his brothers, forever seeking what only the wind shall know. The true heart of the Mistress where his heart was bestowed.*

"*But the day will come...*" her voice had lowered with a mystic foreboding sound "*...when the Wind Mistress shall rise once again. With the strength of the power of the Wind Crystal, her will strong, her heart whole and unscarred by the touch of evil. She will rise, and she will know the truth, the power and the heart laid bare for her to see. But first, she must accept that which she fears the most. She must know that which she has denied the strongest.*

"Until then, she will remember, only in her dreams. She will seek in darkness, and fight without strength and she will know little but the faintest breeze to whisper his name, rather than the full force of the wind which should carry her devotion back to him.

"Beware Mistress, for in his hands does your fate rest. Beware daughter of the Earth, for there are deceptions, darkness and pain. Seek and ye shall find. Deny and ye shall die…"

The winds rose around her then. Howling, screaming in fury and rage as her grandmother's bedroom door opened and her father stood framed in the doorway. She had shuddered in fear. He was angry…again.

"Ariel, I need to talk to you." His voice had been rough, filled with his rage. *"Now."*

And she knew what was coming. She would have pleaded with him not to lock her up again, but then her grandmother would know. And if she knew, then Ariel feared her father would make good on his promise to have the old woman locked away, confined forever in the darkness.

So she left the peace of her grandmother's arms, followed her father from the room, down the winding stairs and to the basement where he pushed her into the foul-smelling closet and locked the door.

"That will teach you to obey me, Ariel. You will always obey me or you will pay…"

Seconds later he was gone, leaving her in the black nothingness with only her screams to keep her company.

"The Wind Mistress can call her warrior. No sound is ever gone, Ariel…" Her grandmother's words had wrapped around her. *"They are there on the breeze. For you to hear, for him to know. Call him, and he will always aid you…"*

And she had screamed out his name. Cried for him until in her fury and her terror, a sudden violet light had lit the way, and the faintest breeze had carried his voice to her… Gentle. Comforting. And she had feared then that she was as crazy as her father had claimed… Just like her mother…

15

Chapter One

ഇ

The winds howled. They screamed in fury, bending trees, stripping the supple branches of leaves and laying young saplings to the ground. Nature in all her glory was ripping through the land, screaming out its rage.

Clouds boiled into a tempest overhead, swirling in myriad shades of black and gray as the forces of nature converged to spill their anger upon the forest below. Lightning flared in brilliant arcs, rain slashed at the ground below, joining the wrathful violence as it pounded the land.

Like demons swirling from hell, the screaming winds and spearing lightning joined with the clash of thunder to rock the mountain with a force that only nature could produce.

Beneath the violently swaying trees, amid the flying bramble and leaves, Ariel St. James moved desperately through the storm. She screamed out in furious fear as a thick limb crashed to the ground behind her, and cursed roughly as she stumbled through the gathering winds, feeling it push at her back, forcing her deeper into the surrounding forests.

She was careful to stay close to the trees, within the shadows, as lightning whipped in the sky overhead. She knew she was being hunted. They had been at the house when she returned that evening, more of them than she could have fought, waiting to catch her unaware.

But she had smelled them. On the softest breeze, she had smelled the stench of death and evil. She would have gotten back in the car. Would have sped back the way she had come, but the wind and the warmth of the crystal her grandmother had bequeathed her had urged her along a different path.

This time, unlike when she had been kidnapped, she heeded the strange crystal at her breast and moved quickly into the forest that surrounded her home. She wouldn't be caught as she had been before, undefended, unaware.

She shivered beneath the onslaught of the rain. Water saturated her short hair, plastered her linen shirt and jeans to her body and ran in rivulets down her face. But between her breasts, heat radiated through her, dispelling the chill of the storm and the fear as she made her way carefully through the forest.

All she had to defend herself was the sword she had been carrying into the house, and the matching dagger now tucked into her jeans at the small of her back. Weapons she had taken from the safe at her shop before leaving, filled with an unexplained need to take the priceless artifacts home with her.

She had never used the weapon she held vigilantly in front of her, yet it felt comfortable in her hands, the hilt fitting into her palm as though it had been created for her alone. It was heavy, but there was no strain to carry it, no hardship to keep it raised in front of her as she ducked beneath slashing limbs and continued the dangerous trek through the foothills.

They were behind her; she could smell them. The wind itself carried the scent of diseased minds and blood-soaked hands. She could feel the death that surrounded her trackers, feel their hatred and their intention to see her dead.

She would not die. She hadn't died when Jonar had kidnapped her months before and she would be damned if she would let them kill her now. He might be the big bad-ass alien terrorist as Alyx Dragon had mockingly called him, but she wasn't going to let him kill her without a fight.

The chilling nightmares she had of the brutal beatings she had endured while locked in his Middle Eastern fortress were enough to assure her that he was dangerous. That he was determined. But so was she, determined to live if nothing else.

Breathing roughly, she paused beside a thick tree trunk, drawing in a calming breath and watching the shadows that twisted around her. She was heading deeper into the forested hills, further away from any added protection that civilization would have afforded.

Overhead, thunder clashed with such force it shook the land below and dragged a choked whimper from her terror-closed throat. The storm raged with the same desperation as the blood pounding through her veins. It rocked the land as her heartbeat rocked her body, filling her with the warning of violence.

Move. A voice, not her own, male and filled with fury, echoed in her head. Her father was right, she thought for one incredulous moment. She was insane.

Goddammit Ariel, run! They are too close! The demand echoed around her, whipped by a wind she knew wasn't natural.

She could feel the demand run through her system though, as lightning above her flashed low to the ground, lighting a slender path through the brush and bramble that littered the ground.

The crystal burned beneath her shirt, a surface heat that would have blistered had it been anything else. She moved carefully, though as quickly as possible, along the path laid out for her, ducking to avoid the flying debris, her heart in her throat as she pushed her sodden hair back from her face and fought her way ahead.

She didn't bother to stem the terrified tears that fell down her face or the sobs that tore from her chest. The storm covered any sound she would make, and she was so scared she couldn't control it anyway.

She remembered the horrifying pain, the nightmares and terror that had gripped her since Jonar had held her captive in that damned dungeon. The beatings had been the worst, merciless, striking at every weakness until she had been certain she would die in her own filth. Cruel, taunting laughter had followed each blow, and haunted her now with the viciousness of the attacks.

But something, someone had saved her. She remembered the heat that filled her, the strength that flowed through her, but nothing else. She knew that it was then that the crystal had come to life once again, warming her, keeping her alive until her rescue. She knew it, because until those fractured memories of strength and warmth, of being held, comforted, the crystal hadn't warmed against her since her childhood.

"Find the bitch, she's here. I can feel her..."

She whimpered at the rough sound of the vicious male voice behind her. Deep, filled with wrath and the intent to kill. This wasn't the same voice that echoed around her moments before. More wisps of air than true sound, this one was evil itself.

"Oh God... Oh God..." The prayer was litany on her lips as she fought to move faster through the storm, and prayed for a miracle. It would definitely take a miracle to save her.

Where are you?

She stopped, flattening herself to another tree as the words seemed to echo through her mind. She shook her head, looking around frantically, certain that she couldn't have heard that demanding male voice as she knew she had.

Ariel, talk to me. Let me help you!

She stared around the darkness in shock. The voice wasn't in her head, it was in the very wind whipping around her like an elemental cape. Strong, gravelly, filled with...desperation?

She bit her lip, fighting back the hysteria rising in her chest. The voice was there, yet it wasn't. It swirled and fractured around her, almost a whisper at her ear rather than the shout it should have been.

She wouldn't answer. She wasn't crazy. There was talking to herself and then there was crazy. This was crazy. Voices didn't echo in the wind just for her ears. She closed her eyes tight for a second, sending up a quick prayer that she wasn't losing her sanity. It would be a really bad time for a nervous breakdown. And she didn't relish allowing her father to win the battle for her sanity.

She ignored the tears that mixed with the rain, and throttled the choked sob that would have escaped her throat. Gathering her strength, she bent low and raced through the storm once again. The fetid stench of the horror following her was growing thicker, closer. She didn't have time to feel sorry for herself or to sift through the differences between fantasy and reality, sound and imagination.

Woman, such stubbornness does not become you. The harsh male voice held a punch of frustration, making her shudder with the latent anger she could feel within it.

She wouldn't answer the whispers, the insistent sound on the wind that shouldn't be there. The middle of a clash of nature with God only knew how many terrorists on her ass was not the place for this.

But she knew that wasn't entirely true. She had heard them before, at least this particular one. As a child, locked in the terrifying darkness of a closet, alone and frightened, she had screamed out her pleas for help until her voice was hoarse. Then, lying on the cold floor, wrapped in misery and certain she would die from the darkness alone, the voice had come to her.

Panic bloomed in her chest now as the stench of evil suddenly wrapped around her, stealing her from the painful memories of the past, gagging her, taking her breath for precious moments as she stumbled, nearly falling, to the rain-slick ground beneath her.

"You die tonight, Mistress of the Wind."

The voice had her freezing in terror a second before she turned, her sword raising to meet the enemy's steel even as the urge to protest the title he gave her vibrated through her mind.

With a quick turn and an overhead clash of swords, she swerved from the sharp blade before jumping back far enough to avoid another blow. Her wrist twirled sharply, bringing the blade defensively in front of her as she faced death itself.

His eyes glowed red. He was taller than she, broad and thickly muscled, his smile feral. Did she mention his eyes were red? For God's sake, people didn't have red eyes; only demons' eyes could glow with such savage intensity. And demons didn't exist, she reminded herself harshly.

"No enchanted sword can save you, bitch," he called through the clash of thunder and lightning overhead. "I'll cut you in two, no matter the power you wield."

He came at her again, missing her by less then an inch as she parried the slicing stroke and danced to the side. How did she do that? How had she *known* to do that?

"Dammit, haven't you heard of guns?" she screamed as sparks flew from the clashing steel. She deflected the blow, braced her knees as she gripped the hilt with both hands and faced the sneering enemy.

Guns were nice, quick and clean, she thought perversely. What the hell was she doing fighting with a weapon she had never handled in her life? Better yet, how the hell was she doing it?

He didn't answer her furious question. His sword descended as she met it, fighting the hysterical laughter that wanted to build in her chest as she used a weapon she had done no more than clean over the years. Maybe her father was right. Maybe she was crazy, she thought with brittle calm as she instinctively swung the weapon to strike out at her attacker or parried another of his thrusts. Only crazy people did stuff like this.

Where had the knowledge come from? How did she know to twist her upper body and parry the thrusts of the stronger foe facing her? To use her smaller frame to throw him

21

off balance, and rather than meeting each blow, dancing away from it as she struck at his undefended body parts?

Blood stained the terrorist's chest, his arms, but he kept coming, growling in rage as lightning struck around them and her own screams of anger blended in with clash of nature around her.

She pivoted as a killing blow was aimed at her midsection, her knees bending as she swung around, sword held low as she thrust it quick and hard into the lower chest of the man preparing to take her head from her shoulders.

Her scream echoed around her as she felt the blade sink past flesh and bone. She pulled back quickly, staring in shock as he went to his knees, his eyes staring back at her in horrified knowledge. He sank to the ground, a hand to the gaping wound that seemed to grow larger and larger before her astounded gaze. A second later, lightning flared, built, converged in brilliant arcs to a single, horrifying streak that sliced through her would-be assassin.

Run, damn you! NOW! The voice was screaming as though the furious male stood by her side, closer, more demanding than ever before as she heard a war cry echo through the forest, savage and ruthless, spurring her to do just that.

She ran.

Chapter Two

෨

Shane felt the berserker rage filling him as he glimpsed the dark forms trying to surround Ariel within the storm-drenched forest. Jonar's men had moved swiftly the moment she had ordered the bodyguards from her property.

Alyx, the Dragon Prime joining the group of psychic bodyguards, had been less than amused when he related her insistence that the protective force leave the grounds. A less than logical female, he had called her, his voice vibrating with irritation. It wasn't a lack of logic, Shane knew, but the bitter realization of the lives that had been lost in the attempt to keep her safe as she lay unconscious.

Damned stubborn woman, he thought, as he cut down the first of Jonar's men that met him, Derek and Joshua as they raced through the storm to catch up with Ariel. She was determined to do it all herself or die trying. And though he suspected the crystal would aid her in fighting to survive, he knew that she could not do it alone. The thought of her attempting to do so filled his heart with dread.

He could feel his commander, Devlin, monitoring the battle through Chantel, his wife, and the crystal she wore. The same crystal that allowed Shane to reach out to Ariel as they followed her enemies into the forest.

Not that she would answer him. Just as she had fired the men who were to watch her, so had she ignored his demands to give her location as he fought to reach her in the storm. Had it not been for Chantel and Devlin's connection to him, then she would have already fallen beneath the swords Jonar's men wielded.

As he rounded a bend in the path that led to Ariel, three of Jonar's warriors blocked his way. Shane stopped, a smile curving his lips as lightning lit up the scene for long seconds. Great, jagged flashes, one after the other, illuminated the area in stark relief.

He lifted the sword before him, his wrist twisting as he twirled it dangerously. The assassins before him tensed their bodies, eyes narrowed, concentration lining their faces as they braced for his attack.

"Well, let's hope the three of you can give a better fight than the last ones," he called out over the din of the storm. "Come on, boys, don't be shy. Let's play…"

He cut through them within minutes, for once glad they had not given a better fight. As the killing wounds to the chest began to disintegrate the evil of their bodies, Shane raced on through the storm. Ariel waited up ahead, and he wanted nothing more to delay the moment that he would hold her in his arms again.

He wanted her out of harm's way. Away from the assassins sent to kill her and steal the power that had caused nature to unleash its fury onto the land around them. Chantel and Devlin would lead him to her when he was finished sending Jonar's men to hell. Then he would ensure that she never placed her life in such jeopardy again.

He tracked her through the raging rains, his eyes narrowed as he made his way through the darkened foothills. He didn't have the gifts the other warriors had. His eyesight wasn't exceptionally strong in dim light; he couldn't use the power of his mind to do great feats of magic. His gifts were in his strength, in the power of his arm, the stamina of his body, and the often cold detachment he used while in battle. Not that he was using it now. The flames of rage fueled him as his sword cleared the path before him of both the enemy and the thickening brush.

She was terrified; he had felt that overwhelming emotion the closer he came to her and the crystal that reached out to him. She was running on adrenaline and fear alone, her strength steadily giving out as the weakness of her body overcame her will to flee. The crystal would not sustain her strength with him near. It would know that he would protect her, that his sword and his life would cover hers and forever draw from her the danger that surrounded her.

He paused as he left the battlefield behind, confident that Derek and Joshua were cleaning out the garbage Jonar had littered the mountain with. He could smell her now. He paused to draw in the rich scent of the woman he had waited centuries for. Her scent was that of the storm mixed with a hint of spring. Soft, inviting, with an edge of danger.

He bared his teeth in a smile. His Ariel had been temperamental, filled with passions that she kept tightly restrained, and a thirst for vengeance against Jonar that he knew would only be quenched at his death. The raping of the child she had been in that first life, as her fragile mother lay dying beside her, had stripped her of any illusion of gentleness.

It had been a time of darkness, of wars and evil and Jonar had swept across the land like a tidal wave of malevolence, catching Ariel in his path. Her powers had drawn him, though at the time he hadn't known why. Unaware that what lay dormant inside her would one day be his destruction. Instead of killing her, he had taken a part of her she could never steal back. He had taken not just her virginity, but her innocence and her belief in herself as well.

Yet, she had been strong. When he had come to her in those dark times, sent by the Guardians to make a pact with Galen, she had been all woman. A woman and a warrioress intent on fighting at his side and spilling the blood of their enemy. A woman whose heart had opened to him, even if she had hid from the power she controlled.

Chantel had warned him to expect differences when he met with her this time. Her soul would be the same, but her life experiences different. She had feared it would cause him to be less than understanding of the woman she had become this time.

He shook his head, flinging back his soaked hair as he drew closer. He could sense her weariness, feel her fear swirling in the winds around him. As he drew nearer, the sensation of her presence became stronger, until he stopped completely, staring around the darkness with narrowed eyes as he tried to catch a glimpse of her through the storm raging around him.

"Ariel, I'm here to help you," he called out, knowing she was near, watching him.

She was silent, the scent of her fear thick in the whipping winds.

There was no answer. He turned, knowing she was within feet of him yet unable to glimpse her in the gathering darkness. But he could feel the crystal drawing him. The link he had established with the enchanted stone was strong within his soul now, in a way it had never been centuries before.

He concentrated on that bond, with everything inside his soul he called out to it, reached for it and fought for a glimmer of knowledge as to where she would be.

As he made a slow circle, the faint glint of light through the foliage caught his eye. He almost missed it, would have if the lightning hadn't stilled for that brief amount of time. The wink of violet light was all he needed.

Shane restrained his smile of triumph as he began to move through the night encased trees, knowing her eyesight would be no better than his right now. The sheer darkness surrounding them was as thick as her tension, his satisfaction.

He lifted his arm and returned his sword to the leather sheath strapped to his back to better free his hands when he moved upon her. He wanted them free, wanted to experience the warmth of her body with all his senses once he had her in his arms.

She was trying to circle him. She held her sword in her hand, raised in preparation to defend herself. She knew he was close; she just wasn't certain where he was.

Steeling himself for what he knew he had to do, he moved in on her. Before she could protest or fight, his arms circled hers, clamping them to her sides as she screamed out in terror and struggled to fight against his greater strength.

"Dammit woman, I'm not here to hurt you," he yelled out over the sudden renewed violence of the storm. "Would you settle down!"

Lightning was striking the ground all around them, sizzling with electricity, protesting the terror raging through her. The winds were barreling through the hills, trees cracking beneath the force as thunder shook the air repeatedly and rain poured down in almost blinding sheets.

His hand gripped hers, breaking the hold she had on her sword as she tried to swing it at his legs. He was terrified that in her rage and fear she would do more harm to herself than to him.

She fought him like a madwoman, her curses blistering the air as lightning struck ever closer to their struggling forms. Shane gritted his teeth, containing his snarl of outrage that his wife, his *wife*, would fight him in such a manner. Her curses were those she had reserved for only her worse enemies in that first lifetime, never for him. He didn't care if she may not remember that life, she should feel it, sense it, feel him.

"Damn you woman, settle down now!" he cursed heatedly as her foot, small as it was, nearly tripped him as she fought him.

At this point, his bond with the crystal would do him no good. She was locked in a kill or be killed state of mind, and the power of her crystal was reacting to this hysterical terror. It was doing as they had never believed it would. Drawing from the Earth Crystal's powers and fueling the natural forces of her sisters that came to her aid. Independent of one another, yet reaching out to each other, the crystals were reacting to Ariel's hysteria and her fears. Her sisters were coming to her aid.

Chapter Three

ဢ

Ariel's eyes widened in shock, confusion, as her back met the drenched trunk of the tree, and the stranger's lips came down on hers. She could have fought him. She would have fought anyone else. And he was more dangerous than any who had tried. But suddenly, the crystal stilled. The raging heat that had lain against her chest as she fought her way through the storm, cooled and the hard, rain-wet lips that moved over hers stilled something within her as well.

It was irrational, unexplainable. She fought to break free of the web of sensations that held her in its grip as strongly as the man before her held her to the tree. Shifting shadows in her mind had her reaching for reality as she fought the shift that slammed around her. She hated this, hated the moments of terrifying knowledge that came and then were gone just as quickly, leaving only remnants of the knowledge she knew she needed.

She whimpered beneath the conflicting impressions, unable to make sense of them, unable to fight him. One moment she was herself, the next she was another, and yet not. But no matter which she was, the kiss was flavored with such passion, such need and a familiar driving hunger, that she couldn't resist it.

Was she crazy, just as her father had always claimed? What else could it be but insanity?

She stared at his closed eyes, feeling the fierce, heated possession of his kiss as his tongue forced her lips open and pushed arrogantly against her own. She whimpered at the onslaught, her lips softening beneath his, accepting his kiss, his touch, as though she had known it forever.

One hand twined in the hair at the nape of her neck as he jerked her head back, restraining her, holding her still for a kiss that possessed, that whipped through her system like a supernova. And all she could do was stare back at him in shock as his lips moved over hers, as she felt the pleasure burn through her body and fought to make sense of it.

She had never known this. She wasn't a sexual person, experimentation had never interested her. No man had ever incited passion or pleasure within her. But this wasn't just passion. This wasn't just pleasure.

She could feel every cell in her body straining toward him. Her head bent back as his hold tightened on her, a strangled groan echoing from his throat as he licked at her lips, nipped them, then returned for another deep, all-consuming possession that had her shuddering with a whiplash of hunger.

"Kiss me," he growled against her lips then, a rough, gravelly sound that had her stomach clenching in pleasure. A man's voice should never sound so sexual. It should never stroke the flesh like invisible fingers of a lover's caress. Yet it did, trailing insidious wisps of sensation through her body that had her staring back at him, dazed, as she ignored the rain still pouring around them.

For a moment, she fought for strength, her utter disbelief that he would dare to attempt to restrain her in this way. That he would use her passion, her need for him...

She pushed her head back against the tree as a frustrated growl of fury tore from her lips. No, dammit to fucking hell, now was *not* the time to remember things that *were not real!*

"No..." She bit at his lips as the hills echoed with the clash of thunder and sizzling bolts of lightning tore through the sky.

Her hands balled into fists, one driving into his hard abdomen as her knee drove upward but missed its intended target.

"My warrioress…" Male laughter stoked the fires of anger and lust pouring through her now.

The tight muscles of his stomach deflected her blow, just as he moved with a grace and speed she wouldn't have expected as he lifted her, insinuating his body between her quickly spread her thighs as the hardened length of his cock pressed against the rapidly moistening mound of her cunt.

She was wet, damn him, and not just from the rain.

His teeth flashed in the night, startlingly bright as he pinned her to the tree, his broad hands framing her face as he took her lips in a kiss that drove the breath from her body. Deep, controlled, his tongue tangled with hers as his thumbs pressed her jaws open, keeping her teeth from clamping down on his tongue.

Tension, albeit a less violent sort, tightened her body now. She could not smell the stench of evil, but what she did smell made no sense. Passion. Arousal. And something so subtle, so unexplained she could make no sense of it. Something natural, elemental, honest and pure. She trembled at that thought just as she trembled with the pleasure suddenly whipping through her.

Burning sensation sang through her veins. Her tongue twined in carnal hunger with his even as she fought against him. Her hips bucked against the erection between her thighs as her hand clenched at his wide shoulders, holding tight as she ground herself against his hardness. She didn't know if she was protesting or encouraging the licking flames building in the core of her body or the hard hands rocking her against him.

All she knew was the sudden shift from violence to passion. A stranger, one so tall and broad that her femininity was forced ruthlessly into her mind. He cradled her to him, keeping her back to the wet trunk of the tree as his lips raided hers, and she could do nothing to stop the answering desire surging through her body. She wanted him. God help her, his kiss was like a fire racing through her veins, her need for him confusing, terrifying, but there all the same.

Before she could stop herself, her hands were buried in his hair, her fists gripping the wet strands. She wasn't trying to force him from her, though; she was trying to bring him closer. Ever closer.

His taste was incredible. Fire and heat, dispelling the icy fist of terror that had tightened in her chest and turning it to a blazing firestorm of need instead. His tongue wrapped around hers, licked at her teeth, her lips, tasted her in turn and she knew, found her pleasing. As pleasing as she found him.

"God help me," he muttered at her ear as his lips slid over her cheek, his breathing rough and raspy as his chest labored against her breasts.

Or was it her fighting for breath, fighting for an anchor amidst the chaotic storm of terror and passion whipping through her system?

Though it had lessened, the rain still fell rapidly above them, the drenched leaves of the tree spreading out above them providing little protection against the fall of moisture. She could feel it dripping from her hair, from his, and it should have chilled her. The heat of his body warmed her instead, a heat that curled through her, heating parts of her body, her mind, which she would have preferred remain cold.

Like her common sense...

"Let me go." She struggled against his hold, though her voice wasn't as strong, or as demanding as she would have liked.

Her ankles were locked behind his back as she unconsciously rode the thick shaft rubbing against her swollen clitoris, bringing it to blazing, fiery life. For all the protests her head was screaming, her body was telling a different story. It loved being held against him, loved the heat and hardness of him. It welcomed him.

"Not this time," he growled in response. "Never again, Ariel. Never will I let you go again."

She started to protest, would have protested virulently if he hadn't bent his head, stroking his lips over the flesh of her chest between the edges of her blouse. The rough velvet feel of his lips over the upper mounds of her breast shocked her to silence. Her nipples became electrified, the fabric of her bra a rasp against them that she wanted gone.

She wanted to feel his lips covering the tormented peaks, sucking them into his mouth, licking and nipping and…

"What are you doing to me?" she cried out then, her head falling back against the tree, her eyes staring sightlessly into the misty, fog-enshrouded night, fighting to make sense of the impressions and sensations roiling within her.

He drew back then, his eyes blazing down, shocking her as the gunmetal sheen glistened within his dark face. He looked like a predator, a hunter, a hungry savage intent on sating the lust that threatened to overwhelm both of them.

"You're crazy," she charged, breathlessly. "Aren't you supposed to be trying to kill me, rather than fuck me?"

A chuckle stroked her senses as she watched the struggle for control in his expression.

"I never was into a dead fuck, baby, so I think I'll keep you alive," he retorted sarcastically as he moved back from her, though his hand wrapped around her wrist like a living manacle.

Stooping, he retrieved her sword from the ground before staring around them with narrowed eyes.

Only then did she notice the small communications device at his ear. It was small, almost undetectable. He tilted his head slightly as though listening to the voice on the other end.

"This way."

She gasped as he gripped her wrist and began to pull her along behind him.

"Are you crazy?" she hissed, raising her voice to be heard above the storm. She could smell the enemy at her back, feel the wind pushing her along with the barbarian.

"I might be," he called back. A flash of a smile, his gaze dark as his pace picked up. "The cycles are just below on the interstate. Let's get the hell out of here."

She could hear them now. Voices raised in the dark, the demons intent on spilling her blood.

"Joshua, Derek, cover our fucking asses," he called out then, his voice furious as he pulled her along. "We have a whole pack following here."

Her breath caught in her throat. She could hear the rage vibrating in the sound of his voice as the voices drew closer. Curses. Demands. The cry for blood echoed on the wind around her.

"Maybe you should have been more concerned with fighting than pinning me against a tree," she snapped furiously, fighting to keep up with him.

"Not near as much fun," he laughed back at her. "Move those long legs of yours, woman, or Jonar's warriors will have Wind Mistress' ass for dinner."

He was crazy. Crazier than her father could have ever imagined she was.

She raced behind him, not that she had a choice the way he was pulling her along with him. Before her was the clean scent of freedom, behind her, the smell of death.

They would be cut in two. The wretched stench that followed them was thickening, massing. There would be more than they could fight.

"Son of a bitch, they're getting too close." His expression was savage in the brilliant arcs of lightning flaring around them as he glanced behind. "Call to the wind, Ariel," he demanded forcefully. "Delay them now!"

Shock resounded through her. What the hell was he talking about?

34

The wind whipped around them, growing in force as though preparing itself...for what?

"Do it, Ariel!" He screamed back at her again as the winds moaned around them more forcefully than before. "Call the wind to your aid."

"Are you insane!" she screamed back. "Kiss them, maybe that would stop them," she snarled furiously a second later.

"Do I look insane?" he yelled imperatively, glancing behind him a second before a wide smile flashed across his face. "Forget I said that. Just call the winds, dammit, or you may never know another kiss."

She had a feeling he wasn't crazy, no matter how he looked, or acted. She could feel a demand rising inside her, the crystal calling out to her as the weak violet aura began to pulse around them. She fought to keep up with his longer stride, running as fast as her weary body would allow, feeling the wind at her back. If only it were pushing the enemy back rather than pushing her forward.

"Command it!" he screamed imperiously, something he saw behind them reflecting in the fury of his dark expression.

Knowing she shouldn't. Knowing she didn't really want to see, Ariel looked back at well.

Demons' eyes, dozens of them reflected in the inky darkness behind them. Glowing red, fiery hot and moving closer.

"Oh God! Oh God!" the prayer was on her lips as the winds swirled around her again.

"Ariel, command those fucking winds before we both die." The impossibly commanding male was lashing out in fury as his pace suddenly increased. Ariel knew there was no way she could keep up. She would get them both killed.

How did she do this? How did she command the winds?

The swirl of forces gathered in strength.

"Push them back!" She screamed out the command as the crystal blazed in heat, as demanding as the man pulling her along. "I command you to push back my enemies…"

The winds screamed, they howled. Like demons from the pits of hell, reluctant to tear themselves from her, furious with the need to do so, the sound rose in volume, a crescendo of fury as it suddenly whipped around her, behind her.

There was no breeze before them, but she could feel its power at her back as they broke the edge of the forests and ran for the nearly deserted interstate below. At first, she knew nothing but the darkness as the winds, lightning and rain stayed concentrated at her back. Then, slowly, other shapes began to emerge. The presence of two others running from the tree line on each side of them, the large black motorcycles below and the figures revving each of them into throbbing life before jumping on their own.

"Get on!" He threw a leg over the nearest crotch rocket as she preferred to call the ultra-fast, streamlined ZX10 motorcycles. They were big, sexy machines, designed for speed and maneuverability.

Gripping his shoulders she threw her leg over the back, crowding in close and gripping his waist as he lay along the front rest and kicked it into gear. She wanted to scream in exhilaration as the machine powered away, closely following the lead cycles. She could feel the wind at her back once again, pushing them along, adding to the aerodynamic effect of the powerful beast between her thighs.

The night zoomed by alongside them as she felt the horsepower increasing beneath her body, throbbing, purring as it was kicked into top speed as it was meant to be. Rocketing through the night, pushed by an unnatural wind, held in place by the strength of the man before her and guided to safety. Finally, safety.

Chapter Four

ಬಿ

Long minutes or hours later, Ariel wasn't certain which, the cycles came to a terrifying, sliding stop, the wind swirling around them, whipping past her ears with the triumphant laughter of the man in front of her.

He was as wild as the wind itself. His laughter filled with excitement, pleasure, the thrill of the chase and that of the fight. Before she could do more than gasp, he turned to her, pulled her across his lap and lowered his head for a kiss that stole her breath. His tongue pushed demandingly past her lips, sweeping along hers with a carnal passion that had every nerve ending in her body flaming in riotous response.

She stiffened in his arms, would have fought him. She wanted to fight him, and yet she didn't. The contradictory impulses confused her, kept her still, kept her searching for a reason why she wasn't trying to rip his face off for his sheer nerve. Flashing memories of other kisses, other touches, laughter in battle and in bed flitted through her mind. She belonged to him.

Her hands gripped his shoulders as his hand splayed just beneath her breast, close to the crystal that now lay silent. His hand was warm through the chilled dampness of her clothing, his body raging with lust if the erection pressed to her side was anything to go by.

"You were incredible," he breathed against her lips as he came up for air. "Absolutely incredible."

Ariel blinked up at him in shock as he stared down at her, a smile creasing his face, his eyes dark as he watched her.

"Thank you. I think." She eased herself up, watching him warily now. "Where are we?"

"Outside Lexington, near the airport."

She looked around, avoiding the gazes of the others watching them as she recognized the area.

"Did we lose them?" She watched a few passing cars suspiciously.

"For now." He shrugged, his rough voice still vibrating with arousal. "We'll take a room for the rest of the night and plan out what we do from here. We need to get you warm and dry. I don't want you picking up pneumonia again."

She glanced at him in surprise. What the hell was going on here?

"Who are you?" she snapped, more angry at herself for her position now than she was at him.

She moved to struggle from his lap and the hard length of his erection pressing into her. She needed to think, to figure out what was going on. It was impossible to do so while his cock was pressing so thick and hard against her.

"Get back behind me," he finally commanded her, as though command came naturally to him. "We've only a short distance to go to the motel and we can talk there."

"Where's my sword?" She ignored the order.

She checked the sheath at the small of her back for her dagger, thankfully it was still there.

"I have your sword, babe," he murmured, the innuendo not exactly lost on her though as he shifted her behind him again before pointing to the sheath at his back. The one that carried his sword, as well as hers.

"That's good to know," she replied mockingly.

"I thought it might bring you comfort," he chuckled as she settled in behind him. "Let's go, the commander's getting testy. He doesn't like getting wet."

He nodded to the silent couple ahead of them who watched them with penetrating, too intent gazes.

"He can join the crowd," she muttered, gripping his waist as he leaned over the motorcycle's chest pad once again.

The cycle shot off, just as it had before, in the center of the strange procession that made their way to the motel on a deserted stretch of interstate. It wasn't long before they pulled into the motel parking lot and cut the engines, everyone dismounting wearily.

"Kanna has our rooms." The dark, faintly accented voice of the one who had been pointed out as the commander struck her senses with its familiarity. "She has food waiting too. Thank God."

She could hear the weariness in his voice, a weariness that the man who stood beside her obviously didn't feel.

"You're getting old, Devlin," her rescuer chuckled. "Or lazy."

"Probably both." Devlin snorted, his arm curling around the much smaller woman at his side.

The woman watched Ariel closely, too intently for comfort.

"Let's find our dinner and our beds for now. We'll meet in the morning to decide where we go from here."

"Come on." A large hand at the small of her back propelled her forward.

"Stop pushing at me," she hissed, becoming aware of the fact that since the moment she had met him in the earlier storm he had either been yanking her forward or kissing her senseless.

"Move a bit faster and I wouldn't have to. God gave you those long legs for more than wrapping around a man's waist, sweetness," he told her, his voice thick with amusement.

"You're dangerous to be around," she told him fiercely. "I should be running from you, not with you."

"There's no escaping this, Ariel, and I know it's in your mind to try. I don't intend to allow that to happen." His voice hardened, purpose filling it.

She glanced up at him, for the first time getting a clear look at his face from the lights outside the motel. His features were harsh, his eyes swirling with myriad shades of gray, rather like an intense, building storm. Long, tawny gold hair fell past his shoulders and he was massive muscle. From his neck to his ankles, the man was built like a mountain.

At over five-foot-ten, Ariel had often felt too tall, too gangly. But he made her feel feminine, petite, and that just pissed her off. She had gone twenty-six years without that feeling; she sure as hell didn't need it now.

As they moved through the back lobby doors and then to the elevators, she watched the men gathered around her warily. There was something about them, something otherworldly and too powerful to be entirely comfortable. They reminded her a bit of Alyx, Lynn Carstairs' lover. He wasn't natural in any human way except perhaps looks. These men had that same dangerous, alien aura.

To be truthful, Alyx was very alien, as Lynn had confided to her before Ariel had more or less fired the group. Too alien. Alien, as in not born on Earth. That knowledge still had the power to shock and amaze her.

The woman sheltered beneath the commander's arm was different, though. Petite, obviously tired, but not weak. She had a bearing of strength, of comfort, which reached out to Ariel, though she wasn't certain why.

Her long, white-blonde hair framed a petite, drowsy expression. And if Ariel thought she was watching the other woman closely, then it was no closer than the woman watched her. A light curl to her lips indicated amused indulgence, and emerald eyes glinted with affection. An affection that seeped into Ariel's consciousness as well. Which made no sense at all.

"Your rooms are ready." Ariel jumped in surprise as the elevator doors opened and the small, brown-haired woman faced them commandingly. "Follow me. I've stocked them accordingly and you should have every thing you need." She stopped a few feet up the hall, waving to the opened doors on each side of the hall. "I'm in the last room. Just let me know if you need anything."

Ariel watched in surprise as each man headed to a different room.

"Come on, slowpoke, I'm starved." That hand pushed at her back once again.

"Imbecile," she muttered as he herded her into one of the nearest rooms and sighed in relief as he closed and locked the door behind them.

"That was Kanna." He nodded to the door, indicating the woman who had met them. "You'll see her again in the morning. The blonde was Chantel, the warrior with her, Devlin..."

"Warrior?" She lifted a brow mockingly as she entered the small suite, staring around the room and wondering how in the hell she was supposed to maneuver herself out of whatever trouble she had managed to get into this time.

"Warrior." He nodded agreeably, flashing a smile of male satisfaction. "Oh good, the food's still hot."

Before she could protest, he stepped into the bathroom, leaving the door wide.

Ariel blinked as she heard the faucet running, watching the doorway until he walked out, drying his hands and face with a hand towel.

"Go ahead and get cleaned up and we'll eat."

"Who the hell are you?" she asked him with what she considered a quite calm demeanor.

Another of those smiles. A flash of white teeth, a curve of male satisfaction, the darkening of those unusual gray eyes.

"Shanar, but you can call me Shane." He watched her expectantly, the harsh features of his face somehow gentled by the incredible warmth of eyes that should have appeared cool.

"Shanar...who?" She pursed her lips and barely refrained from rolling her eyes. Was he being deliberately obtuse or had he just been born so arrogantly male? She ignored the flash of familiarity, the feeling that she *should* remember him.

"Steele." The smooth rumble of his voice as he said the word sent shivers down her spine. "Shanar Steele. Now get washed up, I'm damned hungry and it's been a lot of years since I've had KFC in front of me. I might not wait on you."

Savage... Ariel stilled as the lightest of breezes danced around her, the whisper of it creating a surge of warmth at her ear as the single word had her swallowing tightly.

No one else had ever heard the whispers in the breeze. She had grown used to hiding her reaction to them as best she could. But they were growing more frequent, more intent than before. Her father had suspected it, often aware when the voices teased at her ears. When she refused to admit to it, refused to tell him what she heard, he punished her.

She forced away the memories of the darkness closing in on her, stealing her breath and her mind. It was over, years in the past, she told herself. Her father hadn't driven her to madness, nor had he yet managed to convince anyone that she was crazy as he had convinced the judges that her mother and grandmother were. She was safe from him. Allowing those memories to affect her now would serve no purpose at all.

"Get cleaned up, Ariel. We'll talk after we eat." His fingers went to the buttons of his shirt, releasing them slowly. "Or you can watch me change into something drier..." he finally suggested, his voice lowering until it nearly grated from his chest.

She jerked to attention as the strong, broad expanse of his deeply tanned chest began to come into view. That put her into motion as nothing else could have. Damn him, he was distracting enough dressed and mocking, she didn't need him naked and sensual to reinforce the knowledge that this man was a weakness she could ill-afford.

She moved quickly to the bathroom, but unlike him she slammed the door closed behind her and locked it like the coward she knew she was being.

Breathing roughly, she closed her eyes as the scent of him, stronger here than it was outside, wrapped around her. It was intoxicating, weakening. She hated her ability to both hear and smell things that no one else seemed able to detect. In this case, she didn't know if she should regret it or not. The aroma was dark, like the storm, clean and fresh with just a hint of heat. Male heat. Arousal.

She bit her lip as that particular scent sent her own hormones into overdrive. Her breasts swelled in response to it, her nipples beading tightly beneath her damp shirt.

"I have a clean gown and robe for you out here," he called through the door. "Kanna just brought it."

He knocked on the door then. "Open the door, Ariel. You can't eat or sleep in those wet clothes."

Turning, she laid her forehead against the smooth metal before she unlocked it with a sigh and stepped back to open it a few narrow inches.

The material was thrust into the room. A long gown, robe and a pair of soft, thickly padded socks. She jerked them from his hands as a shiver worked over her, reminding her that she was indeed still dressed in wet clothes.

"Go ahead and shower if you like," he told her as she closed the door quickly. "I'm sure I can hold off on all this chicken long enough for that."

His voice shouldn't sound so gentle, she thought, not as deep and as rough as it was; it should be frightening, nightmarish. It shouldn't bring fractured memories of heated sighs and lust-filled caresses.

Ten minutes later, warm from the shower and wrapped in the cotton comfort of the plain white gown and robe, she stepped hesitantly from the bathroom, her gaze seeking and finding him as she prepared herself for a fight. She could feel the heat, the arousal and lust that emanated from him. She could *see* it.

He was waiting on her. Slouched on the couch, bare feet propped on the low coffee table as he watched the news on the flat-screened television mounted to the opposite wall.

He turned his head slowly, his body tensing before his eyes ever met hers. Instantly, they darkened, heat flaring in the dark centers as she stood hesitantly at the entrance to the room.

"I'm not going to rape you." Irritation reflected in his voice when he shifted as though to get up, causing her to back away a step.

It wasn't that she was frightened; to the contrary, she was too drawn to him. Too aware of him for her own good.

"Good thing," she responded archly. "Because I'm not in the mood to be raped."

He arched a brow in sudden humor, planted his feet on the floor and rose from the couch until she was forced to look up at him.

"Come on, little bit, let's eat. I'm starving."

Little bit?

"What did you do with my sword?" She wasn't about to make another move without the weapon that had saved her life earlier that night. And she wasn't about to accept any of his rumbling innuendoes either.

He flashed her a half-drowsy, sex-laden look instead.

"It's under your bed. You can check it out after we eat."

He moved to the table and her eyes widened.

"The others are joining us?" She really wasn't in the mood for more strangers.

Casting her a surprised look he sat down. "Do you see them here? Get over here and eat, woman. I'm half-starved. I need fuel."

There was a large box of chicken, two potato and gravy sides as well as several other assorted accompaniments. He opened the box, then the large cups and began piling the Styrofoam plate he had before him high. At his elbow, a jug of iced tea waited with two empty cups.

"Sit down and eat. Then we'll talk." There was no amusement in his voice now when he looked up at her. His eyes were a dark, stormy gray without the sense of laughter that had filled them before.

"Do you get your way like that often?" she asked, though she took her seat and selected her food in much smaller quantities than he had.

"Like what?" he growled.

"Like your word is law and I better follow it implicitly?" She gave him a look of wide-eyed innocence. "I don't obey so well, Mr. Steele."

A shadow seemed to cross his expression and for a moment, bleak memory filled the unusual depths of his eyes.

"Eat," he said again, the sound of weary male patience grating on her temper. "We'll discuss your shortcomings later as well. We both need a full stomach and a clear head for that though."

So that was how it was going to be? Ariel hid her smile and did as she was bade, for the moment. She ate. But only because she was hungry…

Chapter Five

ဢ

A thousand years. He had waited a thousand years to hold her, to touch her, to feel the rebirth of his soul at the sound of her voice. God knew he had lived for this day, had prayed for it for so long that at times he thought his soul would shatter from the need. And now that she was here…he swallowed tightly…how was he to find the control to woo her rather than to take her?

His cock was harder than he could ever remember it being. It throbbed beneath his jeans, ached at the confinement and the need to press into the tighter, hotter confines of Ariel's sweet pussy. His eyelids lowered, his chest heaving as he dragged in a deep breath.

She was the same as before, yet different. The sensuality she had kept so carefully hidden in her first life was just below the surface now. Jonar hadn't had a chance to rape or humiliate her. Jonar hadn't stolen the innocence that would always be so much a part of her now. That deep core of sensual femininity that would burn him alive once he tapped into the need that glittered in her brilliant, dark amethyst eyes.

Shanar swallowed tightly. Waiting was a bitch. Could he wait? Could he refrain from touching her, tasting her?

Even now, she was like a wildfire to his system. Time had not dimmed the hunger that surged inside him for her. Only her death had eased the physical need, though the soul had ached more harshly than ever.

For years he had known she was out there. Even during her childhood years after she had first called out to him, he hadn't known this overpowering need. But it had erupted inside him in the middle of that damned storm. The moment his lips touched hers, surrounded by death and danger, he had been unable to stop himself. And now, long minutes after their meal had finished, it only rose.

If only he could have located her then. If only he could have found her when her fears had been strong enough that the winds had first brought her whispers of need to him. He would have found her, brought her to safety, if he could have convinced her to speak to him once again. Yet the connection had never returned.

Midnight had long passed and he knew dawn wasn't far away. There would be few enough hours to sleep before they attempted to put more distance between them and Jonar's dark minions. So much to do and yet he knew there weren't enough hours to do it in.

"So, you were going to tell me just who the hell you are," she announced with studied interest as she began to place the empty cups within the chicken box and the plates in the bottom of the bag that sat on the floor.

She had eaten well. He was glad to see that she hadn't adopted this century's habit of making their women eat only dainty portions. She was tall for a woman, with a light padding of muscle that he could tell was adequately honed. She wasn't a lazy woman, but her life would now demand more from her than it ever had.

"I told you who I was." He restrained his smile, knew he was doing little more than firing her irritation higher.

He had always loved pushing her to anger. To see her violet eyes snapping with ire, her face flushed with emotion. It was only then Ariel had loosened a bit of the self-control that she imposed on herself. It was only then that he had been able to loosen the reins on his own control.

"You're going to piss me off." She placed the bag of debris in the trash can next to the table before using a clean napkin to wipe the small crumbs from the table. "Now isn't a good time to do that. Now tell me what the hell is going on and what you and your buddies were doing in the foothills earlier."

She looked at him directly, and yes, there were the snapping sparks of anger he had so longed to see in her eyes.

Beloved. His mind whispered the word as he watched her. Beloved by his heart, and by his soul.

"We were there to find you," he finally answered as her gaze narrowed on him. "Alyx contacted us and informed us that you had fired your remaining security force. We came as fast as we could after that."

Her lips thinned.

"What business was it of yours?" She stood watching him, one hip thrown out aggressively as she watched him with her elfin features.

He realized then that he did not like her shorter hair. It was too short, and rather than framing her face and shoulders as it had after he rescued her from Jonar, it was now a sleek little cap that barely fell below her neck.

"It was much my business," he grunted, staying in his chair and slouching back in it lazily as he laced his fingers against his abdomen. "Your survival is of vital importance to me, Ariel. As I said before, I'm not into a dead fuck. I need you alive for what I intend."

Crimson heat washed over her face as her eyes widened ever so slightly.

"A little overconfident aren't you?" she questioned him softly, mockery lacing her tone.

He shrugged lightly. "I don't know about that, love. The wind doesn't just whisper to you and bring to you the scents and sounds you need..." He ignored the sudden shock on her face. "But now, it will aid me as well. And I smell your heat like the lightest brush of spring. So I really don't believe overconfidence will be an issue."

She backed away from him slowly.

"You're crazy." A strained smile shaped her lips. "I don't know what you're talking about."

"I'm not your father, Ariel," he said gently, remembering Alyx's report of Markham St. James' attempts to have his only child committed to an asylum. "I've no desire to see you locked away for the gifts you curse. I would see you accept them, embrace them as well as your destiny. There's nothing or no one for you to fear here."

Her petite little nose flared as her chin lifted in challenge. *Yes, by God, challenge me, woman*, he thought in satisfaction. *Let your blood run hot enough to burn us both alive.*

"I don't know what you're talking about." Her voice was mocking, harsh. But he heard the undertones of fear beneath it.

"Yes, you do. You would just prefer not to admit to it." He finally rose to his feet, watching as she backed away, staring up at him in surprise.

He remembered that about her. How she always seemed surprised by his height when he stood before her.

Shane moved to the single, king-sized bed and jerked the blankets down, preparing it for their rest. She would, of course, refuse at first. His blood thundered with the anticipation of convincing her to sleep against his warmth.

"Do you think you can just kidnap me from my home and make such outrageous statements?" she asked him coolly, quickly dragging a cloak of control around her fragile shoulders. "That I'll just accept it and agree with you? Sorry, you should have done your homework better or you would know that is not going to happen. As you said, you aren't my father, and he's been trying a hell of a lot longer than you have."

His brows snapped into a frown at the thought of the bastard who had raised her.

"I merely mentioned your father to reassure you that not all of us would have you hide from your birthright," he growled. "I have a date of retribution with that fine

49

gentleman," he sneered the title. "When your battles are done here. Until then, we shall concentrate on you."

She was so small next to him. Of course, most women were, but he knew this woman, knew her strengths and her fears. It made him protective, made him want to go to his knees to assure her that he would never see her harmed again. But it wasn't his gentleness and his love that she needed at this moment. She would have to be forced into the power she hid from, and it would fall to him to lead her into that which she most feared.

He wouldn't risk losing her in this life. As much as he abhorred forcing Ariel to do anything, he knew he wouldn't be able to merely sit back and hope she would reach into herself for the power she needed. This battle against Jonar would not be an easy one; she would need his strength, more than his protection, when all he wanted to do was protect her.

An incredulous laugh broke from her lips. She was staring at him as though he were an abomination rather than the man sworn to her soul. But the breeze whispered around her, he could feel it, hear its soothing murmur as he watched it brush at the strands of her hair. The wind, the very air itself would reassure her as he never could.

"Do you think I'm going to stay here and listen to these outlandish accusations?" She gripped the edges of the robe together with hands that were turning white from the strength she was exerting. "I can get this at my father's house. I don't have to stay here for it."

"Ah, but Jonar can take you easily from your father's residence, as you've learned. But trust me, Ariel; he will never get past me," he assured her, his voice lowering as he fought to restrain his fury.

He remembered well how he had found her in those dungeons more than a month before, nearly broken, barely clinging to life. He would not allow it to happen again.

"What do you want from me?" she whispered then, and his heart broke at the fear he heard in her tremulous words.

Shane sat down on the bed, knowing that she would find greater comfort in relief from the strength he exuded towering over her. He noticed the slight lessening of the tension in her shoulders as he did so, and something in his soul shattered for her. She should not know such fear, such a deep, encompassing wariness at a male's strength, *his* strength.

"Everything," he told her firmly. "I want everything, Ariel. And I will have it. Perhaps not tonight, perhaps not tomorrow night, but it will be mine. As will you be."

The color drained from her face. Watching that telling reaction had the muscles of his stomach clenching in pain that he had caused the response. She backed up once again as though placing herself closer to the door and freedom. Shane merely watched her, allowing her to see by his expression that he knew what she was doing and that he was prepared to stop her.

"I won't accept this." She swallowed tightly and he hated the resignation he saw in her gaze. "I won't accept you."

"I will grow on you." He smiled back at her, hoping to ease some of the tension from her face. "You will see Ariel; it will be very, very hard to resist me."

Something in her gaze heated, flared, but all he could smell on the light shift of air flowing from her to him, was anger and suspicion. She trusted no one, and he didn't blame her. She had been betrayed since childhood, left alone in the dark and taught that monsters truly do exist—they exist in the form of those who should love, protect and care for you, in the form of friends and the monsters that hungered for her blood in the darkness of the night.

"I've resisted better men," she sneered and his interest flared.

Ah yes, now the fight was on. She would challenge him every step of the way, although she would never be able to

51

hold herself aloof from him. She wouldn't run now. She would wait and see what protection he could offer her against Jonar and think to use his strength while maintaining the ice that encased her heart. He would show her differently.

This time, when he rose to his feet, he did nothing to hide the sheer power that he knew resonated from him. He *was* strength. Power. In its most ultimate form. His flesh was like living steel, his bones unbreakable. He was indestructible and he did nothing to camouflage it from her too perceptive senses.

Her nostrils flared as though drawing in a new, intriguing scent, and he was certain that she was unaware that her head tipped just slightly to the left to allow the whisper of air across her sensitive ears.

What did she hear? he wondered. What secret was her element whispering to her?

He walked to her slowly, watching her tense, prepare herself for attack. But it wasn't a full-frontal assault that he had planned. Nay, he had waited too long, hungered too hard for this time, he wouldn't frighten her now that she was here.

Keeping his gaze locked with hers, he came slowly beside her before finally releasing her eyes to cross behind her. There, he stopped, just close enough to feel the tension humming from her body, to allow her to feel his heat.

"There is no better man than I, Mistress of the Wind," he whispered at her ear, as soft as the air around them, but less subtle in his message. "Not for you in any case. And I will have you, soon, begging beneath me, your sharp little nails gripping my flesh, your thighs opening for me as I come to you. And you will be slick and hot, your juices like warm honey, your sweet nectar calling to me. Yes, love, you will be mine. Just as you always were..."

Chapter Six

ဢ

Satisfaction threaded through Ariel when she jabbed her elbow furiously into the hard-packed, muscled abdomen behind her and felt the soft whoosh of breath at her ear. A tight smile crossed her lips as she moved away from him, putting distance between them as she fought to maintain her composure. Did he have any idea how hot it made her to hear him whispering those words so silkily in her ear? His voice was rough, a rumble of sexuality that had the fine hairs along her arms lifting in awareness.

When she turned back to him, he was watching her with a grin, his large palm rubbing at his stomach slowly.

"Excellent reflexes," he complimented, appearing more proud of her than put out.

She snorted at that.

"Imbecile," she muttered as she plopped down on the couch. "Shouldn't you be going to sleep or something rather than harassing me?"

He lifted his brow archly as he glanced into the bedroom portion of the suite.

"When you go." He lifted his shoulder negligently as he leaned against the doorway. "It is pretty late, you know. I think we should turn in."

She narrowed her eyes on him.

"I don't think so!" she snapped. "If you think I'm sleeping with you, then you're…"

"Right." Something about the change in his voice had her pausing, watching him carefully.

She could see the ready tension enveloping him now, his determination that she would sleep with him.

"No." She kept her voice mild, but firm, a patient sound as though speaking to a recalcitrant child.

"I won't argue with you," he assured her. "You will sleep in this bed, beside me. Period."

"No." She repeated the word as though he hadn't heard her.

She watched his eyes lighten then darken. The gray patterns of color began to shift and move within the pupil as she watched in fascination. Amazing. She had never seen eyes react to emotion in such a way.

"Ariel, do not try my patience in this matter," he warned her then, his voice gravelly, guttural. "It's not up for discussion."

"Then it better get up for discussion." She shrugged in unconcern. "Because I'm not sleeping in that bed with you."

Beloved... She ignored the whisper at her ear.

Keeper of the wind... Mistress of my heart... Only years of control kept her from flinching as the words caressed her senses as surely as the soft shift of air about her ear caressed her flesh. Because as much as she hated it, as much as she wanted to deny it, the voice sounded too much of the man now facing her so determinedly.

"Do you enjoy being difficult?" he finally asked her curiously as she leaned back against the couch.

"Actually, I do." She crossed her legs and smoothed the robe over her knees automatically. "Do you enjoy being an arrogant ass?"

"It's a hobby of mine, actually," he admitted a bit mockingly. "Do you think I will one day perfect the art?"

She snorted at the question. "I think you already have."

"Excellent. I always strive to do my best in all areas." He straightened from the doorway and walked toward her.

Ariel watched him suspiciously as he moved to the couch, then sat down beside her. The small sofa left little room for her to occupy. She cast him a reproving glare as he leaned closer.

"It is a simple matter," he said softly, his breath wafting over her ear, nearly causing her to shiver in response. "You can sleep in that nice large bed with me. A king-sized bed, with plenty of room for the two of us, so that I may be assured of your safety. Or, we can sit right here. But as close as I am to you…" She jerked as he smoothed his cheek over her shoulder. "I will begin to wonder how that intriguing little lobe of your ear will feel against my lips…" He suited words to action, catching the bit of flesh between his lips then swiping it with the warmth of his tongue.

"Stop that." Ariel shot from the couch, staring back at him resentfully as he smiled innocently.

She could feel the caress echoing along her body, causing her vagina to ripple at the sensation, her clit to swell beseechingly. Damn him, he was evil. Pure, black-hearted evil.

"I cannot help myself." He shrugged, unrepentant. "The choice is yours. Come to bed so that I may sleep, or we can play this little game through the night until you falter through sheer exhaustion. It is entirely up to you."

"I don't want to sleep with you," she snarled between clenched teeth. He didn't seem to care.

His expression hardened, his eyes once again swirling with a darker gray color than before.

"But I want you to sleep with me," he replied silkily. "So which will it be, Mistress? Do we play this game through the night, or do we sleep?"

She snarled furiously. "I'm going to cut your heart out. I swear to God, I'm going to take that dagger and dig it out piece by tiny, tiny piece."

Genuine amusement filled his eyes then. "You are welcome to try."

He came to his feet in a surge of strength. That strength seemed to fill the room, wrap around her, make her nearly heady with the intensity of it.

"Bedtime then," he announced. "I will allow you to keep the gown this time, but eventually I think I would want to feel you bare against me."

Ariel gaped back at him. Slowly, she drew in a deep, hard breath then smiled. It wasn't a pleasant smile, and she made certain of it. It was a baring of teeth, a cold, hard warning to anyone smart enough to understand the anger pulsing inside her.

"Do you think you will, Shanar?" she deliberately cooed sensually, lowering her eyelids to half-mast as she watched him carefully now.

What was that? His pupils flared, the color in his eyes turning a light, gorgeous blue-gray that was almost entrancing.

"I think I most definitely want that." His voice was rougher now, no longer the silky rumble it had before.

"And you think all you have to do is ask for it?" She allowed her fingers to toy with the belt to her robe as she watched him from beneath her lashes.

He cleared his throat, his eyes trained on her hands.

"I can be persuasive." He sounded much too serious.

Her eyes narrowed further.

"Ohh, I bet you could be," she murmured, loosening the belt and slowly drawing the robe down her shoulders.

He swallowed tightly, his gaze rising to hers. What she saw then stilled the cruel words that had risen first to her lips. The ones where she would have assured him in no uncertain terms that he would never be smooth enough, sharp enough or quick enough to deserve her nakedness against him. It wouldn't have mattered that they were a lie, that it was no more than a furious parry back at him.

But she couldn't do it. For a moment, she glimpsed such naked, unabashed longing in his eyes that it held her speechless.

"I would never force you." The quaint, almost old world way he had of talking combined with the sudden somber intensity in his gaze had her breathing out with fury. But not fury with him. Fury with herself.

"Oh, just go to sleep," she muttered, jerking the robe from her shoulders as she crawled beneath the blankets. "And stay on your own damned side of the bed, too. No touching. No crowding. No blanket hogging."

She kept her eyes averted, but she caught the flash of bare skin, the more than impressive length of a thick, savagely ready erection jutting out from his body as he walked to his side of the bed.

Her mouth watered. Now that was impressive. Evidently, all of his body was proportional; it boggled the mind.

The bed dipped, the blankets lifted.

"You didn't say I couldn't sleep nude." Satisfaction filled his voice. "You are welcome to crowd me anytime, Ariel. I will make no objections."

Chapter Seven

ဢ

She was restless in her sleep. Shanar lay for a while watching her, seeing the play of emotions across her expressive face, the fear, the confusion. She lay on her side, turned to him now rather than away from him, lying diagonally on the large bed. Moments before she had been on her back, her head in the corner, her feet pushing at his legs in an attempt to stretch them toward the opposite corner. She was never still.

He could feel the crystal trying to soothe her. The threads of energy pouring through it and wrapping around her were maternal in their sensations, attempting to calm what could not be calmed.

If only he could ease her. He reached out, his finger smoothing back a stray lock of hair that fell over her brow and had her swiping at it occasionally. He had taken to moving it himself for her, hoping to ease her in what small way he could.

The coming days would be hard for her, and most likely filled with danger. A danger he hadn't wanted her to face, but if the information they had learned was true, then the third mistress, Caitlin, would show herself soon. The Mistress of the Water Crystal would face a greater danger than even Chantel or Ariel had.

Chantel had felt the force of the rains as Ariel called the elements to her. All three of the sister crystals had connected with the Earth stone to amplify their powers and aid the wind in saving Ariel's life.

Jonar would know that, and he would be searching for the Mistress of the Water Crystal now. It was moving quickly, he thought with an edge of sorrow. There would be no time to shelter Ariel, to ease her into the life she had been born to know. She was being thrown into it, and she would fight it. Fighting it could get her killed.

Shane sighed wearily. Caitlin had been the wife to Derek, the Wizard. An Irish lass who had eyes of sea-green and a fine temper to match. Chantel had been attempting to connect with her third sister since Ariel had been found. She had tracked the Water Mistress to one small area, but could not connect with her fully. As legend told, only Ariel could find the sister who came after her. Just as only Caitlin could find Arriane, the wife to Joshua, the fourth and final sister, and the key to destroying Jonar. Finding their wives and the destinies that were ripped from them were of prime importance. And only destroying Jonar would ensure those destinies.

As he watched her sleep, he moved his hand to the crystal, gripping it lightly, feeling the warmth and the power it contained and infusing it with more of his own. He was strength, his body of the earth, his powers amplified, magnified. There was plenty enough for the crystal to use what it required.

And it drew from him, just as it had been created to do. He could feel it strengthening, feel it taking from his strength what it needed to reach into the deepest parts of her mind and to release all that she had, and could be. He was her strength. The Legacy of the Savage and the Wind Mistress foretold this, just as she was his soul.

"I send you ease... I send you peace..." he whispered, watching her closely. "Rest, beloved, while you can..."

She woke, her body tangled with his, his arms wrapped around her, one of her legs pushed between his as she sprawled over his chest. A warm, hard chest that felt too good, too solid beneath her cheek.

Her lips quirked into a drowsy smile as she realized she was on his side of the bed. She was a greedy sleeper and was prone to sprawl out in the bed after going to sleep. She had no doubt it was more her fault than his that she ended up on his chest. Not that it wasn't a nice place to wake up. It was. Comfortable, warm, peaceful. But highly disconcerting.

Biting her lip, she glanced up, seeing the peaceful relaxation on his face, the charm that hadn't been as readily apparent the night before when she had been so damned furious with him. It was there now. Breathtaking, not exactly handsome, but a hard-boned, weathered face that spoke of life and battles won. His chin was impossibly stubborn, his nose a bit crooked, but mostly straight and arrogant. High cheekbones, wide eyes and a broad forehead. A warrior. Wasn't that what he called the others the night before? It suited him better.

The Savage shall come on the winds, Ariel. He will bring with him danger, blood and hope. He is salvation. He is death. He is the chosen mate…

Her heart slammed in her chest as she moved to jerk away from him. Chosen mate, her ass.

"Stay." His arms snapped into place around her, restraining her effectively, pinning her to the massive length of his body.

"In your dreams!" she snapped, instantly rising to the autocratic tone. "I'm not a damned dog for you to command."

He snorted at that. "Stay still. One moment more. I want to enjoy this."

"Enjoy what?" she questioned furiously between clenched teeth.

He sighed wearily. "The lack of a delicate little foot planting itself in my shin. Woman, you are dangerous to sleep with."

His voice was filled with such male frustration that she couldn't help but almost grin. But just almost.

"Let me go, moron." She pushed at his chest in disgust. "I told you I didn't want to sleep with you."

Before she could do more than gasp, he twisted, bearing down on her, holding her effectively in place by simply pressing his long legs between hers. The length of her gown was now caught between him and the bed, holding her tight as she stared up at him in surprise.

"Now this is much better," he sighed then. "You should return the favor and let me nap just like this."

His elbows held the better part of his weight from her, but nothing could hide the prodding of his erection between her thighs as he rested his head against her cloth-covered breasts.

Shock traveled through her as she had to fight her reaction to him. She could feel her blood boiling in her body, though not in outrage as it should be. Like bonds of invisible steel, chains silken and yet unbreakable, sensation began to bind her to him. Everywhere he touched, he was a familiar weight. She remembered, she knew, she had awakened many, many nights, reaching for this.

She breathed in, a shuddering breath of knowledge that she wanted nothing to do with as she tried to push the memories away. How often had she awakened, convinced it was another place, another life, reaching for someone, knowing he should be there. Knowing this was what she had sought.

"You are so soft, so warm against me," he whispered, his breath hot through the material of her gown as it blew over her nipple.

That traitorous bit of flesh tightened, becoming a hard, aching point of delight at the attention.

"We need to stop this." She had to force the words past her lips, though she wanted nothing more than to call them back.

"Not yet," he whispered. "Just a moment longer."

A strangled gasp escaped her when she felt his tongue settle on the diamond-hard point of her nipple, licking, prodding at it, sensitizing it so fiercely that she shuddered in response.

Lazily, lasciviously, he painted the hardened tip as she fought to find a defense against the pleasure whipping through her. It wasn't fair, she thought, to find this, to need this, at a time when everything in her life had gone insane.

"I have dreamed of this, Ariel," he whispered then, his hands tugging at the neckline of her gown as his lips moved higher. "You, soft and sweet beneath me, warm and welcoming. Just for a moment, welcome me, Ariel."

His voice rumbled, echoed with the same needs she could feel flaring brightly in the pit of her soul. It shouldn't be like this. So intense, so desperate that she couldn't deny it. She shouldn't remember the long, lonely years and the loneliness she had suffered from.

She lay beneath him, fighting for strength. Just enough strength to deny him, to make her body stop arching, her hands to stop clenching on his thick forearms. The familiarity of him to stop permeating her senses.

"You taste of spring," he groaned as his lips smoothed over her collarbone, his tongue painting a trail of fiery sensations. "So fresh and delicate. I want just to taste you, beloved…"

She had heard those words before. A whisper of memory, a bed of furs and this man rising over her.

A whimper escaped her as his lips moved up her neck, along her cheek. His hands framed her face now, his fingers reaching into her hair, thumbs smoothing beneath her jaw to hold her in place. Not that she was fighting. Anticipation coiled in her belly, ran thick and hot along the sensitized lips of her cunt. It caused her clit to swell, her breasts to ache. It held her suspended within a web of gossamer passion and heated kisses.

His lips smoothed over hers, striking a blow of arousal that she couldn't have expected deep into the heart of her womb. It wasn't a touch unfamiliar and surprising. It was a kiss too familiar, too long missed. And that frightened her more than anything.

She opened her lips anyway as a groan of surrender escaped them and her tongue reached out tentatively to touch his. Her eyes closed as she let the sensations sink into her very being. She couldn't fight them, not now, not yet. It was as though something or someone else lived within her, someone who knew this man's taste, his touch. Yet it was her. She trembled at the thought.

God, it was good. Had anything ever felt as good as his hands holding her still for his kiss, his lips moving over hers demandingly, his tongue tangling with hers, stroking a fire inside her she couldn't have imagined existing? Just for a moment, she wanted to relish each pleasure, to immerse herself in a touch given in hunger and in need. And she could feel that hunger, wrapping around her, tightening about her with fierce bands of lust.

Before she knew, before she realized the implications, she lifted herself to him. Her hands were on his shoulders, then at his neck, sinking into his hair as she held him closer. She needed more, deeper, harder. The hungry moan that escaped her throat shocked her, but not enough to stop the demand rising inside her.

She couldn't feel enough. No touch was deep enough, hard enough, strong enough. She shifted beneath him, her hips lifting to the pressure nudging against her gown, pressing against the sensitive lips of her pussy.

He was gentle. Too damned gentle. But he controlled the kiss for now, controlled the movement of her body, how deeply he tasted or allowed her to taste, how much sensation she received.

It was too much.

It wasn't enough.

She growled low and deep, her hands clenching in his hair, tugging at the strands as she used them to try to pull his head closer, to force him to deepen the kiss. That lasted for seconds only. Before she could guess his intentions, his hands left her face, gripped hers then slammed them to the bed before his head tilted, his lips slanting over hers and devouring the passion rising inside her.

This was what she knew awaited her. Sizzling heat exploded through her body, drawing tighter against him as his tongue plundered her mouth, hard, deep groans tearing from his chest as his hips began a gentle thrust and retreat between her thighs.

Oh God. That was too good. She could feel the broad head of his erection, burning hot, pressing into her, nothing but her gown holding it back and she wished he would rip the cloth from between them. She needed more. So much more.

"Yes," he growled as his lips slid from hers to her neck once again.

Stinging little kisses were pressed to the flesh only to be soothed by the heat of his tongue. Ariel fought his hold, twisting beneath him, desperate to feel his lips devouring hers again.

But this, this was different. She moaned, a low whimpering sound of pleasure as new sensations began to whip through her. She opened her eyes, gazing down at where his lips covered the peak of one swollen breast, gown and all.

His teeth rasped against it, his cheeks hollowing as he drew on the tiny point, his tongue lashing it erotically.

For a moment, one long sensual moment, she knew him and she knew what was coming. She knew the expression on his face, drowsy, intensely sensual, filled with hunger. And then it happened. He took her wrists in one big hand as the other lowered to the bodice of her gown. In one strong move, he ripped the material free of her upper body as greedy, unabashed lust suddenly overwhelmed them both.

His hand cupped the hard mound of her breasts, his lips covering her nipple once again and Ariel could do nothing but cry out at the storm that began to rush through her. Her womb contracted, silky warmth spilled from between her thighs to dampen the tip of his cock as it pressed against her. She tightened, her breath catching, caught between reality and fantasy, knowing him and fearing him as heat exploded in the pit of her stomach.

Chapter Eight

෨

Shudders raced through her body, almost ecstasy, almost rapture but not quite. She twisted against him, knowing there was more waiting, knowing yet not knowing where this path of pleasure would lead her.

"Shane…" She wailed his name as the tremors of pleasure shook her body.

She couldn't escape it, couldn't deny it. She had known his touch before, trusted it, needed it. She needed him.

"Easy, Ariel," he whispered, panting as his lips smoothed over the engorged flesh of her breast then. "Just feel, baby. It's okay, I'll hold onto you."

Her head thrashed on the bed. She could feel the perspiration gathering on her naked flesh, the heat of the room, of his body. Her body.

"What are you doing to me?" she moaned as he held her to the bed, restraining every movement, denying her the deeper, closer touch she craved.

She shouldn't want this. His arrogance the night before should have been enough to keep her anger burning. But it wasn't anger whipping through her body.

"I am merely holding you, precious," he whispered as his lips caressed her collarbone again. "Just holding you, just warming myself in your fire. That is all."

The way he spoke, the odd turn of his words, the light accent just below them. They melted her. That had to be the reason she couldn't fight against them, it couldn't really be emotion she heard in his voice. Could it?

And the familiarity of it. That alone perplexed and yet drew her. Each time she fought against the pleasure she was sucked into a pit of knowledge, hazy and distant, that wouldn't let her free.

"It aches," she whispered, her hips lifting to the hard presence of his cock between her thighs.

Ache nothing. It was damned well hurting and she needed relief.

"Aye, I ache as well, love." He was breathing harshly, his voice deeper, rougher than before. "But the pleasure, Ariel. Feel the pleasure the ache possesses. Feel it, love, deep inside you."

Feel it? It was killing her.

She would have berated him, would have screamed her need for him if his lips hadn't covered hers a second later. Deep, intense, it was a merging not just of lips, but something more elemental. Deeper. Stronger.

His free hand smoothed down her body. He ignored her whimpered protest when he shifted, his hips moving back from hers, the pressure against the portal of her sex lifting.

That wasn't acceptable. She strained against the retreat. Then his hand was pushing the tattered remains of her gown to her hips, cool air stroking between her thighs a second before his fingers covered her.

Ariel stilled. Her eyes flew open, caught by his as she felt him part her, his fingers sliding through her wet slit, circling her clit, easing back along the narrow channel to her pulsing core.

She was shaking. His lips still covered hers, his tongue moving against hers, a slow, deliberate thrust and retreat between her lips that only then seared into her mind. She trembled beneath him, caught between pleasure and fear as the wisps of memory invaded her mind. Memories of other touches, other kisses from his demanding lips. His whispered words of need, the lust he inspired in her. Back and forth, memories of a *then* and the pleasures of *now*. They were terrifying her.

"Like that," he growled when he saw she realized the movements he was mimicking. "I'm going to take you like that, Ariel. My lips buried between your thighs, my tongue sinking inside you, over and over again, until I am drowning in the taste of you. Drowning and needing still more of you."

He held her legs apart as his fingers found the small opening to her vagina. He rimmed the entrance, humming his approval as more of her juices escaped to bathe his fingers.

She was burning alive. She strained to lift closer, as he released her hands, shuddering in a pleasure so intense it was overwhelming. She fought to sift through the layers of memories, reach inside herself to make sense of it. Shaking her head, she concentrated on the crystal at her breast, praying it held the answers she needed. The strength she needed. She connected into the power, but there was little strength to fight against him to be had. It only intensified the pleasure, the familiarity and, God help her, the hunger.

"Be still, love..." The soft words were accompanied by a slight, resounding little smack to her pussy.

Ariel's eyes flew wide as her body shuddered, electricity whipping from her clit through her bloodstream as pleasure nearly incapacitated her. The vibration of the sharp little swat sent pleasure racing through her cunt, clenched the muscles of her vagina, sent her clit into near orgasmic shudders before it faded away.

"There..." He watched her closely, his eyes narrowed, his chest heaving for breath. "We're not in a race. Enjoy..."

"Your ass..." She gasped for breath. "Do it again."

He stilled. She saw the look then, a heat so intense, so overwhelming that for just a moment she wondered if he would lose the control he was obviously exerting over himself.

"Again?" His voice was guttural now. Low, intense.

"Again." She was close. God, she was so close to...something.

He smiled then. A wicked, sensual smile that had her catching her breath in response.

He rubbed against the soft, damp curls, his fingers sliding through the slit, glancing her clit, then back down to dip enticingly into the narrow entrance of her pussy.

Ariel could hear her heart pounding, the blood rushing through her veins as he lifted his hand once again.

Oh, yes.

She needed this.

Her hips lifted beseechingly, her lips opening to drag in air as she watched his eyes narrow, anticipation tightening his own body as his cock throbbed against her leg.

A second, that's all it would take, another second...

Raised voices suddenly shattered the atmosphere as the sound of wood crashing inward galvanized Shane into action.

Before Ariel could do more than gasp in surprise, he was off the bed, tossing the comforter aside and jerking the swords from beneath the bed.

"Catch." He threw her weapon to her before she could even make sense of what was going on.

She caught it with a smooth, coordinated movement, the familiarity of which shocked her briefly, then came to her knees as the room suddenly filled with people. Silent, suddenly stock-still, amazed people.

The warriors from the night before were framed in the doorway, among them, the petite blonde who rode with the commander of whatever fighting force they thought they were. Shock rounded her eyes as her gaze went from the blade in Shane's hands then to the living sword between his thighs.

"Oh. My. God," Chantel breathed as Shane cursed, jerking the sheet from the bed as Ariel fought to hold the comforter to her breasts. "Devlin, he's going to split her in two."

Devlin's hand clapped over her mouth. He grimaced roughly as he silenced the woman, wincing at Shane's muttered curse as he stalked to the recessed doors between the two rooms.

"Sorry, Shane." Devlin cleared his throat, his lips twitching to hold back a grin. "Chantel felt Ariel was in…uhhh…distress…" The snickers behind him had Ariel's face flaming.

"Fix the fuckin' room door," Shane snapped, ignoring the information as he slammed the panels together between the two rooms.

He snapped the lock into place before laying his head against the panels and breathing in roughly.

"Well," Ariel breathed out with mocking patience, her sword falling to the bed as she shook her head in confusion. The fragmented memories had slowly dissipated, leaving her drifting in a mix of reality and illusion. "That was interesting anyway."

He turned back to her with a frown. Irritation lined his face, thinned his lips.

"And you come to this conclusion, how?" he growled.

She shrugged slowly, pushing the blanket aside as she crawled from the bed, pulling the ripped sides of the gown over her breasts.

"Well." She smiled back at him innocently as she moved to the clothes he had stacked on the small table at the side of the room. "It's not everyday a girl gets saved just before being split in two. I'll have to thank them. Do you think, maybe, it would be possible to find a less amply endowed warrior? We wouldn't want to hurt me, now would we?"

Her sharp mockery obviously struck just as she intended it to, if the narrowing of his eyes was anything to go by.

She swept into the bathroom before he could reply, but she didn't miss the echo of the curse that rang out behind her. Locking the bathroom door behind her, she breathed in furiously staring up at the ceiling and wondered just how the hell she was supposed to resist him now. More importantly, how had he managed to make her mind work against her? For a small moment in time, while held beneath his body, she had known him, and she had hungered. A hunger she couldn't resist.

Chapter Nine

ഇ

Ariel wasn't certain which was worse—facing Shane after the humiliating episode of having his entire group seeing her naked and nearly fucked, or facing the implications of who and what they could be.

She sat in the small living room section of the suite, after they fixed the door amid the yells and curses of the manager and handyman, watching the interactions between them all.

The one that fascinated her the most, made her the most uncomfortable, was the blonde who sat beside the commander of the group.

Devlin "Shadow" Hunter and his wife, Chantel, were obviously a perfect match. They fit each other, not so much in size, as he was much larger, but more in how well they seemed attuned to each other.

It was the crystal that hung around Chantel's neck that fascinated her most. She was the Earth Mistress. Ariel had known that the moment she walked from the bathroom, dressed in jeans and a T-shirt, and saw the other woman standing by the window, the gems within the crystal glowing eerily.

The central emerald and amethyst stones were brilliant. The sapphire and ruby less intense, but still bright. She knew then that the legends her grandmother had told her were true. That meant the evil she faced was worse than she could have ever imagined. It was true evil, dark and destructive.

To this warrior, whose heart and soul was most pure, the Earth Mother gifted to him, a most precious daughter...the Wind Mistress. The one who possessed and controlled the Wind Crystal.

Ariel possessed the Wind Crystal. But if Shane was the Savage legend told of, then he was... No. She wasn't even going to consider that. She couldn't consider that and stay sane. If Shane was indeed the Savage, then her own destiny was most likely entwined with his. A destiny dependent not just on her belief in the impossible, but her belief in the unrealistic.

"We don't have very many options left at this point." Devlin leaned forward as one of the others spread a map out on the table. "According to Chantel, the third crystal has to be in this vicinity." He pointed to a region of mountains in Washington State. "But, she can't connect with the crystal as she did with Ariel's." His black eyes locked onto Ariel's, holding her mesmerized for long seconds. "That will be your job."

She blinked in confusion. "That will be my job?" she questioned him, amazement thickening her voice. "You're kidding, right?" As she thought, impossible and unrealistic.

"No, he isn't." Chantel watched her quietly, the eerie green of her gaze making Ariel want to look away, yet unable to. "You have to know what the crystal is; otherwise you couldn't have called the elemental forces to you the night before. That means you can connect with the next crystal."

"Whoa! Hold up here!" She laughed incredulously, coming from her chair as she cast Shane a fulminating glance. He could have at least warned her that this was coming. "I didn't do anything. That storm was not my fault."

She didn't like the way they were watching her now. Chantel tilted her head thoughtfully as Devlin's eyes narrowed on her. The Irishman, who wasn't bad-looking, sighed wearily. And the crazy amber-eyed warrior smirked. Now that one she didn't like at all and she couldn't figure out why. Shane merely watched her quietly, keeping his expression clear, his opinion, thankfully, to himself.

"Ariel, you know better than that," Chantel finally replied quietly. Relaxed and calm, the woman just exuded confidence.

She wore her crystal outside her dark gray T-shirt, and Ariel couldn't keep from noticing how the emerald sphere in the center of it occasionally brightened. Like it was now. "There was no storm as you neared your home," she related then. "The sky was clear with no storm warnings. Yet, what happened when you realized Jonar's men were waiting on you?"

Ariel stepped back. "Freak storms happen all the time," she pointed out in a brittle voice.

"And when you were running for the motorcycles and Shanar realized they were following too close? He told you to order the winds to push them back. That they would obey your direction. You did that. Didn't you?"

What could she say? She cast Shane a look of silent retribution.

He spread his hands as though innocent, a smile tipping his hard lips.

"Loose lips can get you in a load of trouble, Shane," she sniped furiously as she propped her hands on her hips and faced him, outraged.

"I was wearing my comm link." He shrugged a little too innocently. "They could hear everything."

"Great," she muttered, remembering the helpless, yearning little sounds she had made when he held her against the tree, his lips consuming her, burning her alive with a need she had never known before.

"Ariel, you don't know how thankful we were to have found you," Chantel said then. "But surely even you realize the power you have at your fingertips? That power is more far-reaching than you know. And only you can connect with the next crystal. You have to do so before Jonar finds her first."

Ariel shivered at the thought of that.

"That's why he wanted me dead," she whispered. "For the crystal?"

"He couldn't kill you and take the crystal," she said then, her expression filled with pain. "You had to remove it yourself and give it to him. Don't you remember what happened to you in his fortress, Ariel?"

It was as though they were holding their breath, waiting on that answer.

"Not much." She shrugged. She figured she was better off not knowing. "I have a few nightmares sometimes, things that make no sense..."

She dropped her arms, shoving them in the pockets of her jeans as she paced away from the group. She didn't want to think about those nightmares. Didn't want to remember the darkness and pain, and the confusing shifts of reality and fantasy that had merged within her head.

"You know you controlled the elements last night, regardless," Chantel continued. "You are connected to the crystal and through it, to its sister stones, enough to draw on them for aid. If you can do that, you can find the next in the circle of four. You have no other choice. If we don't find her first, then Jonar could instead. Would you want her to suffer the same fate as you?"

She rounded on them furiously then. "Don't lay that on my shoulders," she snapped harshly. "I wasn't at fault for my own kidnapping and I'll be damned if I will accept fault for another's."

"You have the power." Chantel's voice never rose, but her eyes snapped with her own anger. "You have it and you deny it. Trust me, Ariel, you will learn one of these days that you cannot hide forever from what you don't want to face. It would not rest on your shoulders if you truly didn't have the power to reach her. But I know you do."

"Did you have the power to reach me?" she cried out. "Where the hell were you when Jonar was beating the life out of me?" Those nightmares she did remember. The pain vibrating through her, agonizing, hellish in its intensity as she hung suspended from a chain in the ceiling.

She remembered the cell, dirty and as dark as her father's closet, until Jonar opened the door. And she knew when that door opened that more pain was coming.

"I came to you when you called to me." Naked pain flashed across Chantel's face as she laid a hand on Devlin's chest to prevent the flash of fury in his expression from having voice. Ariel had a feeling she wouldn't have wanted to hear whatever was building behind that lethal black gaze. "I had no choice. And if you would face who and what you are, you would remember it."

"Enough. From both of you." Shane came to his feet then, staring down at Ariel fiercely when she would have said more. "Enough, Ariel," he repeated. "This will get us nowhere." He reached out and would have touched her cheek if she hadn't flinched away from him.

She had no desire to be touched by him or anyone else.

"I'm not hiding from anything," she told him furiously. "I don't know how that happened last night, Shane. I don't know what happened."

She needed him to believe her, even if none of the others did.

"She's no different than she was before." Dark, brutally cold, the amber-eyed warrior rose to his feet as Ariel stepped away from Shane.

He watched her with a smirk around those sensual, cruel lips, his long-lashed eyes cynical and chillingly insulting.

"What the hell do you mean by that?" she snapped, watching as the others rose as well.

"Just as I said, Mistress." Censure filled each word. "You denied your power the first time and hid behind your fears when it may have aided in saving others' lives. Now you do so again."

"Joshua, that's not true," Chantel snapped then. "Don't make this harder than it is."

"Isn't it?" He arched a brow mockingly, ignoring Shane's growled order that he cease. "I remember it well, Chantel. She hid in her room cleaning her sword when the Snake worshippers visited Arriane's room. And she hid even further after your death. Just as she will hide now. You go too easy on your sister, Chantel."

Ariel's gaze flew to Chantel's. She saw naked disgust and pain on the other woman's expression.

"As we all hid," she snapped. "At least we tried to find a way to ease Arriane's life from the misery you made of it. I'll hear no more of this. If you have recriminations, turn to yourself first, Mystic. I'll hear no more against her."

He opened his mouth to speak, but no words came out. He cast Devlin a furious stare as the other man stared back at him sardonically.

Joshua snarled, snapped his lips together and threw himself back in his chair. Thick, devil's-black hair flowed around him, creating an impression of... She drew in a deep, hard breath. A Mayan warrior. That was what he reminded her of.

"He comes to heel so charmingly." The Irishman chuckled then, his accent deep, throbbing with power. She felt that power now, on the very air around them, reaching toward her, flowing around her.

She stepped back quickly, surprised to find Shane there, his arms coming around her instantly. Derek watched her closely, the blue of his eyes intense, brilliant.

"Get him out of here," she whispered. "Get them all out of here. I've had enough."

"What's wrong?" he whispered, his lips at her ear. "Let me help you, Ariel. I'm behind you, as I will always be. Let me aid you in this."

Why couldn't he feel it? Why couldn't they all feel it? It was thick, pervasive, as though something were trying to sneak into her very soul. She stared back at the one called Derek, cautiously, wondering why no one else could sense the waves of power pushing at her. Or did they?

Her gaze went to Chantel. She could feel the power emanating from her, reaching out to her as the other woman's eyes watched her closely.

"Make him stop," she whispered bleakly. "Now."

Confusion filled Chantel's gaze. "What?" She leaned forward suspiciously. "What are you talking about, Ariel?"

She drew in a deep hard breath. No help there. There would be no help, because no one else could sense what she herself felt. Nothing unusual for a crazy person, she thought. Wasn't that what her father told her, each time he sensed the voices whispering on the air around her? That she was crazy?

"Ariel, what is going on?" Shane's voice was soft at her ear, though filled with strength. She could feel that strength inside her, allowing her to draw upon it to find the calm she needed amidst the whispers of warning, not truly words, but a hiss of danger at her ear.

She was aware of everyone watching her carefully. Everyone but Derek. His eyes were too brilliant, too cold…

She drew herself straight, edging away from Shanar, watching as Derek's eyes followed her. Did he have to see her to do whatever he was attempting to do? She thought perhaps not. She could sense him, probing at her, locking onto her unique aura, rather like a vampire, determined to suck her dry.

Her gaze swung to Devlin.

The leader commands all. The hiss slowly formed words, information needed as she fought against the tendrils of power attempting to force themselves into her mind.

"Make him stop!" she ordered Devlin harshly. "Now!"

He frowned heavily, turning his head to look at Derek. But Shane beat him to it. Before anyone knew what he intended, he was across the room, his fist clenched and plowing into the other man's face. Ariel watched in shock as Derek literally flew across the room to crash into the abused door on the other side.

"I warned both of you." He turned to Joshua, gray eyes snapping with fury, his voice so rough, so gravelly it was horrifying to hear. His expression was tight, cheekbones more pronounced, his sensual lips pulled into a snarl. "Use your powers where you will, except on my woman. You destroyed your own, I'll be damned if you'll destroy her."

Across the room, Derek eased to his knees, rubbing slowly at his jaw, shaking his head as though as addled as he well should be.

"Damn," he grunted, a look of disbelief quickly replaced by ire as he glared at Shane. "It was just a little probe."

"Damn all of you!" Chantel came to her feet again, fury flushing her face as her crystal began to glow dangerously. How Ariel knew that throbbing glow was a sign of forces no one wanted unleashed, she wasn't certain.

She turned to her husband, her fists clenched, nearly shaking with fury. "They're your stupid men, do something with them."

Her finger poked demandingly into Devlin's broad chest as she stood fiercely in front of him. Dressed in jeans, flat boots and a dark T-shirt, a black ball cap pulled over her head, she looked like an ill-dressed sprite challenging a dark warrior. But that dark warrior, dressed all in black, despite his fierce expression, looked upon her with a glimmer of emotion so intense it confused Ariel. Tenderness, an affection so intense it defied her understanding, and longing. In that moment she had no doubt that Chantel commanded that warrior as easily as he commanded his men.

Joshua rose to his feet then, shifting his shoulders as though the weight he carried on them was suddenly trying. He stared back at Ariel, compassion glittering only briefly in his eyes.

"The next crystal is worn by his wife, Ariel. And she, unlike you, has few defenses if Jonar snatches her. She must be found, quickly." His gaze went to Shane then. "You would have done no less."

"Wrong," Shane snapped. "I would have done no such thing. You cannot force what all of you want, and I'll rip the head off the next one of you who tries. Now get the hell out of here. We'll meet you outside on time, and head to the cabins as we agreed. But you will not force her. Not any of you. Try it again and you'll gain much more than a sore head."

He turned away from them in disgust then, stalking back to Ariel, his lips thinning as she stepped slowly away from him. She turned to Chantel instead.

"They remind me of the *Three Stooges*," she said clearly, crisply. "If this is what the next owner of the crystal has to look forward to, I say we find her ourselves and hide her. We'll be doing her no favors in letting him find her." She nodded to the one slowly rising to his feet, working his jaw carefully.

Chantel sighed. "Unfortunately, Ariel, I have to agree with you. And you have no idea how much it pains me to admit that."

Chapter Ten

ဢ

"The *Three Stooges*?" Shane bit out incredulously as the door closed behind the rest of the group and he faced her once again.

Six and a half feet of offended male pride watched her, his eyes stormy, his long mane of hair flowing around his face. "Do you think I don't know who they are? Woman, that was a low, dirty insult."

"But more than appropriate." She crossed her arms under her unbound breasts and faced him, just as angry now. "What the hell is with you guys? You're supposed to be a group. Working together. Teammates. Ya know?"

He pushed his fingers roughly through his hair, sighing wearily as he plopped down on the sofa and stared back at her in resignation.

"These are trying times for us all, Ariel." He grimaced. "Much is riding on finding the owners of those stones, such as yours. Not just our lives, but the fates of many. They are all that can defeat Jonar's madness."

So she had heard. Too long ago to really remember the exact legends and the warnings that went with them.

"What was he doing?" she finally asked him. "Couldn't you feel it?"

She had felt it. The bands of power wrapping around her head, attempting to find a way to sneak into her mind, to steal whatever it was he sought. It was insidious, disturbing and it damned well creeped her out. She didn't need anything creepier than what she was already facing.

"Not at first." He shook his head negatively. "I felt nothing until you moved. Then, as though you had displaced or displeased the air around you, I felt it pass by me. I know his powers, the gifts he was given. I knew instantly what he was doing."

"And that was?" She sat down slowly in the chair beside the couch.

Leaning forward, Shane braced his arms on his knees, turning his head to watch her closely.

"He is the Wizard. His powers are that of illusion and the art of stealing secrets. He is a thief of sorts…"

"A psychic vampire, in other words?" she snapped.

"Not as much so as Joshua, but yes, more or less" he agreed, frowning slowly. "I do not know what happened with his wife. Much was going on at that time. But from what I understand, for some reason, she turned from him after their marriage. Derek was devastated. So he stole her memories of whatever it was she held against him, and forced her to remember only the love she had first felt for him, instead. It…weakened her…" He shook his head as though bemused by all that had happened. "As I said, it was a long time ago. We do not know if she still suffers from this loss and its weakness, or if she remembers. Whichever it is, she is either in danger, or a danger to him herself. She must be found."

"When did this happen?" She asked the question that she knew she really didn't want to know the answer to.

Shanar paused, regret shimmering in his eyes. "This happened nearly a thousand years before, Ariel, as I'm certain you suspect."

She knew it! She didn't want to know.

"So…" She breathed roughly. "You remembered all this stuff? After you were reborn?"

His head lowered, a grimace twisting his lips as he shook his head, resigned. She wasn't going to like the answer.

"I and the other warriors never died, wife," he said then, spearing her with his eyes, trapping her in a truth she didn't want to know. "We have lived, knowing, regretting the death of each of you, every day of our existence. We never died, but unless we triumph now, it will be our curse to see your deaths once again."

Wife… The word echoed through her.

Ariel felt her lips part in shock. Though why she was shocked she wasn't certain. Somehow she had known, had remembered a vague tale of the warriors who walked time, who searched years everlasting. Immortal, her grandmother had told her. Always seeking. But she hadn't believed it. Not really. And she didn't want to believe it now.

"You know, I really think being crazy would have been a hell of a lot easier," she sighed as she leaned back in the chair and closed her eyes wearily. "I think I would have preferred it, actually. Just think, three meals a day, happy drugs, a life of ease and peace. It might be easy to get used to."

But she knew better.

He grunted, though his lips tilted in amusement.

"I cannot say I blame you. It is not an easy fight we are facing, nor is it one that can be called sane. But, it is our battle, and we must triumph." His gaze turned suddenly bleak. "You have no clue, Ariel, what awaits this world if we fail. It is because of this that everyone looks to you now for the answers. Just as they looked to Chantel before you."

"Oh, now that's just screwy enough," she grumped, leaning back and staring around the small suite in exasperation. "Shane, I am not having fun here."

Or was she? She should be screaming, freaking out, on the verge of a nervous collapse. Instead, she could feel the knowledge sinking into her, hear the whispers of truth on the air around her.

Beloved... Wife to the Savage... Mistress of the Wind... Soft as a breeze the words whispered around her, his voice, broken, filled with pain...

"You are merely denying the fun at hand," he pointed out then. "Just think of all the excitement you have faced in less than twenty-four hours. Admit it; at least you are no longer bored."

"Who said I was bored before?" She glared back, determined to ignore the little voices that shouldn't be whispering around her. "I had a perfectly nice life. I enjoyed my life. Boredom was the least of my problems."

A smile touched his lips. It was sexy, wicked. "You know you were bored," he chuckled. "Even I could feel your boredom, even if you did refuse to hear my calls to you. And I know you heard them, Ariel. You deny it, but you know they were there, whispering to you."

She swallowed tightly, suppressing the tears of helplessness that clogged her throat. Yes, she had heard them and she had ignored them, just as she ignored them now. "You're as crazy as the rest of them."

Amusement and joy glittered in his eyes. There was something about sparring with her that brought him pleasure, aroused him, made him hot. She didn't want to admit it, but it did no less to her.

"I am the sane one," he informed her archly, but that glitter in his eyes warned her that he could possibly be the most dangerous one of all.

Shaking her head, Ariel leaned forward, covering her face with her hands and breathed in deeply.

"I don't like this," she whispered then. "It's been hell, living with this, not knowing what it is or how to control it."

"And this is what we will fix for you," he promised her then, reaching out to her, touching her cheek with the pads of his fingers. "You will learn your power, Ariel." His voice hardened, his expression turning savage. "I will not lose you again. I will not ever watch you die in my arms, bloodied and whispering my name in pain, ever again."

Ariel felt the breath leave her chest for long seconds, felt her shock deepen at the ragged pain that filled his voice, and once again was reminded that Steele wasn't just his last name and Savage wasn't just a codename.

"And I won't be dictated to," she whispered just as painfully. "You won't control me, Shane. No man ever will." Her father had tried to control her, even as a child, and she would be damned if she would give into another's control now. "And neither will this power that I may or may not have. I'll help you and the others all I can, but I won't be forced into a role."

"You will learn your power," he fairly snarled. "No matter what I must do, Ariel, no matter what it takes, I will allow you to hide from it no longer. So be prepared, wife. This time, you will accept my claiming of you, just as you will accept who and what you were meant to be. You will accept it, or I just might end up paddling your ass as I should have a millennium ago. Now get ready to leave, we ride in an hour."

Chapter Eleven

ᵴᴑ

The summons to Devlin's room was made by psychic call. A demand that Shane clearly recognized after a thousand years. After leaving Ariel to finish getting ready, he made his way to the room across the hall, stepping into the suite to join the others gathered there.

"How is she handling it?" Chantel was the first to question him. Her emerald eyes were dark with worry and filled with concern.

Shane snorted. "As stubbornly as ever, but at least now she admits to what she hears in the air around her." Smug satisfaction filled him then. "She admits it enough that her crystal is able to share it. I could smell the evil of Jonar on the winds this past night and heard the presence of the whispers she hears around her. She is opening herself to the powers and this is what matters."

"What about Caitlin?" Derek stood on the other side of the room, his eyes dark with the thoughts of his wife.

"That has not yet come to her." Shane shook his head firmly. "And I tell you now, Derek, you attempt to steal into my wife's mind again and there will be nothing left of you for Caitlin to care if you live or die. I'll take you apart myself."

Derek's full, sensual lips lifted in a wry grin as he massaged his jaw.

"Aye, I have felt your determination to do just that, Savage," he grunted in amusement, then sobered. "But I warn you now. By the time we reach our destination, have you not learned of her location then all bets are off. I will know where she is, one way or the other."

Shane knew he could expect nothing else, no matter how it grated. For all his faults, Derek was a good man, and he had waited, perhaps not as faithfully as Shane had, but in as much torment, for the rebirth of his wife.

"We'll travel on the cycles," Devlin informed them all, stepping forward to ease the tension that filled the room. "It will place her directly within the winds, keep her in constant contact with it. Chantel will use her powers to amplify the call that Caitlin's crystal will send. We have five days before we reach Newhalem. Hopefully, we're going in the right direction, and if not, then Chantel will be able to at least detect that much if we are off course."

"We won't go off course," Chantel spoke up then, her voice crisp and filled with her own knowledge. "I've been able to track the power coming from her that far. The storm last night held more information than I could have hoped for. For the time the rain fell, I was able to sense her, and to assure myself of her general location. But only Ariel can connect with her and bring her out of hiding. Until she does, we're helpless."

"Why would she hide if she knows she's needed?" Shane questioned her roughly. "Surely she would know her legacy if she is deliberately hiding from us?"

Chantel shook her head at that. "It could be unconscious, the help she's given Ariel so far. We can't be certain. I don't sense her except during the few times she's reached out to obey the command for help that Ariel's crystal sent out. She may not know anything. Or she may know everything. I won't know until we get closer or until Ariel connects with her."

"Ariel's a strong woman." Joshua spoke then, surprising them all, his voice dark, pitched low.

Shane turned to him questioningly, wondering at the strange note in his voice.

His eyes were eerie; there was no other word for it. The amber color wasn't so much brilliant as it was deep, swirling with the color as power moved inside him. Joshua was always the strangest of the warriors, and Shane often wondered at that otherworld appearance he sometimes had. If he did not know better, he would swear the other man was Guardian.

"She fears the dark," he said softly, dangerously. "Being locked away in it for answering the wind, for acknowledging who and what she is. Her mother and her grandmother before her lost the fight to prove their sanity. Ariel is determined she will not lose."

Shane clenched his fists at his sides, fury moving through him. The bastard who raised her had much to answer for.

"Is she Galen's blood?" He looked to Chantel, knowing that the crystals had first been bound to blood alone.

Galen had sired the four girls in that first life, as well as Chantel in this life. It was suspected, based on the investigations into Ariel and her parent's pasts, that he may well have fathered Ariel in this life as well.

"She's Galen's child," she sighed. "Though she is unaware of this. Galen is in Boston now working to prove paternity and to break the hold St. James has on her. Let's hope he accomplishes this before her father convinces the judge in Lexington to sign the papers requiring an evaluation based on her experiences at Jonar's hands. Her hysteria in the hospital won't help her."

"I told you she should not have been sent back alone," Shane snarled, remembering well the report he had read in the plane.

Weak, in pain, Ariel had awakened believing she was on that battlefield where she had died in that first life. She had seen her blood, had watched Shanar become mist as the Guardians stole him away, and had raged at the Fates, Destiny and Mother Earth. She had believed the orderlies and nurses to be Jonar's warriors and nearly injured herself further attempting to escape them.

"There was no other choice, Shane," Devlin reminded him bleakly, staring back at him compassionately. "You have her now. You can heal her. If you can break past her reserve."

"I shall do more than break past it," he assured his commander confidently. "I will destroy it. I will not allow her to hide from me any longer, I promise you this."

"Excellent," Devlin nodded. "We'll meet in the parking lot within the hour. Kanna left at daybreak for our next stop, just this side of Kansas City. She'll meet us there with supplies and more clothing for Ariel. Until then, she managed to purchase the leathers she needs for now." He nodded to the clothing Joshua lifted from the desk beside him. "Get her dressed and let's roll. No helmets. No hiding. You'll ride between the rest of us to afford her protection in case of accidents or attacks by Jonar. Though I doubt he can secure the power to attack in daylight."

Shane took the leather, his cock swelling, hardening at the thought of seeing his woman once again in the clothing that had shown her lithe body to advantage. He accepted the soft doeskin, specially prepared for her once Kanna had managed to track down her measurements. His hands smoothed over it, imagining her behind him, pressed close on the Harley that had replaced the super-fast ZX10 from the night before.

"We might meet within the hour," Derek drawled in amusement. "As hard as our Viking's getting over there, we might not head out until next week."

A smile creased Shane's face at the thought of that.

"I could only get so lucky this day," he finally snorted, knowing well that Ariel would lead him a fine chase. He was looking forward to it. Anticipating it. "We will be there," he finally promised as Devlin watched him suspiciously. "This ride, I would not miss for the world."

Chapter Twelve

ക

"So why don't I have my own motorcycle?" Ariel paused beside Shane as he led her to the monster machine rather than the sleek speed demon they had ridden the night before.

Dressed in the softest leather she had ever felt in her life, she felt a confidence that she knew could well knock her on her ass. Her dagger was strapped to her thigh, her sword placed inside the flat scabbard that ran down the side of the motorcycle. She had never seen anything like it. On each side of the powerful black cherry pearl machine were slender, hard plastic scabbards that locked each sword into place. In the metal saddlebags were extra clothes and daggers, and several high-powered pistols.

"Aren't you guys a little over-prepared here?" she asked him cautiously as he placed her dagger in along with his and locked the lid in place.

"Not hardly," he grunted as he pushed her hair aside and attached a small receiver and mic to her ear. "This is your comm link. It's set to private communications with mine, or you can press the button on the earpiece and you'll be in a shared link with the group if needed. We'll ride during the daylight hours with stops in between to eat and rest, but we need to make our destination within five days. We'll stop outside Kansas City tonight to rest."

"What about helmets?" She didn't see any and no one else was wearing them.

He gave her a horrified look. "What good is immortality if you can't throw away the helmets?"

Her eyes widened. "Listen, Bub, I'm not immortal. I need a helmet. Thank you very much."

He grinned slowly, his gaze once again going over the lace-up vest that was only just barely decent. She loved it.

"From the moment I found you in that storm, Ariel, your life was assured for this time. Only Jonar and the technology he possesses can kill you now. That crystal and the winds you command will ensure that."

"Yeah. Right," she snapped out sarcastically. "Just what I need now. Immortality. Plenty of time to be tortured. How pleasant."

"Or plenty of time to be pleasured." His large hand cupped her hip, pulling her close to his big body, so big and hard that it made her breath catch in her throat as his head lowered, making her feel enfolded, protected. "When this is done, Ariel, I will show you how special immortality can be. The many, many hours spent learning all we do not know about touching, stroking, hearing your screams echo around me in pleasure."

Her breasts swelled, her nipples hardening and poking into the soft leather encasing them. She could feel her pussy clenching, aching, sweet moisture dampening the inner lips where the butter-soft leather caressed them. Her breathing altered, increased, blood rushed through her veins.

"You'll be lucky if I don't castrate you first," she snarled weakly. "Imagine that one. Eternity without, Shane. That would suck."

His eyes narrowed thoughtfully. "It would be best not to say 'suck' in my presence," was his only retort. "It's been a long time, sweet wife, and the fantasies have been many."

He turned away before she could reply and straddled the powerful machine before glancing back at her. "Mount up, sweet thing," he drawled wickedly. "Time to ride."

The motor flared to life, hard, pulsing, a masculine growl of power that somehow suited him.

"Just what I need," she muttered. "A horny immortal with delusions of pleasure. Just my luck."

She settled into the seat, her legs straddling his wider body, the position not lost on her by a long shot. The backrest wrapped around her securely, holding her in place as they moved out.

"You know, I need to call home soon." She tested the mic that lay against her cheek. "My partner will worry."

"We've taken care of that." The smooth rumble of his voice sent shivers of pleasure down her spine. "Your partner and attorneys are aware that you are now in hiding with your security force until this matter can be taken of."

Her hands gripped his waist, though with her snug balance and the comfort of the backrest she knew there was no need. It felt good though. Secure.

Find her. She's crazy... Ariel flinched. Was it memory or words she heard in the wind? How many times had her father accused her of insanity, threatening to have her locked up, put away and kept safe from herself?

She has the dagger... A voice so frightening, so filled with evil that Ariel only wanted to hide from it.

I won't be found... Soft, musical, filled with bitterness, the unknown voice was a wisp of sound past her ears.

I must be found... Another stark with pain, her voice thick with tears.

And it continued. Words that made no sense, others that would have terrified her if she allowed herself to believe in them. She tried to stop, to hide her head against Shane's back, to keep the wind from brushing past her head, but nothing seemed to stop the steady flow of sounds that came to her, barely heard, yet there all the same. Like ghostly voices, snatches of conversation, and with them, brief flashes of memory that she knew could not be her own.

She had awakened like that in the hospital. Convinced she was someone else. Somewhere else. She had seen blood, watched a man — tall, strong — disappearing before her eyes.

"No... Don't leave me..." she had screamed out madly. "No...not in the dark, Savage...not alone..." And the darkness had tried to swallow her. A forever darkness that she knew she would never escape from.

The psychiatrists had arrived the next day. A week in evaluations that she had only just managed to pass. Weak, in pain, knowing that her father would use any excuse to institutionalize her, Ariel had fought every instinct inside her to ignore the voices that drifted in the air around her.

She had slept lightly, secretly disposed of the sleeping aids she had been given and fought the betraying weakness of her own body. And she had prayed. Nearly unconscious, battered, terrified of dying, yet even more frightened of what could await her if she lived and her father won, she had fought the power building inside her.

Weeks later her attorneys had finally prevailed and the security force they had hired had carried her from the care her father had set up and taken her home. If only that had ended her problems.

Ariel...

The wizard's tears...

I will not be found...

We must have that dagger...

Insane... She's crazy...

Find her...or kill her...

It was never-ending, just as always. It made no sense, and she was certain she didn't want it to.

"Are you okay?" Shane's voice came to her through the comm link, gentle, filled with strength as she rested against his back.

"Just tired." She didn't know how long they had been on the road, but she knew it was well past noon.

"We'll rest soon," he promised her, his voice inordinately gentle as he reached back to wrap his hand around her leg for a long moment.

That touch, strong and secure, filled her. Why it mattered, she wasn't sure, but it gave her the strength she needed to go on. Just as she had always done, with voices, pleas and gasping cries echoing around her, she continued on...

Chapter Thirteen

ဢ

It was well after dark before Ariel found herself showered and well-fed, lying limply on her stomach across the king-sized bed in yet another expensive motel. This time, Kanna had a damned banquet set up in their room. Trays of fruit, hot roast and potatoes, freshly baked bread and a variety of side dishes.

Shane, of course, ate the better part of the meal with a gusto that amazed her. After eating, he had been kind enough to give her the shower first as he tossed her another gown. She remembered the tatters the first had been left in and fled to the bathroom before he could comment.

Now, she drifted sleepily, almost content, as the bed cushioned her weary body. If it wasn't for the arousal that still pulsed inside her, she could have slept. It was irritating, and if she wasn't exhausted it would have been terrifying. But it wasn't going away.

Her breasts were swollen and sensitive, the flesh between her thighs aching and wet despite the fact she had spent several minutes drying it after her shower. Even the light coating of talcum powder she used hadn't helped. And Shane wasn't making things easier.

He had taken every opportunity to touch her, to have her touch him, refusing to allow her to space herself away from him.

"You need to let me massage your thighs for you," he spoke from behind her, his voice rough, heavy with sensuality. "You'll be sore otherwise."

Her thighs clenched in anticipation.

"No thanks, I'm fine." Her weary body protested that statement almost violently.

"You won't be able to walk tomorrow without it," he warned her, sitting down on the bed by her feet, one large hand circling her ankle. "Come on, I promise you'll like it."

She would like it too much.

"Go bother someone else," she muttered. "I just want to sleep."

She had to bite her lip as that strong hand began to knead her lower leg.

"I have a special salve, just for sore muscles," he said absently as he continued to massage her. "It will make you more relaxed, your muscles better able to endure the long ride."

If she got any more relaxed she was going to rape him, she thought violently, shivering as his thumb pressed against the tight muscle and rubbed soothingly.

"Come on, Ariel. You aren't really afraid you can't resist me, are you?" Smooth and blatantly amused, his whisper had her stiffening at the challenge.

"I can resist you fine," she snapped, though she was too tired to give it much heat. "I don't need a massage." Then she betrayed herself with the minute whimper that escaped her lips as he continued to work her calf muscle.

"Don't need one, huh?"

She sighed in regret when he stopped and moved away from her.

A part of her was screaming at her for being so aloof, for not rolling over, opening her thighs and demanding that he attend to the ache he was building, touch by touch, between them.

Her cunt was weeping, moist and slick, hot and aching.

"Here we go." His hands brushed aside the gown that lay to her ankles a second before his hands smoothed from her ankle to her knee, spreading a cooling, silky emollient over her skin. "Alyx gave me the salve. He said it would help your muscles after being confined to bed for so long."

Alyx. That damned alien, she thought hazily before her mind snapped in gear and a frown crossed her brow. It eased away as Shane continued to massage her lower leg, drawing a low, pleasured moan from her throat.

"That's illegal," she mumbled. "It feels too good."

He chuckled. "Not near as good as it could feel," he answered wickedly before moving to the other leg and creating magic there.

She drifted in a haze of relaxation, her muscles slowly loosening beneath the cool wash of the salve, only to warm pleasurably moments later. She drifted on a cloud of contentment that was marred only by the slow, intense ache centered in her pussy.

"Your skin is so soft," his voice sounded strangled as his hands moved slowly beneath the gown, one on each leg, his thumbs pressing into her skin smoothing the salve onto muscles that ached in exhaustion. "Perfect, silky skin. I have long remembered how soft your flesh was, Ariel."

Her lower stomach clenched, her womb convulsing as his fingers pushed higher, closer to the pulsing center of her body. Warmth gathered like hot syrup between her legs, spilling slowly from her vagina as it wept in need for his touch.

"I can smell your heat." The gown inched up further, pushing to her upper thighs as his hands continued to massage her flesh with wicked strokes. "Sweet and warm, beckoning me to taste."

She couldn't stop the small cry in response. It spilled from her lips as her thighs parted at his urging. The air around her throbbed with lust, scented with the smell of Shane. A hot, aroused, fully ready to fuck her into oblivion, Shane.

"God, Ariel." His voice was thick with hunger as her gown moved further up her thighs, finally stopping just above the rounded curve of her buttocks.

She was bare to him now. She should fight, she should push him away, demand he stop, but she couldn't. She was enthralled, held in a grip of anticipation and need unlike anything she could have imagined.

"You're wet for me." His voice was so deep, so rough, it was guttural. "I can see it Ariel, glistening on your sweet pussy, thick and heavy with your need."

She shuddered with arousal, her thighs clenching beneath his hands as he notched them further apart. Then his hands were smoothing up her back, pushing her gown ahead of them until they met her neck. The loose neckline cleared her head and she bit her lip against the tremulous cry that would have escaped as his hand urged her to her back.

Dear God, if she had the strength to say no to him before, it fled then. He stared at her, his eyes such a dark gray they were nearly black, his expression so hungry, so drowsily intent that it left her trembling.

He pulled the gown from her arms, dropping it to the side of the bed before his gaze consumed her body. Her swollen, hard-tipped breasts, her stomach, between her legs. His gaze was almost a physical caress as one hand tucked between her thighs, pulling them further apart, his eyes devouring her.

"Do you ever pleasure yourself?" he whispered then, shocking her.

"What?" Her eyes rounded as his hand cupped her inner thigh. His gaze came back to her, heavy-lidded, starkly male and filled with such a dark sensuality it nearly took her breath.

"Pleasure yourself," he whispered again. "Have you ever done this?"

She swallowed tightly. "What does it matter?"

His eyes narrowed, darkened, his nostrils flaring savagely.

"Did it feel good?" he whispered thickly. "When you touched yourself, did you enjoy it? Did you find your release with it?"

She was shaking, held in the grip of an eroticism she couldn't explain or fight.

"None of your business..." she gasped as his fingers moved higher, his warmth barely feathering the wet curls that lay there.

"I would know," he whispered, his voice low but so rough it was nearly painful to hear. "I would see you do it now, if you have. I would have you show me your pleasure."

Her hands clenched where they lay above her head. She was not going to do this.

"You're crazy," she gasped. "Just do it and be done with it, before I ache to death."

A smile, rueful and sexy, crossed his lips.

"I will not rush this," he denied her command. "I would treasure it. Make it last. Gorge myself on every sweet cry from your lips, every erotic passage we can make together. This I have fantasized about for so long. Longer than you can know. Seeing you abandoned in your pleasure, seeing those things that you know bring you pleasure."

His voice cut through her shame, her embarrassment. It washed over her soul, and left her gasping at the brutal hunger in his voice.

"Pervert," she accused him roughly.

"Aye," he agreed with a sensual quirk of his lips. "In ways you can never guess. Do this for me, Ariel. Allow me to see your pleasure, to see you before me, wet and wild. Tempt me to take you."

Her gaze flickered from his face to the erection pressing tight beneath the lacings of his leather pants. It was thick and hard, pressing so tight against the soft leather pants that she could see the imprint of the thickly flared head.

Tempt me to take you. The words pulsed around her as his hands went to the laces of his pants. He released them slowly, loosening them until the material parted and she could glimpse the hard stalk of his cock rising from between his thighs.

Slowly, he eased her thighs further apart before moving between, his legs spreading her further as he watched her.

"Touch your lips," he urged her roughly. "Think of my kiss, of how hot and hungry we become when we kiss."

"Just kiss me," she moaned, clenching her fists tighter to keep from doing as he asked.

It was too erotic, too sexual. But she wanted to. She wanted to watch his face as she did as asked, see if his eyes could get darker, hotter.

"Not yet," he whispered. "This time is for you. So I can see what brings you pleasure. See with your hands how you wish to be touched. Do this, Ariel. Touch your lips."

Her hands uncurled. Just her lips, she assured herself. She would touch only her lips.

She watched him, dazed, her body on fire as her fingers moved to her lips. She touched two to her lips, her tongue peeking out to dampen them, to ease their movements along the warm curves. His eyes narrowed, his broad chest rising and falling harshly now as his hands flexed on her thighs.

What was he seeing? she wondered, as her fingers caressed her lips, feeling the swollen, passion-filled curves. They were plumper than they should have been, ready, prepared for his kiss.

"I love kissing you," he whispered. "Feeling you move against me, growing hungry, devouring my passion as I consume yours."

Oh God. This wasn't fair. His voice was thick, his face flushed and heavy with sensuality as his eyes followed her fingers.

"Suck them into your mouth," he groaned. "Let me see your lips wrapped around them."

His hands were flexing on her thighs, his fingers stiff, taut with the effort it took not to dig into her flesh.

Her lips opened slowly, her tongue pushing beneath her fingers as she pressed them into her mouth. Closing over them, she watched him as she suckled at them, her breathing harsh as she imagined his cock pushing into her mouth, the hunger she would know as she tasted his lust.

"Sweet Heaven," he groaned, his hands moving, lifting her thighs as his legs spread further apart, laying hers against them. "Would you take my cock as sweetly, Ariel? Open your lips for me so hungrily?"

She would. She would do it now if he gave her the chance, she was so hot for it. What the hell was he doing to her?

"Use your other hand," he breathed roughly. "Cup your breast. Let me see you pleasure your breasts."

There was no hesitation. Her fingers cupped the swollen curve, her finger and thumb gripping the hard nipple as she rasped it roughly. Her hips jerked convulsively as he grimaced tightly, baring his teeth in the effort to hold onto his control.

"Yes," he hissed as the pleasure flooded her. "Show me what you like, love. Show me how to take you."

She needed no further urging.

Her fingers left her lips, the wet tips painting a trail of fire down her neck to the other breast as the hand cupping the opposite curve began to stroke along her upper stomach, her abdomen, moving ever closer to her throbbing clit.

She was so close, closer than she had ever been before. The heat was whipping through her body and she wanted nothing more than to feel the tremors of release that she knew would quake through her body.

"God yes," he groaned as her fingers neared the throbbing flesh of her cunt. "Touch your sweet pussy, Ariel. Show me your pleasure."

She was so wet. She arched closer as her fingers slid into the narrow slit, running along the crease between the plump lips until she touched the aching opening to her vagina. She circled it slowly, her finger dipping in, feeling the fiery heat of her own lust.

Her juices coated her fingers as she opened herself to him, two fingers parting the flesh as the third stroked it tremulously.

He was panting now, his breath sawing in and out of his chest as his eyes followed every movement, his tongue licking his lips in hunger as he watched.

"Touch your clit," he growled. "It's so swollen, baby, I can nearly see it throbbing with the need to feel your touch. Touch it for me, Ariel."

She was going to come so hard it was going to take her head off, she thought distantly as she followed his command. Her fingers stroked around the sensitive knot of nerves, explosions of sensation shuddering through her body as she found the spot, just to the side of her clit, that she knew would trigger her climax. Heat built in her body, pleasure lashing at every nerve as she began a tight, circular rhythm guaranteed to send her head spinning.

"I'm going to fuck you so hard," he whispered as her eyes nearly closed, her heart racing as the sensations increased. "And you will watch. You will watch as my cock parts those pretty pussy lips, opens you to my penetration and pushes inside. You will see as it pulls back, your juices covering my flesh, clinging to me as they now cling to your fingers. Come for me, Ariel." Gravelly, deep, his voice was so rough it was an added rasp of pleasure against nerve endings already sensitive past endurance.

She felt her womb convulse at his threat, more of her juices spilled from her cunt and a second later, her fingers stroked her clit to an explosive release.

"Oh God..." Her throttled scream echoed around her as she shuddered, jerking in the grip of an orgasm she had never achieved at any other time.

As he watched, his intent to take her any second clear on his face, her fingers lifted to her lips, her tongue snaking out to lick at them erotically as she watched his control shatter.

Before she could do more than gasp, he pushed her fingers aside and took her juice-covered lips like a man starved for a woman's taste. His hands were tearing at his pants, pushing at them, desperate to free his cock as hers lowered to help him.

She was so damned hot she was ready to scream for his possession as his tongue plunged past her lips, thrusting between them, creating a heat so fiery, so intense she feared she would burn alive within it.

Then the world shook around her. Ariel's eyes flew open as she felt it, heard it. That wasn't just her, was it?

It wasn't. It happened again, a blast of energy a second before the building felt as though it were rocking on its foundation.

Shanar's head jerked up, at first in confusion until he heard the screams outside, then livid in fury.

"I'll kill the fucker!" he snarled as he jumped from the bed and hurriedly retied his pants before bending to jerk his sheathed sword from beneath the bed as he threw her gown to her. Slinging the strap to the hard scabbard over his head to rest across his bare chest, he yelled, "It's Jonar. Get dressed now and prepare to fight."

Chapter Fourteen

𝕊𝕆

Prepare to fight. What?

Minutes later Ariel stood outside the motel staring into the black velvet sky as the motel rocked once again.

"Earthquake," one woman wailed in fear. "This was why I left California. They're following me."

The earth rocked beneath Ariel's feet, but the tremors weren't originating in the ground beneath her. She stared around the crowded parking lot, her sword lying along her back, her dagger strapped to her thigh.

She could feel Shane, caught his scent on the breeze as he searched for Jonar. But Jonar wasn't here.

She lifted her head, drawing in the scents around her. There was no taint of blood and death, only a whiff of power. Her eyes narrowed as she turned, following the direction of the winds as they tugged at her.

"Find them," she murmured, a compulsion she couldn't ignore. "Seek the destroyers."

She felt the air around her thicken, ripple with power. There were no whipping winds, and a second later she saw why. As she stared into the sky around her, focusing in the direction of one of the warehouses across the block, she saw it. Like a shimmer in the air, a force building, tunneling through the air until it blasted into the motel.

"Shane, what kind of technology do these bastards have?" she asked, amazed at the calm that seeped through her as she watched the destructive waves slam into the building.

"We're not certain. We destroy what we can find, but we've never had a chance to truly observe or experiment with any of it. Each time we manage to save a piece, the Guardians claim it."

She tilted her head, her eyes glued to the dissolving force in the air above her head.

"They're directly across the block from me," she told him then, knowing that he and the warriors were on the opposite side. "They're aiming some sort of power at the room we were in."

She slid her sword free of the scabbard at her back, aware that no one seemed to realize she had done so. Too frightened? Too focused on what they believed was an earthquake?

"No way." Joshua finally spoke through the link. "I could feel it if that were true."

Ariel shrugged as though he were there watching her, making her way carefully from the perimeter of the parking lot, across the street and toward the three-story warehouse.

"I see it," she kept her voice calm, still.

"Where?"

"Watch the air above us." She kept her eyes in the direction she knew it would begin. "Toward the tallest building on the next block..." She waited, watching until the air began to ripple, the hazy effect of the disturbance building. "See it?"

She picked up her pace, certain of the location now. The top floor and a broken window. The lights from the streetlamps were dim, the outer buildings casting long shadows that she used to hide within.

"Where are you, Ariel?" Shanar snapped then. "Stay within the perimeters of the motel."

"They're building in power." She gripped her sword tighter as she made her way to the small side door of the building. "They'll bring the building down this way and God only knows who will be hurt."

"Better them than you." He snarled through the communications device. "Do not enter that building, Ariel."

"Too late," she murmured, uncertain where she was finding her courage. "Don't worry, Savage, I trust you to get here in time."

The words came easily from her lips, the trust flowing through her mind. She could feel her own amusement, her familiarity with him in a way she couldn't believe possible. She could see his expression, eyes narrowed, anger flashing in his strange gray eyes.

She heard him curse and let a smile cross her lips as she moved along the wall, her gaze narrowed against the darkness. She could feel the air around her pulsing with tension, buffering her against whatever evil resided within the walls. Shadows moved to aid her, a small, almost undetectable breeze pushing her in the direction she needed to go.

The winds will aid you. Give them their due. Whisper to them your commands.

"Ariel, command the air around you for protection," Chantel's voice was calm through the link. "We'll be there within minutes, but you can expect at least a small force of his men."

The warriors were quiet for the most part, though Ariel was aware of the sounds of them running, muttered curses and even a snarl of rage.

Breathing in deep, she felt the crystal throbbing, heated and demanding where it rested beneath the snug vest.

Two voices, one in the air, the other at her ear.

"Surround me," she whispered, allowing the tension curling in the pit of her stomach to rise and encompass her. "Protect me. My life is yours…"

Her eyes widened as she felt something unfurl around her. As though the air itself was a physical force, a shield that encompassed her body. Shaking her head, she fought the voice in her head, her father's voice, sneering, assuring her that only madness would be found within her mind.

She wasn't mad.

She balanced the sword in her hand, feeling it. A trusted weapon. She could feel a knowledge shifting within her mind, glimpses of memory that she knew couldn't be possible, yet she recognized was surely a part of her. She had battled before. She knew her enemy. She knew herself.

Over the past days, the fragmented memories had become as familiar to her as Shane was. The better part of those memories was the knowledge of battle. She had trained in that first life, trained hard and with a determination only exceeded by her hatred and desire for vengeance against Jonar. A vengeance she would have now as well.

She moved lightly up the stairs, pacing each step, controlling her breathing as she worked her way to the third floor. She wouldn't have much time. The foundations of the three-story motel had shuddered with the last blast of energy. Soon, it would fall.

"We haven't seen the bitch. Surely she would have shown herself by now," a rough voice echoed along the empty top floor. She ducked and moved to a nearby support column.

"She's in the crowd. She won't leave the area. She doesn't know her power yet."

"But she's with the warriors. That Earth whore will tell her the powers she may have."

"It won't matter. I remember her well. She despised the power and she does so now. Her father did his job well. She believes herself insane."

Ariel smiled. A cold, hard curl of her lips as she moved to the next post.

She could see the machine now. A thick, dull-colored barrel with a wide, serpent head-shaped end and balanced on a triangular, adjustable base. It moved easily as the operator placed his eyes at the sights, a large rectangle that glowed with the image of the motel.

"She's not there, I tell you. Your source was wrong."

"My source is excellent," the other growled. "If you cannot find her, blast the building again. The warriors are there, we just have to flush them out."

The operator's hand moved to the side of the display, gripping the controls and preparing to fire.

There was no longer any time to wait. Ariel felt the force of that knowledge rage through her mind, her body. Without thought she moved into that part of her mind that she knew held the power and the strength.

The sword came above her head swiftly, descending with a soft whoosh and slicing through the hand that gripped the controls. Whirling, she brought the weapon in an arc at her side before sending it slicing through the slender tentacles that led from the barrel to the base of the weapon they were using.

"Whore!" The leader screamed, coming back at her with his own blade. "Do you think us alone here?"

No, she hadn't and it was a damned good thing she was prepared, she thought, as she jumped back, placing enough distance between them to avoid the figures that moved from the sides of the cavernous room.

"Aww, it was a party," she sneered sweetly. "You should have invited me sooner. I would have brought gifts."

The link crackled at her ear.

"Get the fuck out of there, Ariel," Shanar screamed.

She faced the enemy, knowing there was no place left to run. She would have to fight her way free.

...yours to command...command the winds...

How? She could feel the protection like a thick layer of power that lay over her flesh, but she had no idea how to command more. And there was no time to figure it out.

She jumped back as swords converged on her.

"I like guns." She met the first with a clash of steel. "Why can't we use guns?"

Surprise registered in the inhuman eyes that glowed back from a demon's face.

"Stupid bitch," he snarled. "No gun can harm us."

"Oh yeah. Right." She jumped back behind a column, wincing as his sword tore chunks of cement and plaster from its side. "I should have known that."

She ducked and slid to the side as two others rushed her, their swords whipping in the air above their heads.

Command them…

Use your power…

…They are your protection…

"Goddammit, get out of my head," she yelled as she deflected another blow, sparks striking from her sword as she kept the blade from slicing her in two.

There were too many. No matter where she moved or how she ducked there was another to hold back. Snarling in rage she kicked out at the nearest one, catching him between his thighs as he squalled out with a high-pitched girlish sound she loved. Before he could move to protect his vulnerable balls, her sword sank into his chest, directly through his heart.

"Bastard! Give me my sword back!" She jerked at the weapon as he gripped the blade with his hands.

She grimaced at the gurgling sound he made as she pulled it free of his body and turned to meet another. They were out for blood, but so was she. They would have killed innocent people to reach her. Women, children, mothers and fathers, it made no difference to them.

"You want me so bad, here I am," she laughed as another took a swipe at her head but only barely missed one of his buddies as she threw herself across the floor.

She ripped the dagger from the sheath at her thigh, and now doubly armed, she waded into the fray.

"We're on the stairs, Ariel," Shane screamed in her ear. "Stay clear, damn you. Don't you fucking jump in the middle of it, woman."

"Too late, Savage," she laughed, the dagger burying itself in a vulnerable back a second before she placed her foot on the stiff, dying warrior's ass and pushed him free of the blade directly in line with another sword that sank through his chest.

Curses raged through the darkness, eyes glowed red, and Ariel felt an energy, an exhilaration she could never describe. It whipped through her veins, rushed through her head and sent her spinning in delight as she met another of the enemy. She was alive. Pulsing, filled with power, her very flesh electrified with the surging forces raging around her.

"Come to me..." She screamed at the winds then, feeling the enemy gaining ground, moving closer. "Come to me... Destroy my enemy..."

Voices were screaming in her ear, around her head, lightning snapped and exploded in the night beyond the warehouse as the winds began to storm, shattering windows, whipping through the warehouse with tornado force as the elements gained in fury.

Lightning arced and sizzled around the huge weapon that would have killed dozens, shattering the base, splitting the barrel. Bolt after bolt aimed through windows jagged now with glass, tearing through the bodies of Jonar's men as the winds ripped them from their feet.

Clashing forces raged in the air as the warriors joined the elemental battle whipping around her.

Voices raged in the winds that surrounded Ariel then, isolating her, protecting her from the battle. Her arms raised, her sword held high as she gripped the dagger with her opposite hand. Eyes closed, her lips parted in wonder she let out a war cry that hadn't been heard for a thousand years and with a leap, sliced an enemy in two that would have charged Shanar's back.

Like a fairy, an elemental ballerina, she danced with the wind and in all her glory became the warrior that only the Earth Mother could have envisioned.

Chapter Fifteen

❧

"Woman! You are insane…"

When the battle was done, death and carnage from the enraged warriors and the forces of the Earth lay around them as they fought for breath and stared back at Ariel.

She was like a luminous light, smiling in excitement, her amethyst eyes shining with power as she slid her sword and dagger quickly into their sheaths with a twist of her wrists.

"My God! That was so incredible." She was almost bouncing with energy as she stared at the slowly disintegrating bodies of the enemy. "How the hell do they do that? Just go away?"

Within minutes the soft breeze dispersed the dark, powdery remnants.

"Ashes to ashes, dust to dust," Chantel said sadly as the last body disappeared. "The Guardians managed to steal the blaster, Devlin." She nodded to where the weapon had sat.

Like the bodies, it was gone as well, but there was no ash or dust to mark its passing. Only a charring of the floor where it had once sat.

"Not that Ariel left much of it," Joshua growled as he stalked over to the window, his long, black hair whipping around his body. "How do you control the lightning as well? Only the Mistress of Fire was said to know that secret."

Shane heard the anger pulsing just under his voice, dark and deadly as he stared back at Ariel. He could see the fury that beat in the air around the other man, a threat, a danger to whoever had caused it.

Ariel laughed, a low, sarcastic sound that had Joshua's shoulders tensing.

"I controlled the wind, nothing more, big boy. Anything else that joined in wasn't of my doing."

He watched her head tilt as though to catch the slight sound on the breeze. For a moment, just a moment, he sensed that sound. A voice thick with pain, filled with warning.

Shane moved to Ariel then, desperate to touch her now, to make certain no harm had befallen her.

"Did you see me?" She nearly jumped in his arms, surprising him as he caught her, pulling her against his body as her knees gripped his hips, her hands on his shoulders, her head tipped back as excitement spilled over from her. "Did you see me, Shane? I wasn't crazy. They did what I told them to do. They destroyed my enemy. They did it."

She was burning bright and hot. He could feel it inside her. The clash of who she had been and who she was now. It merged in her eyes, shadows of knowledge, but not clear memory, and he thanked God for that.

He couldn't answer her. The emotion sweeping through him then was too intense, too filled with needs and desires he had never known. He had not seen Ariel fight like that, even when her own life had been lost. Twisting, gliding, her eyes shining with triumph, her light body moving like an avenging goddess as she covered his back, her sword slicing through the enemy with no hesitation.

"Woman! You will make me insane..." he growled a second before his lips covered hers, his hands holding her hips in place as he pushed her against the wall behind her, devouring her.

He couldn't taste her enough. Couldn't get close enough. Couldn't find a way to assure himself that she did indeed live. But she moved against him. A moan vibrated in her throat, her breasts pressed against his chest and her hands gripped his hair to pull him closer, deeper.

His cock was a swollen ache of hunger as he pressed against her hot pussy. He was dying for her. Aching for her. And he had no time now to take her.

Gripping her hair, he pulled her head back, seeing the flare of excitement that the little pain caused her.

"You are mine!" he snarled in her face, watching her eyes narrow.

She jerked at his hold, nipping his kiss-swollen lips with a fiery caress. Adrenaline still pumped through her body. Lust, fiery hot, fueled by her triumph and her need for his touch had her giving in to the desires that pulsed just under her flesh. The desire to tempt, to tease, to test out her newly found sensuality on the man who had awakened it.

"Prove it," she dared him with a throaty murmur that had his teeth clenching against the lust rising within him.

Aye, he would prove it, he promised himself. The next time he had her naked and slick beneath him he would make certain he proved it. Jonar had best have a weapon more effective than an energy canon the next time he attacked.

"Kanna has the van packed, Shane," Devlin called from the darkness then. "We ride. We can't stay here."

He tensed, breathing harshly, everything inside him clamoring at him to take her now. To sink his erection into the tight, wet grip of her hot cunt. To lose himself in her heat and the power he could feel swirling around them.

"Soon," he rasped, his lips curling back from his teeth in feral promise. "Soon, Ariel."

He released her slowly, feeling her slump against him for the smallest second before she straightened. And to his shocked horror, his once very circumspect wife lowered her hand, cupping the heavy weight of his scrotum within it before pursing her lips slowly in a silent kiss.

"I can't wait." Her throaty little growl spiked his lust and frayed his control.

Had she not released him when she did, moving away slowly, brushing her swollen breasts against his arm, he feared what he might have done. No matter who was watching.

Let me hide, Ariel... Don't let him weaken me again...

The words drifted over her as sleep would have claimed her. Hugging close to Shane's back, a leather jacket dwarfing her body, the motorcycle throbbing beneath her as they sped through the night, she let the voices come to her.

It was raining, and Ariel considered riding in the rain the height of stupidity, but she knew distance needed to be placed between them and where they had been. Besides, it was the strangest rain she had ever known.

She wasn't wet as she knew she should have been. Insulated, somehow protected from the wet drops, she wasn't protected from the sound of it falling around her and the whisper of tears in the sound.

Whose voice was she hearing? Drifting between sleep and reality, she reached out with her senses, looking for the source of the sound.

He will destroy me...

Sadness filled her soul as tears whispered around her.

Turn back, Ariel... Make them turn back...

She opened her eyes then, seeing the man who rode at their side, wet, rain drifting like tears down a haggard face and the pain of it engulfed her.

Derek didn't look at her, seemed unaware that she watched him. He lifted a weary hand from the handlebars of the motorcycle and wiped his face tiredly. His expression was stoic in the reflective glow of the gauge lights.

"See him." She surprised herself at the whisper, and Shane as well if the tensing of his body was anything to go by. "He sheds tears as well."

A wizard's tears, the voice scoffed, though she heard the fear beneath it. *An illusion for all to see, for trapped inside the stone of his land, did he hide his tears of shame. The Wizard knows no tears...* The voice faded away as Derek moved ahead of them, alone, swallowed by the dark landscape, the rain as tears on his face. An illusion...

"Shane?"

"You should rest, love," his voice answered through the link. "We'll ride 'til daylight and rest 'til the next morning. But you need to rest now as well."

"Do you know anything about him?" she whispered. "The Wizard."

Shane sighed. "I know much of him, Ariel. I know him to be an honorable warrior, a fine man, and a true brother. But I know not the man who played the role of Caitlin's husband. As I told you, those were dark years; years that even now can strike at us with the sharpest fangs are we not careful. Only Caitlin knew that man."

And if Ariel wasn't mistaken, whoever Caitlin was, she would destroy him...

Chapter Sixteen

ᔕᓂ

The motel they arrived at that night was right next to a tattoo shop and a honky-tonk. At first, Ariel paid little attention to the Harleys parked outside the large building. She heard the music, loud and pulsing, the roar of the engines and the sounds of laughter but she paid little attention to it.

Once inside, after dinner and a shower, she sat on the bed, her head tilted, hearing the whispers of information that came to her. The raucous glee, innuendoes and liquor-slurred voices.

She had never gone to a bar. She had rarely drunk a beer, let alone liquor. She knew her father had people watching her often and had refused to take many chances with her freedom. Now, as she listened, her eyes closed, it was almost as though she heard something else.

A different kind of music, freer, filled with joy. The voices rougher, the clang of swords, the neighing of horses. When the memory washed through her mind, it wasn't a hard slam or a slap into her brain. It was a gentle, sneaky wave that took long minutes before her eyes flew open in surprise, her gaze finding Shane as he watched her from the end of the bed.

"There was a bar," she whispered. "In France. I know it was in France. A dirty little bar…" A smile spread across her face. "We went in for a drink and dinner, the others were too tired, they were bedding down in the stables." She tilted her head, the details slowly coming together in her mind as soft laughter filled her voice. "We got into a fight, didn't we?"

Shane snorted, though she read his delight in his eyes. "You started that damned fight, woman."

She smiled slowly. "He was a bear of a man. A loud-mouthed bastard who thought I should be under him rather than beside you…"

She chuckled, closing her eyes, remembering the brash, piggish prig who had come up to them.

"I knocked him out."

"He was an influential member of the town." He was chuckling as well. "Several of his guards were there as well."

Bittersweet joy filled her as her eyes opened once again.

"I'm not crazy, am I, Shane?" she whispered. "It's real. Truly real?"

He knelt on the floor in front of her, his hand, so large and strong rising to cup her cheek as he stared into her eyes.

"I have lived, Ariel, for one thousand years. In France, we inhabit a castle from the first century, and there you will find artifacts preserved through the ages, as beautiful now as they were then. Objects that you found great joy in during that time of darkness and of war. And you, my love, were the greatest warrior to ever strap a sword to your hips. Your eyes were brighter, your joy like a flame when you fought by my side. No, dearest heart, madness is not a part of your mind. Truth. Honor. Courage. Those are all a part of you. But never madness."

God, she could remember him. *Remember.* Not just sense the truth, but she saw him in her mind's eyes, a memory as clear as those she had of yesterday. Dressed in leather and furs, his hair longer, his eyes gleaming as he laughed while she fought.

He had toasted her with a mug of ale as she struggled with one of the guards. Drained the mug then used it to brain the man.

She should be terrified, she thought. She should be screaming, disbelieving, she should be checking herself into the nearest institution. Instead, she stared back at him, wonder filling her.

"I want a tattoo," she said then, something inside her exploding with joy. She wasn't crazy. There was nothing wrong with her.

His eyes widened though laughter gleamed in the mercury depths.

"You want a what?"

"A tattoo." She grinned. "Of this." She reached out, her fingers gripping one of the runes he wore about his neck. "I want it, on my shoulder. The other...on yours..." She smiled as something inside her shifted into a joy she couldn't explain.

His head lowered. The runes lay in her hand. Strength for her shoulder, protection for his.

He looked up at her once again. "You're certain?" he asked her then. "Runes are not to be taken lightly, beloved. It will tie you to me for all time."

Her other hand slid from his shoulder to the strong column of his neck.

"I thought I was already." She knew she was. There was no question of it.

"Aye," he smiled back at her slowly. "You always have been, and you always will be."

"There was a tattoo parlor beside that bar," she reminded him. "It was open. I saw the sign."

He cast her a knowing glance. "Devlin will have our heads for this, Ariel."

"Do you care?" She could feel the excitement rushing through her.

For years she had restrained herself, pushing back the least hint of impulsiveness, hiding the need inside her to have fun, to make waves. She had hid from herself, and she was only now beginning to realize that.

"Did I ever?" His lips quirked in amusement. "I think we could sneak away for a bit. It's been a long time since I've experienced your brand of trouble, woman. And I must admit I've missed it nearly as much as I missed you."

There were so many emotions she heard in his voice then. Pride. Tenderness. Caring.

"Was I a good person, Shane?" She couldn't stop the question that whispered from her lips. Despite the returning memories, she still feared so many mistakes at that time. "Did I make you happy?"

She hoped she had.

He ducked his head for a moment. A strong, brave man. One who towered head and shoulders above others, whose strength was unrivaled by any. When he lifted it again, his expression was tender, his gaze soft with memories.

"You made me very happy, Ariel," he told her then. "So happy, that in a thousand years, I could not forget you or your unique touch. There has never been another for me. And there never will be."

She leaned forward and touched his lips with hers, staring into his eyes as she let a smile curve her own.

"Let's go play," she whispered.

He grunted, but caught her lips in a quick kiss even as his eyes flared with hotter passion.

"Come then." He jumped to his feet, tugging her along with him. "We'll go play."

She thought getting the tattoo was a weird experience. The tattoo artist looked like a stalker reject, with a beard nearly to his oversized belly and more decorations on his bare chest and arms than she had thought a man could have.

His needles were clean though, as were his hands. The gloves he used were an added protection that assured her that he might even know what he was doing. She was in the mood to be adventurous, but not infected.

Shane went first. He bared his incredibly muscular shoulder, snickering when the artist bitched and moaned about the toughness of his flesh. But the rune design went on without too much difficulty, and she had to say, it looked incredibly sexy on him.

She sat down next, pulling the slender strap of her shirt down her arm and baring hers then. She almost flinched at the first prick of the needle, and though it burned like hell for a minute, she felt a glowing excitement infuse her. Shane carried her mark now. That of protection. The winds would always wrap around him, protect him for her. And his symbol of strength would now grace her body as well, giving her a measure of his unique abilities too.

How she knew they would now share this bond as well, she wasn't certain. Like the memory before, it just flowed over her, through her, became a part of her. It was a whisper in the air around her, a glowing warmth that invaded her soul.

She glanced at him with a smug smile when the artist finished, flashing him a teasing, sex-filled smile that she knew would make him hard. Make him want her. And she succeeded.

"You two be careful if you're headed to the bar tonight," the artist warned them as he turned his back to them, cleaning his instruments. "We've had a different crowd in lately. They've been causing some trouble. Mean bastards."

"How so?" She heard the casual inquiry, almost innocent voice that Shane made.

Uh-oh, she knew that voice. Her eyes narrowed on him.

His gaze had sharpened with a flare of danger, or excitement. As though he was looking forward to whatever danger presented itself.

"Just different," the artist shrugged his wide shoulders as he turned back to them. "Usually, we don't have much trouble here, but this new crew that rode in makes a mockery of any we had before. Two of our girls were almost killed the other night." He cast Ariel a warning glance. "I'd hate to see yours get hurt. I'd just go back to the motel and hope they don't cause too much ruckus if I were you."

Shane flexed his sword arm. He wasn't wearing his sword, but she had a feeling that wouldn't matter.

"You know, there was once a time when such trash was easily dealt with," he sighed in regret for those bygone days. "Now, we must be politically correct and pretend to be the little pussies this world would make of us. No offense intended, beloved." He flashed her an endearing smile. "While disease such as your new crowd sneaks through the night and destroys all we are sacrificing our manhood for."

"None taken," she choked back her laughter. "But I haven't seen you sacrificing any of your manhood lately."

"Only to you, Precious." His teeth flashed wickedly. "But I will regain it here in just a bit. I promise you this."

The tattoo artist chuckled roughly. "She looks worth sacrificing to," he said, though without offense, his hazel eyes admiring. "Keep her away from that bar, though. Or she may not be come morning."

Shane frowned, clearly insulted by this.

"I can protect my woman should there be a need." Shane frowned fiercely at the other man.

The tattoo artist tilted his graying head, his eyes sharper now, having picked on something in the way Shane spoke or perhaps the confidence in his voice.

"They own the cops," he warned them then. "It could be more trouble than you want."

Shane shrugged. "Some men don't always remember so well. They will have to remember us to describe us."

Surprise crossed the other man's features.

"You would be damned hard to forget, and her even harder," he chuckled. "Watch your ass."

"I will watch her ass." Shane's smile grew brighter. "I have found it to be one of my greatest joys."

Ariel felt the flush that washed over her face as he cast her a heavy-lidded look filled with innuendo as she shrugged her jacket on over the light tank top she wore with her jeans.

He chuckled at the reproving look she cast him before paying the tattoo artist and escorting her from the shop.

Chapter Seventeen

∽

"Maybe we should just go back to the room," she said after they entered the warmth of the night, glancing at the bar regretfully. "I'd hate to get Devlin too pissed with you."

She had noticed the easy friendship he shared with his commander. The two men were more than just brothers in arms; at times they acted more like brothers—period. Actually, the whole group somehow gave that impression.

He laughed lightly, curling his arm around her back as he led her to the bar.

"Devlin doesn't control me, Ariel," he told her easily. "He's my commander, not a puppet master."

She loved the confidence in his voice. There was no loud blustering, no exaggerated claims. Just easy strength and dedication.

They stepped up to the wide porch that stretched across the front of the bar, the rough wood planks uneven beneath their feet. Years of neglect had created a harsh, weathered appearance that suited the atmosphere perfectly.

As they entered the smoky interior Ariel was aware of the breeze that suddenly wrapped around her, as protective and enduring as Shane towering over her. The large hand now splayed against her lower back was a warm weight that added to the confidence filling her, the strength she could feel building within her.

Voices lowered when they entered, curious stares following them as they made their way to the bar.

"Two beers." Shane leaned against the long smoothly polished bar as Ariel took a seat on one of the high barstools.

She ignored the looks leveled her way from the men gathered in the room. She could feel a knowledge gathering within her, a sense of confidence, memories of training that she knew she hadn't had in this lifetime.

She wasn't weak as she had once thought herself to be. She had been a fighter, a warrioress, a woman that men had feared at one time.

She accepted the cold mug the bartender set in front of her; he was bear of a man with a braided beard and a tattoo of a skull and crossbones on his upper arm.

"Drink up, wife," Shane spoke at her ear, his voice a rough murmur of laughter that sent shivers of pleasure chasing up her spine.

She lifted the mug to her lips, taking a long drink of the bitter brew as she remembered another time, a rougher, dangerous era and the taste of smooth, dark ale. And the same tensions prevailed then, as they did now. Ariel was aware of the thickening of it behind her, the way the air pressed in against her, surrounding her as though to insulate her from any danger there.

"Should I be worried?" She glanced at him from the corner of her eyes as she murmured the question.

From the long mirror behind the bar she could see the looks she was getting. One group in particular, a table of eight shaggy, unkempt miscreants watching her and Shane with an edge of resentment in their gazes.

"Naw, nothing to worry about, love." He grinned, though his expression was expectant. "I've got your back. Remember?"

Ariel snorted at that as she turned back to her beer, watching the men from beneath her lashes through the mirror.

They were gearing themselves up for trouble. She could see it in the way they moved, and if she wasn't mistaken, they were carrying guns.

She sighed in resignation.

"You know, bullets are hard to duck past," she pointed out conversationally. "And they have guns."

"Hmm, weren't you the one bitching because your enemies weren't using guns?" he asked softly, the laughter in his voice contagious.

She should have been scared. She should have been running.

She sighed instead. "If I was this reckless in my first life, it's no wonder I ended up dead."

She tipped the mug back, finished her beer then watched as three of the men at the table she was watching rose to their feet. Danger whispered in the air around her. A breeze blew in from the opened doors, wrapping around her as though in protection. Between her breasts, the crystal heated with a surge of power that had her breath catching at the punch of energy her body seemed to take.

What the hell was that?

"You folks must be new around here." Rasping and cruel, the voice had her glancing at Shane, and almost grinning at the anticipation in his face.

They turned simultaneously, and Ariel barely restrained her grimace at the stench coming from the three.

Instantly, air wavered before her, carrying the smell away from her.

They were dirty, corrupt in mind and body, diseased in morality. Damn, she wished she had her sword.

"And why would you think that?" Shane's voice rumbled from beside her, filled with mockery, challenge.

Ariel almost winced at the tone.

Beady eyes narrowed on him.

"We have a rule here," the dirty little pig snapped then. "You want to drink in our bar, then you pay the price."

Shane dug several bills from his pocket and tossed them on the bar.

"That should cover any damage," he murmured to the wide-eyed bartender. "To the bar at any rate."

"That's a good start." The taller of the three leered at her while reaching between his thighs and gripping his parts there lewdly.

Some things never changed, she thought in resignation.

"The price is your woman," the third sneered. "She's a pretty little piece. And we'd like a taste of her." He licked his fat lips in anticipation.

Ariel let her eyes drift over the three men thoughtfully before she lifted a brow at them archly.

"Bathe first," she drawled. "Then we might discuss the matter."

Was that a groan she heard from Shane?

"Ariel, shame on you," he teased her then. "These are our hosts. You should use your manners here."

She shot him a dark look.

"I have to use my manners here? Why?"

"They are our hosts." He spread his hands to the three men as though to ask what he should do with her.

"We'll teach the bitch manners," the piggish little man in the front snapped.

Ariel frowned.

"They aren't using their manners. Why should I?" she pouted mockingly.

She had obviously lost her own mind. This had to be on the same scale as baiting alligators. Actually, she bet baiting alligators was safer by far.

Suddenly, she felt the air around her shift, thicken at her midriff a second before one smelly male wannabe aimed his fist at her stomach.

"Whoa!" She jumped to the side just before the blow landed, staring back at him in shock. "That wasn't nice."

He smiled, causing her stomach to turn with the sight of decayed, unbrushed teeth.

"Bitch, you'll be screaming for mercy by time we finish with you," he snarled, advancing on her slowly.

"Do you need help, honey?" Shane called out the question as he leaned back on the bar, watching her with darkening eyes.

Need his help? She snorted at the thought. Memories of her training filled her, she knew how to fight, knew how to kill. Through this lifetime she had kept her body well-honed, her muscles in peak condition, somehow sensing she would one day need the strength. She was the woman she had been a thousand years before.

"I should be done in a minute," she grinned back at him carelessly. "You might want to get me another beer though..." She blocked the next blow a second before her knee came up, delivering a powerful punch to undefended balls at the same time her right arm cocked and flew forward to hopefully break the already crooked nose in line for it.

Blood spurted around her, dissipated by her unspoken command to the air around her.

She could feel the crystal at her breast, her needs telegraphing to it before she had time to even focus them clearly within her thoughts. A hard breeze aided her opponent in his flight across a table, spilling beer and assorted drinks as the bikers jumped back, chairs scraping then flying across the floor as he landed at a heap on the other side.

And then all hell broke loose.

Ariel couldn't believe herself, or the fight that resulted. Fists were flying, and suddenly Shane was at her back in the middle of the fray, his war cry echoing around them as her laughter spilled to the winds whipping through the room.

A fist caught her in a sideways slug to the mouth, busting her lip and sending her anger boiling.

"Bastard!" She turned on the assailant but Shane had him in his grip instead, shaking the tubby little man like a pup before tossing him across the room.

"Have you had enough yet, wife?" he called out to her as he picked her up with one hand, sweeping her to his chest as his strong arm blocked the chair heading for her back.

Jumping from his embrace, her fist plowed into the man's face as the winds followed her aim and threw him backward along the congested floor. Yelps and screams of rage were echoing through the room, to be joined by the sudden discordant sound of police sirens.

"Uh-oh." She laughed back at her warrior as the winds screamed around her. "Time to go?"

"Time to go." He grabbed her hand, his fist swinging out at the bruiser standing in his way, sending him staggering backward with the force of the blow.

They made it outside the door, laughing, running. Ducking behind the tattoo shop, they waited until the police cruisers sped past and came to a squealing stop outside the bar.

Adrenaline pounded in her veins; excitement, the heady rush of danger and triumph sensitized her heightened nerve endings. She was alive, more alive than she had ever been in her life.

"You two are as wild as you ever were."

In tandem, she and Shane both turned, crouched to fight, the fury of the fight still upon them as they faced the Wizard who had managed to come up behind them.

"Life is for living, Derek," Shane laughed as he straightened, pulling Ariel to his side in a swift, hard hug. "It was merely a bit of exercise."

Derek grunted, his gaze seeking Ariel's then.

"We're riding back out immediately," he reported.

"Why?" Ariel felt Shane tense, but suddenly, she knew why. The winds whispered the knowledge to her, caressing her ears, her hair as she heard it.

"Caitlin called to you," she said softly.

Derek inclined his head subtly. "She did," he answered coolly. "A challenge I believe."

I await you, Wizard. Catch me if you can before the Wizard's Tears are mine once again…

Ariel wanted to roll her eyes at the words that lingered on the air around them. Caitlin hadn't been prone to melodrama, unless she was pissed. She must really be pissed.

"What did you do to her?" Ariel drawled mockingly.

He cleared his throat, glancing away, but not before Ariel caught the almost hidden quirk of his lips.

"I'm the Wizard." He shrugged. "I deal in illusion, in magic if you will. Shall we say, I may have brought her a vision."

"Oh hell…" Ariel lowered her head, shaking it slowly as she suddenly remembered the Wizard's ability to mess with minds, both on a large and small scale. "Didn't you learn your lesson the first time?"

"Of course I did." He acted too surprised, and much too innocent. "I didn't steal her mind, Ariel, I merely caressed it a bit. Quite a little bit…"

"Great," Shane snarled suddenly as he pushed past the other man. "You diddle with a furious wife and ruin my plans for the night. Remind me, Derek, to repay you in kind at my first opportunity."

Ariel snickered, but there was little else she could do as she was being dragged behind Shane. Back to the motorcycles, another ride, another communion with the winds, and none of the hot, heated sex she was determined would soon, very soon, be hers.

Chapter Eighteen

ଛ

His control was next to nothing, and Shanar knew it. When they arrived at one of the little towns just off the highway that Devlin had chosen later that morning, he was a throbbing mass of lust ready to explode, despite his lack of sleep. If he didn't manage to sink his cock between the sweet thighs that had hugged his hips all night long, he knew he would be resigned to at least jacking off in the shower to keep from raping her.

She had slept for most of the ride, resting against him, her head pillowed on the back of his shoulder as he guided the cycle through the night. The rain had eased after she finally dropped off, the short, sharp bursts of lightning fading into the distance.

He would never forget watching the elements invade that damned warehouse after she called them to her. Lightning, rain and wind had whipped through the building, leaving a mess that he knew would raise questions when the workers returned there the next morning.

In the middle of it, sword flying, a smile on her face and her war cry echoing around them had been a vision of Ariel he had thought he was never to see. Here was the warrioress he could glimpse in her eyes all those centuries before. The one restrained, cut off from her power, distant from what she might have been because of Jonar's cruelty and treachery.

They dragged themselves wearily into the motel, ate the breakfast Kanna left for them and Shane could only watch in frustration as Ariel collapsed onto the bed, still dressed, and fell asleep.

He grimaced painfully, shaking his head at his arousal and the hard-on that refused to go away.

"Come on, sleeping beauty," he sighed roughly as he unlaced her vest and began undressing her. "You can't sleep in your clothes."

She mumbled something that had his brows rising in surprise.

"Grouch," he chuckled, stripping the vest from breasts so round and firm it made his tongue ache to taste them.

Gritting his teeth, he tossed the vest to the chair by the side of the bed and eased her boots and pants off before jerking the blankets over her and releasing a guttural growl. Dammit, ten fucking centuries living like a celibate so he could watch her twitch her ass around him and fight like a little hellion, only to have her sleep when his need was so great.

Shaking his head, he moved for the bathroom and a cold shower. An hour later he pulled a small bottle of complimentary whisky from the mini-bar and downed it in two drinks. His dick was still as hard as iron and throbbing for relief.

And Ariel still slept.

Damn her hide.

He plopped down on the couch, staring at the bed, his eyes narrowed as his fingers wrapped around the stiff shaft thrusting from between his thighs. How many nights had he laid in his bed at the castle, eyes closed, jerking off to the remembered scent of her, the sounds of her breathy little gasps as pleasure finally overwhelmed her?

No matter how long the centuries or how deep the loneliness went, he had remembered her. Her taste, her touch. Those luminous amethyst eyes, the passion that would rise within them.

He leaned his head back against the couch, gritting his teeth as his hand tightened on his cock. His balls contracted, tight and aching, to the base of the shaft, pleading to release the seed they contained.

He was not going to get off like this, he told himself, refusing to give in to the need to stroke the pain away. He would wait. He could wait for her. Surely she wouldn't deny him much longer. She knew she belonged to him. Knew she was his wife. Would she make him wait indefinitely?

His hand clenched on the erection, realizing that the state of arousal he was in would only grow worse if he dared to attempt to sleep in the bed beside her. There was no way he could be so close…

"You should have woken me."

His eyes flew open, then narrowed at the sight his wife kneeling between his spread thighs. She was naked, her breasts swollen, her nipples hard and thrusting forward, demanding attention.

His eyes went to hers then. There, he saw not just the temptress, but the innocent woman kneeling before him. A glitter of nervousness shone in her dark eyes, in the way her tongue dampened her full, luscious lips.

Her hands pressed against the inside of his thighs and he shifted them apart wider, making room for her to fit herself before him.

"Do not tempt me," he growled in warning. "I will not be able to let you go a second time."

"Did I ask you to let me go the first time?" she asked him as she lay her head against his thigh, her warm breath drifting over his scrotum. "I watched this movie once," she whispered as her hand smoothed up his other thigh, her fingers reaching the taut sac. "I watched it over and over again, and knew if I ever met the man who could make me hot enough, wet enough to need him, then I would try it."

She looked up at him again, and he saw her need for this, for the choice to be hers, the decision all her own.

"I'm more than just a fighter, or a Mistress of the Wind," she whispered. "I want to be a woman too, Shane. Your woman." There was no hesitancy, but he could sense her trepidation, her womanly fears.

Oh God. This would kill him. He could hear the curiosity in her voice as well and feared he could never hold onto his control long enough to allow her whatever play she desired.

"Ariel, I have waited too long," he groaned as her fingers moved to support the heavy weight of his scrotum. They were soft, so silky, so perfect.

"Why don't you have body hair, Shane?" she asked him then, her breath licking over the bare, sensitive flesh like flames.

He gritted his teeth against it. "The healing units," he breathed out harshly as he attempted to explain. "We must use them each century. They prevent body hair from growing."

"Hmm." The explanation seemed to satisfy her. If it didn't, at least she was waiting before saying more.

"Sweet heaven, woman!" His hips jerked as her tongue stroked slowly over the tight flesh, his hips arching, nearly coming out of his seat at the pleasure.

He would have thought she would go slow. That perhaps she would have taken that sweet mouth and covered the head of his cock, instead, her head dipped lower, her tongue lashing at his balls as her lips created a heated, erotic suckling along the flesh and nearly sent him into climax.

He could not endure it.

His hand tightened on the base of the erection, fighting to hold back the sudden, fiery demand for release. The other hand sank into the strands of her hair, his fingers clenching in the strands to hold her in one place, but it didn't stop her. She moaned as she tugged at his hold, a throaty, hungry sound of pleasure that had him pulling at the strands anyway, knowing it aroused her.

She had never wanted the little pain before. She had feared it. But now, there was no fear, no memories of pain and helplessness to sway her passions. She was beauty. She was heat and fire. She was the dream that had haunted him for a thousand years.

Her tongue was a fiery little demon, washing over his balls again and again, laving flesh that grew more sensitive with each stroke. Her hand brushed his out of the way as she finally, thankfully, began to move along his cock. Up. Up. He restrained the agonized gasp that fought to rise from his chest as the pleasure became so deep he was certain he could never stand another moment of it.

But he did. He held his breath. He recited runes in his head. He called upon God for strength and finally, when he could bear her exquisitely slow pace no longer, he gripped her hair, raised her head and pushed the head of his cock between her willing, parted lips.

"Yes," he hissed as she closed her lips over the near bursting head, her tongue stroking sensually along the nerve-laden underside. "Suck it, Ariel. Take me deeper. Deeper, baby."

He watched through narrowed eyes as she took several inches, moving her lips slowly along the thick stalk, her eyes dark and gleaming back at him wickedly. The woman was a vision of sex, of beauty.

Her firm, warm breasts pressed against his upper thighs now, swaying and flushed from the tight strokes of her mouth along his cock.

His head ground against the back of the couch as he fought to hold onto his control.

"Your mouth is so hot," he snarled between gritted teeth. "So tight and hot I do not know if I can hold back, Ariel. Cease this at once if you are not prepared…"

His cock jerked tightly as he felt his release building in the base of his erection.

Her eyes were ever darker, excitement glittering within them.

"Is this what you want?" His voice was guttural, demanding. "My seed filling your mouth, Ariel?"

She moaned, the sound vibrating along his flesh and sending agonizing pleasure whipping through his system. Even the air stroked his body with exquisite sensations, so sensitive was he. He could feel it, curling around the hard points of his flat nipples, twisting around his arms.

His eyes widened, his lips pulling back in a snarl of ecstasy as he realized what she was doing. How well her power was adjusting to her every desire.

"Damn you, Ariel," he groaned, feeling the fragile tendrils of air move to his balls, wrapping around them, touching him with heat and a pleasure he could not deny.

Her suckling mouth moved on him faster now, the soft sounds of moist pleasure filling his ears, mixing with his hoarse groans until he knew he couldn't deny her any longer.

Electric impulses of sensation surged up his spine, back down, then raced to the base of his cock to produce an explosion that had him fighting to keep from shouting his pleasure to the world.

Hard, desperate pulses of his semen began to jet from his cock, filling her mouth, causing her to tighten further on him as she swallowed each hot stream of silky fluid as she hummed her approval at his taste.

He convulsed with the pleasure racking his body, every muscle drawn tight as she milked him of each violent spurt of his seed, until he was gasping but still hard. So hard he knew that it would take years, it would take forever to relieve his hunger for her.

Chapter Nineteen

ℬ

Before Ariel could do more than lift her head from the still swollen erection that had filled her mouth, Shane was on his feet. He picked up her up in arms that strained with tension before he stalked to the bed, tossing her to the mattress before he came over her.

"You would push a man too far," he growled as he restrained her hands, holding them to the bed as powerful thighs encased her legs. "Control is a fragile thing, Ariel. You have destroyed mine."

She stared up at him, knowing she should be concerned, worried about the sudden lustful flames that burned in his eyes. Shadows coalesced in her mind, an edge of worry, a fragile thread of nervousness that dissipated beneath her own burgeoning desire.

This was how she wanted him. Out of control. Straining with hunger for her.

"What are you going to do?" she taunted him then.

She had always restrained herself, had always played by someone else's rules. But something rose inside her then, something she wouldn't have expected, couldn't have known. She *knew* Shane was capable of much more than he had shown her so far in regards to his passion. He was a large, muscular man. His strength would require great control over each touch. She wanted that control gone. She wanted the warrior and the man, the lover and the Viking. But most especially she wanted what she knew he had never allowed himself to give her in that first life they had known each other.

She was naked, lying beneath as she watched him fight to rein in his lusts. But he was hungry, she could see it, greedy for every taste, every touch. That fire burning in his eyes threatened the hold he had on his lusts.

"Sweet Ariel." Rather than answering her, his head lowered, his lips smoothing over hers. "Do not bait me now, beloved."

She snapped at his lips. Her teeth nipped at the full lower curve, causing his eyes to narrow with the promise of retribution.

"You do not want what you are tempting," his voice was a hard, rough rasp, torn from the very depths of his chest. "It has been too long."

She ran her tongue over her lips slowly, her lashes lowering as she stared back at him.

"Don't I?" She focused on the air around her, a small smile tipping her lips as she commanded it to do what she couldn't.

She watched his expression change, watched his face flush as ecstasy washed over it. She knew the touch was featherlight, curling around the base of his cock, creating just enough pressure to tease, just enough touch to tempt.

"Let me touch you," she whispered, tugging at the grip he had on her hands.

"I think not," his voice was strangled, a harsh growl as the very air teased him in her stead. "I think for this, you must be punished. Tempting me in such a way is not wise."

Before she could gasp or anticipate his next move, he had flipped her over on the bed, pushing a pillow beneath her hips as he straddled her thighs once again. He trapped her hands at the center of her back, effectively leaving her helpless beneath him.

"Lord, what a pretty ass," he whispered then, smoothing his palm over the flesh.

Ariel's breath caught in her throat at the pleasurable caress. Her buttocks clenched as she fought to keep her mind on what she was doing to Shane through the air around them.

If he kept this up, there was no way she could continue to torment him in such a way.

A low groan vibrated behind her as she had the air press in against his cock, imagining the feel of her hands stroking him, milking the thick, hard flesh.

"Bad girl!" His hand landed on the cheek of her ass, sending a flash of heat singing through her veins.

Her eyes widened as she arched, pleasure rushing over her in a wave that sent her juices spilling from her pussy.

She could feel her clit swell instantly, the small slap sending vibrations of sensation washing over it.

"Do you know how I once longed to do this, Ariel?" he whispered roughly, his hand smoothing over her rear once again. "To hold you still beneath me." He leaned closer, placing a delicate heated kiss at the nape of her neck. "And watch your luscious ass turn red from my hand, feel you writhing in pleasure beneath me. And it is pleasure, is it not, my sweet?"

Another blow landed. It sent her senses spinning. Pain should not be pleasure. But was it truly pain? Her clit was throbbing now, her cunt convulsing with pleasure, weeping with hunger.

"Shane, I'm going to kick your ass," she gasped as another blow landed, sending heat washing through her vagina, tightening around her clit.

She wasn't going to come like this, she thought in horror. Surely it wasn't really possible?

Desperate now, she felt inside herself for her own power, calling to the crystal, the air around her.

"Fuck!" She felt him arch as the breeze moved about his scrotum, tightening, stroking like ghostly fingers along his sensitive flesh, as she commanded it to do.

His hand fell again. Again. A series of light, heated little blows that had her twisting beneath him, gasping, on the edge of a pleasure so intense she could feel her womb clenching with the overload.

"Do you know what I'm going to do with this pretty little ass, Ariel?" If the sound of his voice was anything to go by, his control was hanging on by a thread. But she had already lost hers.

"Looks...to me..." A little scream escaped her throat as he shifted, relaxing the hold on her legs long enough to push his hand between her thighs, his fingers suddenly cupping the soaked, slick curves of her pussy. "Oh God. Shane..." She arched her hips closer, feeling his fingers close, so close to the aching bud of her clit.

But he gave that throbbing little bundle of nerves only a glancing caress as he gathered the juices along the slit of her pussy, pulling his hand back, back, until his fingers were pressing at the tight, flexing entrance to her anus.

Ariel stilled, her eyes opening wide, dazed as she felt the tip of his finger begin to part the tiny entrance. Slick and hot from her own juices, she felt it spread the tight muscles there, easing in, stretching her with a slow delicious burn that she could do nothing to push closer, incoherent pleas whimpering from her throat as she lost her mind to the pleasure.

It was decadent. It was forbidden. It was the most sensually erotic thing she had ever felt, feeling his finger slide into her, filling her ass with its broad length, stretching her, burning her alive with pleasure.

"You're tight, love." He was breathing hard now, his voice growing rougher by the minute. "So tight and hot I could come just fucking your ass with my finger."

So could she, if he would just push her a little bit closer.

Her muscles tightened on him, the forbidden pleasure/pain streaking through her anus, vibrating in her clit.

"You like that don't you, baby?" he asked then, his voice guttural. "That little bit of pain streaking through your nerves, driving you higher."

She was loving it.

He chuckled then, sliding his finger free as she cried out at the loss, pressing back, desperate to keep him there.

"Not yet, love," he groaned, moving to turn her onto her back once again, sliding between her thighs as her legs opened eagerly, her arms reaching for him.

Shane came to her, his lips taking hers then in a kiss that struck her to her soul. Hot, out of control, a meshing of lips and tongues filled with hunger, with unstated needs stronger than either of them had known before or since.

Slipping into her mind, sensations filling her were small, disjoined memories. His care of her before, in that first life, almost as though both of them feared the passions that simmered deep inside them.

She had held back, frightened of losing him, of disgusting him with the carnal urges that flared in her when he touched her. And he, always so determined to take her gently, even though she often caught him watching her with hot, lust-filled eyes.

Not so now. Now his body strained against her, his cock pressing between her thighs as his lips tore from hers, traveling down her neck, across her upper chest until he could fill his mouth with the tip of her breast.

A cry tore from her throat at the feel of his hot mouth surrounding her, the head of his erection parting her. Too many sensations, too much pleasure. How was she to endure it?

"Shane, do something," she whispered desperately, feeling the opening of her cunt clench, hugging the smooth width of his cock as it nudged at her.

Flared, heavy with lust, thick and hot, his cock throbbed at the entrance to her body, his hips moving in small, tight circles, caressing her with no more than the burning crest of his erection.

"So good..." he groaned, his mouth moving from one breast to the other, his hair damp with the perspiration building along both their bodies now. "I don't want to hurt you, Ariel..."

He was breathing roughly, stroking her nipple with his lips, his eyes closed, expression tortured as his cock opened her further.

Ariel lifted her legs, her knees clasping his hips as she fought the building fire storming through her body. Taking her over.

"Hold on," he groaned then, one hand clasping her hip, the other bracing his weight on his elbow as he shook his head, fought, then lost the battle to take her as he wanted to. Slow and easy.

But she didn't want slow and easy.

It wasn't a hard driving thrust that he took her with, but neither did he ease in. She felt him penetrating her, possessing her, until he reached the thin membrane that proved her innocence.

He whispered her name, prayed for control, pulled back and thrust through it in one heavy stroke of his erection that carried him deeper, deeper into the tight clasp of her body.

Ariel arched in delicious torment, a strangled cry echoing around her as she felt him fill her. Stretching her impossibly, stroking nerve endings she never knew she had, burning through the feminine channel with such fierce hunger that she felt devoured.

"Shane..." She was trembling with the sensation. So full of the hard length of his cock that she wondered if she could survive.

"God. I'm sorry, baby." His head moved to rest beside hers as his hips bunched, retreating, the friction alive with burning electrical charges of pleasure. "I'm so sorry."

He didn't stop. Pulling back he thrust home again, then began a building, rapturous rhythm that had her shaking, shuddering beneath him, her hips lifting as she fought to take him harder, deeper. And he gave it to her.

Holding her close to him, driving into her with jackhammer thrusts that quickly, violently, sent her exploding in an orgasm she couldn't have imagined, and hadn't expected.

Her eyes opened, widening in sudden surprise and fear as it washed over her. Her pussy tightened, her clit throbbing then exploding in tandem to the deep contractions that fisted her muscles around his driving erection.

As the pleasure slammed through her body, Shane came to his knees, taking her, fucking her with a desperation that kept the rhythmic pulses of release climbing in her body until she screamed with the rapture of it.

One last hard thrust buried him deeper than before, his groan harsh, so guttural it seemed torn from him as she felt his semen spurt from his cock, pouring inside her with hard, hot pulses that shook his body as hard or harder, than her orgasm was shaking her.

They collapsed together. Shane fell beside her, pulling her close as he fought for breath, his hands gentle now, soothing her through the aftershocks that vibrated just beneath her flesh.

"How I love you," he whispered hoarsely then. "With my soul. With my heart. With the very breath that sustains my body, Ariel. I love you..."

Ariel opened her eyes slowly, blinking against a sudden rush of tears as he whispered those words. Love. She wanted to shake her head, wanted to tell him that it didn't exist, that it was just the dream he had needed to survive the long, lonely centuries he had lived.

The bond they shared wasn't love, she told herself bitterly. Love didn't exist, it couldn't. If love had truly existed in this world, then she wouldn't have spent countless days and nights locked in the endless blackness of a cellar closet.

She wouldn't have had to fight for her freedom all these years, and she wouldn't have been forced to hold herself aloof, distant from any friendships for fear that they would be used against her as her father had used false friends in the past in his attempt to prove she was insane.

True love, real love, she had seen no proof of. There was affection and caring, but even those qualities of human emotion could be bought and sold with the right price. She had learned that lesson the hard way. Twice. And nearly paid for the lesson with her freedom. Twice she had cared, reached out and tried to believe in love. First with a new friend she had made in college. Soon after, she had returned to their dorm room, heard her father's voice through the door and listened as he paid her to find ways to prove Ariel was insane.

The second was a young man, several years later. Quiet, studious. He had needed money for school, of course—it took a lot of money to pay for a degree in archaeology. The check her father had written him had been dislodged from his checkbook when a hard breeze had swept through the room and pushed it from his desk. Of course, the reason had been the same.

Markham St. James thought his daughter was *ill*. A family affliction he told everyone. Her grandmother had suffered from it, as had her mother. He was certain Ariel was insane as well.

What he couldn't convince her of through her youth, he tried to convince others of through her adult years. It hadn't mattered that Ariel had learned to ignore the sounds in the wind, that she had strived to be completely normal in all things. Still, she had been distrusted, watched closely, suspected.

If love existed, there would have been proof of it in her life, somewhere, somehow. Love didn't exist.

She lay against Shane now, a bitter, consuming pain ripping at her soul as she wished she could believe. If only love did exist. She would have given it to him, said the words

144

and eased the sudden tension gathering in his body. But she couldn't lie to him. She wouldn't lie to him. So she stayed silent instead...

Chapter Twenty

ဢ

The merging of two lifetimes inside her head wasn't a comfortable feeling, Ariel thought the next afternoon as they continued their ride toward their destination.

The winds whipped around her unhelmeted head, filled with so many voices as memories began to slowly emerge from that dark well in her mind that she had always known existed.

It wasn't déjà vu, it wasn't visions or dreams, it was memories slowly unfurling within her mind.

My warrioress... Shane's voice, filled with devotion.

That emotion in his voice struck her. Deep inside a hidden part of her soul, she could feel it burning her alive. He had always spoken to her in such a way, a way no other ever had. His rough voice holding a hard, masculine rasp, deeper than normal, his gray eyes swirling with an emotion that had always made her heart swell.

Woman, your courage often outdistances what little common sense Mother Earth selfishly bestowed on you! He had been enraged when she had slipped from him that night, taking vengeance for a young woman who had been mercilessly raped. She had shown the attackers the same coin in mercy, rendering one incapable of ever raping another woman.

But she had seen the pride warring with the fear in his eyes when he came upon her, breathing heavily, wounded herself. He had carried her to their camp, bathed her with gentle hands, and held her through the night as he whispered his fears of ever losing her.

I have never known such love, my heart, he had whispered in her ear. *It fills my soul and leaves my insides shaking with fear at the thought of ever losing you. What, Ariel, would I do without you to warm my soul?*

That word again, love. And she had responded. She *remembered* responding, and though she didn't remember the words, she remembered the happiness that consumed her, that filled her with joy each time he said it.

She sensed her emotions from that earlier time. Her shock that he could say such words to her. Her knowledge that somehow she was scarred, broken inside, but she knew Shane had healed the pain of it. Somehow, he had done the impossible, and made her believe in him. How had he done that?

They were disjointed, those memories, and she knew something important, something tragic was missing from them. But she drew strength from them. Drew comfort from them.

The few memories she had of their passion left her confused, though. Shane, touching her with the utmost gentleness, as though determined to cause her no fear, no excessive pleasure such as he had shown her the night before. And Ariel knew she had hidden a part of herself from him as well, though she wasn't certain why.

"Stop thinking so much, Ariel," his voice came through the comm link she wore at her ear as they passed the third state police cruiser in an hour.

The patrol officer didn't even glance at them and Ariel knew they were exceeding any speed limit allowable on the powerful cycles.

"We're going to get a ticket," she informed him darkly, ignoring the softly voiced order he had given her.

"As far as that officer is concerned, we're doing the speed limit." He shook his head in denial, his body tense.

He had been tense all morning. Hell, it had begun last night.

"Nice trick," she drawled. "How did you manage it?"

Her hands smoothed down his back as she leaned into the padded rest behind her. She was tired of him ignoring her. Tired of his dark silence that morning. He had barely spoken to her through breakfast, and had said little on the ride.

"I don't manage it." He sounded as though he were speaking through gritted teeth. "That is Derek's job."

"And what's your job?" she asked him curiously, her hands tugging at the material of the soft cotton shirt he had tucked into his leather breeches that morning.

"Keeping you out of trouble?" There was just an edge of mockery to his voice.

She chuckled at that. "Did Devlin rip your ass for the fight the other night?"

He snorted at that, though he seemed to tighten further as her hands slid around his bare waist, loosening the shirt from the front of his pants as well.

"Devlin wouldn't dare," he growled. "No harm was done."

"Hmm…" she murmured, spreading her hands along the flat planes of his abdomen and feeling them flex with tension. "According to your opinion of harm I guess."

A hiss sounded through the link as her nails scraped across his hard-packed flesh.

"Behave," he growled, though she heard the rising lust in his voice.

"Do you know what?" She leaned closer, smoothing her cheek along his back as the wind whipped around them. "I remember another ride we took once. There was this huge horse that you insisted I ride with you…"

He groaned as her hands dipped into the snugly laced waistband. Instantly, his hand covered hers, lifting her fingers as she smiled against his back.

"Stop," he growled. He almost sounded as though he meant it.

"Do you remember the gown I was wearing?" she whispered. "You lifted it so easily, and made me ride you instead. Perhaps I should find a dress to wear tomorrow. If the cops can't see we're speeding, could they see if we were fucking?"

She could feel the effect her words had on him, not to mention the vague memory that was slowly driving her insane.

"If you do not stop this madness, I will not care who sees me fucking you." He was snarling, she could hear it in his voice.

Her hands snuck between his thighs before he could stop her, her fingers curling around the thickness of his cock beneath the leather breeches.

"Have you ever done it on a Harley, Shane?" she asked him a second before she allowed her teeth to rake across the material that covered his back.

He shuddered. A hard flexing of muscles as she tempted him. She hated his silence, hated it more than anything she had ever known. Something inside her was smothering, hurting with a hollow, violent ache she couldn't explain.

"I told you," his voice was darker now, deadly. "I have taken no other woman since your death. Not in a bed, on a horse, or a Harley." He lifted her hand from his cock, placing it instead on his waist. "Now, unless you wish me to scatter our bodies along this highway, I suggest you keep your hands above my waist."

He was pissed. She could hear it. Hell, she could smell his anger on the wind around them.

"I won't let you be angry with me," she said then, pushing back the hurt the thought of it filled her with. "Why are you angry with me, Shane?"

But she was afraid she knew why. This was her punishment for not returning his words of love. She breathed in deeply, refusing to let it hurt her. She had known her refusal would come with a price.

Didn't it always?

It shouldn't hurt either. It shouldn't feel like a dagger was piercing her chest and ripping her soul wide. But it did. That was exactly how it felt, and she didn't like the sensation at all. It meant he mattered. She couldn't afford to let anyone matter to the point that they could wound her so severely.

But Shane did.

"I'm not angry with you, Ariel." She couldn't see his face, but she knew he was lying to her.

Slowly she moved her hands back from his flesh, almost whimpering at the loss of his warmth as she eased back, placing the distance between them that she thought he needed. She could feel the fear rising inside her now. Like a dark specter, it inched through her mind, reminding her of a dark, enclosed closet, the smell of her own fear.

He could hurt her now. She hadn't expected that to happen in such a short amount of time.

She took a deep breath, her hands clenching on her thighs, fisting against the sudden bleak agony that filled her. It wasn't so much his anger but the distance she felt from him. She had no fear of him, knew he wouldn't hurt her. He loved her. Didn't he? He had said he loved her.

She had no experience with that emotion, but she knew he wouldn't lie to her. He had to believe he loved her. But what if his definition of love was similar to her father's? Would he punish her for some imagined slight, some wrong she had done him?

She remembered her Grandmother whispering she loved her. Remembered a sense of warmth, but not enough to use as a basis for love.

"I need to stop." She was going to be sick. The darkness rose inside her until it boiled in her stomach, clashed within her head and made her dizzy, weak from the effects of it. "Stop, Shane. I need to stop."

She wasn't going to lose herself at this point, she couldn't. But she could feel it in her head, the twisting, demon-filled darkness coming closer, ever closer. Darker than the closet her father had locked her in, darker than the pain...

It struck her abdomen first. A fiery strike of remembered agony that lashed at her flesh and sent her grasping for purchase amid the insanity boiling in her mind.

Her hands locked on Shane's waist, nails digging into him as the motorcycle suddenly swerved, then picked up speed and began to race forward. She could hear his voice in her ear, but the winds blocked it. Screams echoed around her and they weren't her own. If only they were then she might have endured it. Memory couldn't really hurt, but this, this was more than just memory.

She was gasping for breath when she felt the motorcycle jerk to a stop, her eyes wide, dazed, as Shane jumped from his seat and jerked her from her own.

"Make it stop now." He shook her harshly, his eyes blazing down at her as she stared up at him, dazed.

The screams continued, hollow and almost broken. Were they hers?

"Ariel, listen to me," he snapped furiously. "Hear me now. It is over. There is no more pain. Do you hear me? No more pain."

She shook her head, gasping for air. She had to breathe, but God, it hurt so bad.

A memory, demonic, deadly, seared her brain. A face of such beauty it was inhuman, and eyes evil, glowing with hatred, with rage as an arm drew back, energy building between his fingers, white-hot, blistering as he aimed it and let it strike.

The winds screamed. Or was it her? Lightning slashed at the sky above them, dark clouds moving in, heavy with the threat of rain.

"Help her!" he was screaming at someone as her body arched. The pain was horrendous, deadly. She would die beneath it and she couldn't even see it.

She reached out to the crystal that lay burning hot at her breast. It spoke to the winds for her, she thought desperately. It was her protection. Why wasn't it protecting her?

Then it came, like a healing touch, warm, blessedly warm where she was cold. Cool where she burned. The pain no longer blistered. It no longer attacked with such brutality that it stole her breath.

She slumped in Shane's arms, realizing only then that somehow he had managed to get them onto a secluded back road before pulling into a hidden canyon.

"Make it stop," she whispered, realizing only then that tears wet her face, perspiration soaked her body. "I can't make it stop."

But it was going away. The darkness in her mind was slipping back, back into the hidden recess that it had been secreted into.

"God! Fuck!" A line of curses, some she had never heard began to leave his lips as he held her tighter to his chest, his head bent over her, his body still, tense with whatever emotion filled him. Fury? Pain?

Her hands gripped his arms, her head held to the spot above his heart, hearing it beat with a rough, driving rhythm that matched her own now.

"Don't you ever do this to me again, woman." He held her away long enough to stare into her face with her dark, pain-ridden eyes before jerking her to him again. Holding her closer, tighter.

"Shane, let her go." Chantel's voice was soft, concerned, her hand touching Ariel's shoulder. "Let's make sure she's okay. Let me see her."

He eased her back again, lifting her until she sat crossways on the seat of the motorcycle, staring up at him in confusion.

"Ariel, I need to check something." Chantel stood before her, her green eyes glowing. "I want you to lift your shirt and let me see your stomach. Just for a moment."

Confused, Ariel watched as Shane nudged the other woman aside, gripped the hem of Ariel's shirt and pulled it above her abdomen. Her gaze followed five other sets, then widened in horror.

Bloody tracks were showing in the flesh, not deep enough to scar, but there all the same, crisscrossing over her abdomen. She raised her hand, touching the long, thin marks with trembling fingers. Pulling back, she stared at the blood before raising frightened eyes to Shane.

Her lips trembled, her body shuddered. There was blood, enough to drip down and stain the leather pants she wore. Enough to cover the tips of her fingers.

"This isn't insanity," she said hoarsely, realizing only then she had believed her father's warning. "Shane..." She heard the plea in her voice and was helpless against it. "This is madness."

Chapter Twenty-One

ॐ

The horrible lashes were gone hours later. If Shane and the others hadn't seen them, hadn't been able to assure her that they had indeed been there, Ariel would have lost her mind then.

She stood in the middle of yet another motel room, staring down at her bared stomach, her expression blank as Chantel touched the unmarred flesh lightly, her green eyes glowing.

"Something's wrong," the other woman whispered, her voice so soft that Ariel knew none of the men in the other room of the suite could hear her. "Do you remember how it happened?"

Ariel shrugged, the motion jerky, betraying the nervous energy that filled her, the realizations she couldn't run from any longer. No, she wasn't crazy. She sighed wearily at that thought. She would have almost preferred the insanity.

"It just happened," she finally frowned, trying to remember the exact moment she felt the dark power swirling around her.

She moved away from Chantel, uncomfortable with the subtle effects of her crystal reaching out to the sister stone Ariel herself wore. It was — odd — was the only description she could find for it. Not exactly uncomfortable, but unfamiliar perhaps?

She turned away from the other woman, straightening her shirt before crossing her arms over her breasts.

She wished Shane didn't feel so far away from her.

Ariel shivered at the thought. She could feel the distance between them and for the first time being completely alone was more frightening than ever before. She needed him.

She swallowed tightly, her throat thick with emotion, with hurt. She couldn't understand it. It made so little sense that he would suddenly become so angry with her.

"Ariel..." Chantel hesitated behind her. "Nothing just happens. Especially not where Jonar is concerned. The crystal should have protected you. With Shane's strength, it can keep Jonar from attacking you at anytime, anywhere. Something had to have happened."

"Nothing happened," she forced the words past her lips as she shook her head fiercely. "We were just riding. I was teasing him when I shouldn't have been." She blinked back the tears as she remembered the coldness in his voice. "I shouldn't have distracted him, I guess." She tightened her arms, holding herself closer. But there was no warmth in her own embrace. "I don't know, Chantel. One moment everything was fine. The next..."

The next minute hell had whipped through her mind.

Ariel drew in a ragged breath at that thought.

"I can feel it," Chantel muttered then. "I just don't know what the hell I feel."

Now that made sense, unfortunately. Ariel could feel it herself. The air was constantly shifting around her, pulling itself into thick, warming threads that wrapped around her, making her suddenly conscious of just how heavy air itself could become. As though gravity had become heavier.

"Is she all right?" Shane's dark, brooding voice sent a hard shudder down her spine as he spoke from the doorway.

She turned slowly, facing him, as Chantel did as well. He looked so much larger than he ever had before. His chest was bare now, the hard-packed muscles flexing beneath the tough, bronzed flesh. The waistband of his breeches rode low on his hips, emphasizing the lean hips, the bulge between his thighs.

Her mouth watered at the size of his erection, her pussy heated. Which was sad, she thought, very, very sad considering how angry he appeared to be. She should be ready to spit in his face rather than fuck him silly.

"As far as I can tell," Chantel finally sighed. "The marks are gone, and her crystal seems very active. I just don't understand it. I can't figure out how Jonar got to her."

Ariel nearly flinched at the dark look Shane cast her then. As though Chantel's comment had somehow angered him further.

"We'll figure it out." She didn't like the brooding sound of his voice. If Chantel's expression was anything to go by, she didn't think much of it either.

"I'm sure we will." She turned, giving Ariel a long, concerned look. "Will you be okay?"

"She'll be fine," Shane answered for her, surprising Ariel as much as he did Chantel. "I think she needs to rest for now. We'll see the rest of you in the morning."

There was no mistaking the command in his voice. Chantel turned back to him as Ariel tensed, anger churning inside her. What the hell was his problem?

"I see," Chantel murmured then, her voice cool.

"Shane's right, Chantel." Ariel tightened her fingers on her crossed arms, staring back at Shane, knowing the challenge that glittered in her eyes. "I might just need to rest." Or hit the brooding Viking with a very thick, very long board.

Turning, Chantel moved to her, hugging her quickly, taking Ariel by surprise. The comfort, the consolation in that small embrace had tears dampening her eyes.

"I'll see you in the morning then," Chantel whispered at her ear. "Call me if you need me, Ariel. You know how."

A sudden flash, a dizzying shift of reality, washed over her as she suddenly saw the other woman, her face pale, tear-streaked…dying.

Ariel pulled back, fighting to distance herself from this new, flashing bit of knowledge. Past? Or future? Was she seeing what happened or what would happen? God help her, she couldn't handle seeing the future as well as a past that she should have no knowledge of.

"Good night, Ariel." As though she understood better than she should, Chantel touched her hair gently before turning and moving back to the sitting room where the others awaited.

"I think we've been asked to leave," she told them coolly as she passed Shane. "Are you ready to go, Devlin?"

"More than," Devlin grunted, his voice soft, though Ariel picked up on the disgruntled rumble. "It's like visiting a caged lion in here."

Ariel stood still, her lips pressed together, fighting to control the anger pouring through her as she held Shane's stormy gaze. As the door closed behind the others, Ariel felt the air around her thicken further, growing heavier. At her breast, the crystal warmed, a sudden shift in the power sending chills chasing down her spine.

She didn't know this Shane.

"Do you have something to say?" she asked him then, arching her brow mockingly as she stared back at him, meeting him glare for glare.

"I have a lot to say," he nearly snapped. "I'll start with this."

Before she could evade him, avoid him, he moved to her, his hand gripping her arms as he jerked her to him, his head lowering, his lips slamming down on hers.

Shock. Surprise. For a moment, the sheer power behind the kiss rocked her system. Desperate hunger, surging passion, a riot of conflicting emotions surged through her with chaotic violence. She could feel it building in herself as well as Shane. A mix of conflicting needs, desires...angers.

"Damn you, fucking touch me." He jerked back from her, pulling her arms from across her breasts and forcing them to his shoulders as she gasped for breath, her eyes wide, her breasts rising and falling harshly from the adrenaline, the surging lust.

His hands gripped her hips, jerking her against him, lifting her until he could press the surging length of his erection against the soft pad of her pussy.

He was hot. Thick and hot, pressing into her, creating a firestorm of lightning fast sensations that barely allowed her to breathe for the pleasure and the hunger rising inside her.

"Feel me," he growled, his head lowering, his teeth scraping over the sensitive flesh of her neck as he ground his cock between her thighs. "Feel what you do to me, Ariel."

His hands flexed on her hips, his fingers digging into her flesh with almost bruising strength as her head fell back, a moan tearing from her throat.

It shouldn't feel so good. His hands were rough, his kisses hot, filled with a hunger that seemed more compulsive, desperate. Almost angry.

"Shane…" She wanted to soothe him, wanted to still the storm raging inside him, but the passion, the lust burning between them overwhelmed her.

"God, you're beautiful." The words were spoken a bare second before the shirt she was wearing was ripped from her back.

Powerful hands tossed the shreds of material to the floor as she tensed, staring back at him in surprise. His eyes were almost glazed, dark, his expression intent, consuming as he stared down at the full mounds of her breasts. Her nipples strained toward him, hard and peaked, the full curves of her breasts swollen, engorged with pleasure.

His hips bucked against her, pressing his cock firmly against her aching, drenched pussy.

"Do you think I'll ever let you go again?" he snarled, fury and lust whipping in the thunderhead color of his eyes. "Do you think I'll ever accept less than all you are? Ever again?"

She shivered at the sound of his voice, the roiling emotions his words evoked within her.

"Shane..." She shook her head, fighting to make sense of the sudden shift of emotions within him.

This wasn't the gentle giant she had come to expect. This wasn't the lover who had eased her through each adventure. This was the Viking. Ravenous, out of control of his lust, his emotions. And he was making her so fucking hot, her pussy was dripping with it.

"Don't tell me no, Ariel." His voice was ragged as his grip eased, his hands moving from her hips only to jerk at the leather cord that laced the front of her pants. "Get these damned things off before I rip them off you."

Ariel moaned, trembling, staring back at him in dazed fascination as she felt his hands pulling at the snug leather, pushing it over her hips as he turned her, tumbling her to the bed as he abandoned the pants to quickly remove her boots.

"What are you doing, Shane?" She gasped as he flipped her over before jerking the pants the rest of the way from her legs.

"Lay still." His hand landed heavily on the cheek of her ass.

It should have enraged her, that demanding little punishment. She should have come up fighting. Instead, her cunt creamed violently, spilling along the swollen curves and heating her further.

She pressed her face into the bed, listening to the hard bellow of his breaths as moved behind her.

"Shane, I don't understand this." The turnaround was too abrupt. The shift from gentle lover the first time he had taken her, to ravenous lust was exciting, arousing, but confusing.

"That doesn't surprise me," he growled.

159

A flare of anger filled her at his tone. Her lips thinned as she jerked at her legs, determined to roll over and confront him.

"I said, stay still, wench!" His hand landed on her rear again, and despite the anger in his voice she couldn't help but laugh.

Wench?

"Shane, you're slipping." She ignored the fiery heat in her bottom as she felt his hands slide over the curves, spreading her legs further apart. "It's the wrong century for the word 'wench'."

"You are as tenaciously determined now as you ever were then," he fairly snarled, moving back as his hands slid down the backs of her legs.

Taking the opportunity, Ariel quickly rolled to her back, kicked out at him, catching him off-guard as her feet planted in the hard muscles of his stomach and managed to push him back.

He fell hard, right on his ass, his eyes narrowing on her with a glint of retaliation in their depths. His oddly colored eyes were almost a quicksilver now, turbulent with emotion, intensity. It sent a chill up her spine and a ripple through her pussy. This was the Viking. The pillager. The rough, sexual, take no prisoners male she had researched before opening her antiques store in Lexington. This was the Berserker!

"You *will* pay for that." He rose slowly, tall, strong, tension tightening his body as she jumped naked from the bed, her eyes wide as her glance centered on the swollen bulge beneath his leather pants.

She swallowed tightly, her eyes lifting to his face.

"Whenever you're ready to try, big boy." She arched her brow mockingly as she stilled the quiver of lust that rippled over her nerve endings. "Here I am."

Chapter Twenty-Two

✍

He caught her as she attempted to jump from the other side of the bed and rush for the doorway that led into the dressing room before turning into the sitting room. One long arm wrapped around her waist, her struggles ineffectual as he pressed her against the wall, his hard thigh slipping between both of hers as he forced her legs apart.

With her face pressed to the wall, unable to see his expression, she had only her senses to guide her. Senses that were rioting, filled with pleasure, adrenaline and the rush of lust that thundered through her system.

He felt so big behind her, overwhelming her. She could hear his breaths sawing in and out of his chest, feel his cock pressing against her lower back. This was a side of Shane she hadn't seen. One that excited, aroused and sent nervous anticipation whipping through her senses.

His arms were hard, his chest cushioning her back as one broad palm pushed demandingly between her thighs, his fingers sliding through the thick, rich cream that leaked from her pussy.

A low, rough groan echoed against her back.

"You're drenched with heat," he growled at her ear. "Your pussy is dripping for me, Ariel. So hot and wet you'll drown me in your fire."

How was she supposed to speak when he did that? Talked to her with the ruined, rough voice of his. The sound of it slipped over her senses, driving her higher, causing her breath to catch as her womb convulsed with arousal.

A low, harsh cry escaped her as his fingers slid lower, two clamping together and pushing past the tight entrance to her vagina before filling her, penetrating her with a rough, sudden thrust that had her going to her tiptoes, her head tipping back against his shoulder as fire streaked through her body.

"Spread your legs," he snarled at her ear as the limbs in question trembled in excitement.

She spread her legs as he pressed her cheek to the wall.

"Wider." He gripped her wrists, forcing her to flatten her hands on the wall above her head. "All the way, woman. I'll have none of your reticence this time."

She shuddered in near orgasm. He was forceful, dominant, unwilling to take no for an answer or to accept the slightest hesitation.

"Good girl," he crooned, his voice dark as he rewarded her by pulling his fingers back and thrusting in deeper, harder, causing her to cry out at the fire that streaked through her cunt.

"You're close." He didn't sound pleased. "Too close. You won't come yet, Ariel. Not until I allow it. And I intend to enjoy this fully."

His fingers pulled free of her.

"Damn you," she whimpered, pressing her cheek harder to the wall as she fought for her own control.

"Now, let's see just how much of my cock you're willing to take, beloved." He jerked the chair from beneath the nearby table, pulling it close. "Prop your foot here."

He bent her knee, raising her leg until her foot rested in the seat, completely opening her, leaving her undefended, her juices dripping down her thighs as lust hit her squarely in the deepest reaches of her pussy.

Behind her, she could feel him loosing the leather breeches he wore, releasing the straining length of his cock. She couldn't imagine anything more erotic than the thought of his erection straining from the loosened edges of his breeches, aiming for her vulnerable vagina. Unless it was seeing it straining toward her. She shivered at that thought.

"You're so tight, so fucking hot." She trembled as the tip of his cock rested at the opening. "Now feel me, Ariel. Feel every inch of my cock fucking you...fucking you..."

She screamed as he powered into her. A hard, mighty thrust that sent him spearing deep, deeper than he had ever gone before. Harder. Thicker.

Her fingers curled into claws as she fought for something, anything to hold onto. She wanted to be free, she wanted to be penetrated deeper. She wanted him harder, yet she felt stretched to her limits, bruised by the steel-hard flesh impaling her.

His hands gripped her hips, rough, animalistic growls vibrating from his throat as he began thrusting inside her. Long, slow thrusts, demanding, intent on penetrating her to her very soul.

The friction was driving her insane. The hard throb of blood rushing through his cock vibrated through her pussy until her womb rippled with the sensation. The head, thick, pulsing, fiery hot, stretched her impossibly.

She was gasping for breath, certain she would never survive, yet more than willing to fly into the very heart of the death awaiting her. Fire flamed through her, heat filled her, consumed her with each long thrust that pierced her pussy, sinking to the very depths of her, nudging, stretching her further, making her scream out at the pleasure pain of it.

His hands slid up her ribs, covered her swollen breasts. Hard fingers massaged and pulled at her peaked nipples until lightning hard streaks of pleasure were ripping from her breasts and tearing into her core. She was on fire. Blazing out of control.

"Now!" she screamed hoarsely, poised on the edge of release, dizzy with the whiplash of sensations whipping through her.

"Now," he agreed, his voice hot, sensually, sexily rough as his hands moved back to her hips.

He began to move harder, faster. His cock hammered into her with desperate lunges, filling her, releasing her, filling her deeper, harder, faster...

The cataclysm that swept over her was destructive. Bones and muscles tightened with brutal force as the sensitive tissues of her pussy began to milk him, clenching around him tighter than before, until she heard his hoarse shout in her ear and felt the fiery blasts of his semen erupt inside her.

Ariel collapsed against the wall, held in place only by his hands on her hips, his erection jerking inside her. Exhaustion washed over her as she fought to recover her strength, her breathing.

She felt him pull from her then, slowly. An almost imperceptible shift of the air swirled around her then, making her shiver with the strange foreboding she could sense within it.

"I have to go for a while."

She started in surprise as he moved away from her. No kiss. No gentle words. Nothing to ease the sudden darkness that seemed to swirl around her.

She turned slowly, watching as he jerked his pants on, lacing them roughly. He wasn't looking at her, his expression was closed, tense.

"What did I do?" She couldn't help but ask the question. Couldn't control the fears rising inside her.

"You didn't do anything." He shook his head tightly as he jerked his soft boots over his feet and tightened the laces quickly. "Go to bed. You need to rest."

She stood silently, watching as he jerked a T-shirt from the duffel bag beside the bed and stomped from the bedroom. Minutes later, she flinched violently as the door to the suite slammed closed with enough strength to rattle the frame.

"Shane," she whispered his name as she felt him moving away, not just distancing himself physically from her, but mentally, emotionally. Drawing away, leaving her alone in ways she had never known before.

The crystal warmed at her breasts, the air swirled around her.

Beware, Ariel. Beware the disturbance.

She blinked at the sound of the weakened voice, the weariness that filled it.

"Arriane?" she whispered softly, feeling the strange mix of sensations that alerted her to the other woman's psychic presence.

Be careful, sister, she whispered again. *Beware the Savage...*

Just as quickly she was gone.

Ariel firmed her lips, stilled the tremor that would have shook them before slowly straightening her shoulders and taking a deep, steadying breath. Beware the Savage. She rubbed her arms slowly, attempting to warm herself against the sudden chill that chased over her. Shane wouldn't hurt her, she assured herself. She knew him, remembered enough about that life before to know he loved her. He had worshipped her. He had been tender, caring...

Her breath hitched in her throat. As much as she had relished the more forceful touch, the hard, lustful possession, she knew it was something he had never before lost control of. The Savage had never been present when he touched her. Until tonight.

Beware the disturbance...

She could feel it in the very air around her.

Shuddering, she turned and strode quickly to the shower. The water was hot, the pressure pounding, and suddenly, she had a horrible, frightening need to be warm.

* * * * *

Lightning flickered in the distance as rain clouds thickened in the night sky. The elements were unsettled, the air thick with an unnatural tension as Shane stepped from the hotel and drew in the scents of the night.

Since finding Ariel, his own sensitivity to the air around them had increased. His gift from the Guardians had been that of physical strength, yet Shane found himself now sensing things he had never known before. It made him feel…unbalanced.

He shook his head, pushing his fingers roughly through his hair as he paced around the side of the building, searching for a darkened area to hide within, though he knew there was no place he could hide from himself.

God, what had he done?

He had pushed her against the wall and taken her like a camp whore, uncaring of her delicate body, pushing her past limits he would have never pushed her past before. The anger rising inside him had been overwhelming, the rage that he had always controlled so easily, working free as though it had no restraints placed around it.

There had been a time, centuries before, when the Berserker rages had tormented him. It had taken a while to accustom himself to the mental and physical changes his powers had given him, to find the control it took to push back the physical responses to his anger. It had been more than a millennium since he had been tormented with them. And never had the dark anger risen in Ariel's presence. Not until she had denied him her love.

There was no excuse for it.

He sighed wearily as he found a bench beneath thickly leafed trees and sat down heavily. He was angry at her, yes. Worried. In that life before she had denied her powers, but she had never denied her love for him. Now, it seemed she was accepting the powers as they came, but not the love he had waited so long to give her.

His fists clenched at the thought. A thousand fucking years he had waited. Never touching another woman, lusting after nothing but the dreams he had of Ariel each night. Tormenting, lust-filled dreams, but nothing like what he had just done to her.

He wiped his hands over his face, breathing out roughly. Surely the payment exacted by Fate and Destiny for this second chance wouldn't be the love Ariel had once felt for him. It was a price he couldn't pay, he thought savagely. He had lived for her, lived for her love, her touch. And now, he would be forced to push her further, harder than even he thought he could.

Thunder vibrated in the distance as lightning crossed the sky once again. It was closer now, the smell of rain thickening in the air. Her sisters were coming to her aid. Against him? He growled at the suspicion that they would dare to interfere.

They had been close in that first life. The four women had shared their strengths, bolstered each other's weaknesses, and drew solace from the bond they had shared. Chantel's death had destroyed a part of them, weakening them further than they had been due to the lives they were born into.

Chantel lived now though. And she strengthened them. Drew them together, made them stronger. But they wouldn't interfere in his relationship with Ariel, he would see to it. And he would be damned if he would allow Ariel to deny him much longer. There was no way to save her without that emotional bond. No way to open those final powers that would lead her to Caitlin. No one to ensure they would be together for all time without the mating of the spirit, as well as the body.

"Shane." He raised his head as Derek stepped from the shadows, moving to lean against the thick trunk of the tree, beside the bench.

He carried a bottle of his favorite Irish whisky, sipping from it pensively as he stared into the sky above them.

"Caitlin's tears," he whispered quietly. "You can feel them in the air."

The very Earth itself was unsettled. Unusually so.

"Any sign from Caitlin?" Shane asked then, accepting the bottle Derek passed to him.

"Not since your and Ariel's little battle at the bar," he grunted.

"Arrianne has yet to call to Joshua for aid, perhaps it was merely a game your wife plays," Shane growled before tipping the bottle to his lips and taking a long, burning drink. "They delight in playing with us. In keeping our nerves on edge, our hearts bound to their chilly breasts."

He ignored Derek's surprised look, turning from him instead to stare into the darkness.

"Ariel and Chantel were the most devoted," Derek said quietly as Shane glanced back at him, seeing the wearing sobriety that haunted the other man. "That love and understanding is more precious than gold, Shane. For as exasperating as females can often be, there is much to be said for a loyal heart."

Shane grunted at that. "How are we to know such devotion survived death and rebirth?" he snapped. "They are different…"

"No, my friend, your wife is as she always was in many ways." Derek shrugged then. "You are the one now acting differently. She is a woman and a warrior to be proud of, not one to be chastised or reviled. Perhaps you should think about that."

Shane narrowed his eyes, anger rushing through him, but before he could challenge him, the other man turned and stalked away heavily, hands pressed deep into his jeans pockets, his head lowered as a misty, dampening rain slowly began to fall.

Chapter Twenty-Three

ഗ

"We've rented cabins here." Devlin pointed to the small, red X just outside Newhalem, Washington. "If Chantel and Ariel are right, then Caitlin is somewhere in the general area. Finding her might not be easy, though. She's parked herself in one of the most bloody, rainy areas in the States. We won't be able to depend on tracking her element to find her."

"She's more than aware we're coming, too," Ariel pointed out as she leaned against the wall, watching the four men gathered around the maps Devlin had spread out on the long coffee table. "We're not moving in on someone ill-prepared to deal with the surprises of the power she holds. She's more than aware of this power, and she's learned how to use it, especially since Chantel's powers awoke."

She ignored the brooding look Shane cast her. His ill-assed mood was starting to piss her off.

"She's called out to me once, when she thought Ariel was in danger," Derek observed, raising his head to stare first at Chantel, then at Ariel. "Is there any way we can use that? Any way to make her believe she's needed?"

Ariel thinned her lips, restraining the sneer she would have cast him.

"Trickery is what got you into trouble the first time," she told him, tightening her arms where they were folded beneath her breasts. "She won't let you trick her again."

"Because you refuse to aid him." Shane's look was as cool as his voice as he stared at her now.

Gray eyes were chilling, his big body tense, it was easy to see the anger slowly growing in him once again.

"It doesn't work that way," she informed him, her voice just as cold. "The elements can't lie to each other, Shane. Unlike people, nature knows only honesty." The mockery she injected in her voice wasn't lost on him.

Just as the thickening of the tension in the air wasn't lost on her. She would have sighed in weariness if so many eyes weren't centered on her.

"I wouldn't ask you to lie, warrioress," Derek said then, leaning back in his chair, his expression somber as he watched her. "As you said, it is deception that caused her fury to begin with. It was merely a thought."

She heard laughter in the air around her. Caitlin's laughter. Just as she could sense another's pain. Arriane's pain.

She tilted her head, staring at Derek, then Joshua.

"Are you two aware that your wives see each move you make, hear each word from your lips?"

She saw their surprise. She saw Joshua's shock and knew that he had inflicted the most pain.

Ariel, I do not need your protection... Fury echoed in the minute whisper that reached her ears.

Not her protection, her truth... Caitlin was amused, filled with laughter.

Narrowing her eyes, Ariel pulled the air close around her, surprised herself now at how easily the other two women were connecting to her. She turned, saw Chantel's carefully blank expression, and knew that she was aware of it all.

Why hadn't she told them? Why didn't Derek and Joshua know the truth?

The other woman arched her brow mockingly, her emerald eyes glittering brilliantly.

As though she had done it all her life, Ariel lifted her hand, drew a tight circle in the air around her, and sent the silent command to her crystal to hold the words spoken in the room within the room. They would never escape, would never know freedom unless she released them.

"Caitlin knows well how to connect to the crystals." She moved away from the wall, placing the protection about it, assuring herself that neither Caitlin, nor Arriane could know any pain from any words spoken now. "She's learned how to be patient, silent, how to use the moisture in the air to conduct the information she needs. She won't be tricked."

"Ariel," Chantel's voice urged caution then.

Ariel tilted her head, closed her eyes and sent out the command for the knowledge she needed now. Chantel seemed unwilling to allow her to go further; even now Ariel could feel the connection between the two stones, sense Chantel's hesitancy.

"What do they know, Mistress?" Joshau's voice. This warrior had sides as different as the two names he carried. One was primitive, dark, a force to be reckoned with, a power that allowed no refusal.

Her eyes opened then and she knew the reason why Chantel had urged that caution. This man had known no loyalty, no fidelity through the centuries, but she saw something she knew Chantel didn't. Suspicion. Pain.

"You two are without redemption." Pain filled her heart, her soul. "One who deceived and stole another's will. Another who knew no fidelity, no loyalty. What a sight the two of you are."

"You judge us unfairly, warrioress." Derek stared back at her broodingly, dark brows lowered over brilliant eyes.

"Enough, Ariel." It was Shane's calm, dispassionate order that sent waves of tense silence rushing over her, not to mention the anger that began to fill her.

"Enough?" she asked him carefully, ignoring Chantel's concerned look, just as she ignored the crystal's warning at her breast. "Maybe it is. Perhaps in reality, Caitlin and Arriane are the lucky ones. At least they knew the assholes they're getting ahead of time. I had to be surprised by mine."

She ignored the looks of shock that spread across the other men's expressions, just as she ignored the anger that flared in Shane's eyes. Turning from them, she stalked to the door and flung it open.

"Where the hell do you think you're going?" he snarled behind her, a breeze whipping around her, warning her that he had shot to his feet.

She turned to look back at him, a cold smile twisting her lips.

"Away from you. I'm starting to think Jonar might be the lesser of the two evils here."

She didn't give him time to reply, no time to strike back at her with his rough, commanding voice or the thread of dark fury she could feel building in him. Her own anger was growing in ways she had never expected, in ways she couldn't control within herself. Like a dark cloud boiling, roiling inside her, it grew larger, darker, each time she glimpsed the unaccountable accusation in Shane's eyes.

It was too reminiscent of her father and his rages and that came close to the memories of the dark. She shuddered as she ran lightly down the deserted stairs that led to the lobby of the motel.

The expensive suites the warriors used were on the twelfth floor, and by time she reached the lobby exit, she could feel the tightness in her lungs, the exhaustion she was fighting in her body. Lack of sleep, the long days on the road and the tension she had been living under for so many months were beginning to build up on her. She could feel it, wearing her down, weakening her. A weakness she had been able to combat those first days in Shane's presence.

As she reached the first floor, she leaned against the wall, closing her eyes wearily as she fought to catch her breath. She could feel the crystal fighting to aid her, to lend her the strength she needed.

I feel him, Ariel... The voice was amused, a sweet melodic sound filled with mockery. *The Wizard seeks even outside himself now, hoping to follow the waves of power on the very winds...*

Ariel opened her eyes slowly, as she felt the breeze in the small stairwell increase, the air thickening around her.

I know you can hear me... The voice sighed. *Just as I know how foolish it is to speak to the one who searches so hard for me. Would it do me any good to beg you to turn them from me?*

There was such sadness in her voice.

A light breeze teased the hair at her temples, carrying the voice to her, lingering around her caressingly as she waited for whatever the other woman would reveal. As she stood there, a glimmer of a memory coalesced within her mind. The fiery-haired woman, her eyes an ocean green, staring out at the world unseeing, dazed where once they had been clear and bright.

*If only you remembered what he did to me...*the voice whispered again. *He was a demon and we never knew it. Reviled even by his own family and we were never told. Our father lied, Ariel, he was no savior, he was evil itself...*

Ariel wanted to shake her head in denial as an image of Derek, his blue eyes watching the delicate woman with such sadness, such inner pain, that Ariel had turned her head from the sight each time she saw it.

They had all been hurting then, though she didn't know why. She could feel it, a grief of such proportions as to weigh the very soul.

"Without you, we all die, Cait..." She commanded the winds to carry her voice, to seek out the one speaking to her so softly, the voice so filled with fear and pain.

There was silence, the air suddenly thick with oppressive fear.

A demon's lie... The voice wavered. *He would tell you anything...*

"A warrior's mistake, a man's pain," Ariel whispered what she remembered of the Wizard's legacy.

It had been so long ago when her grandmother had whispered the ancient legends to her.

"A child chosen by the gods, marked by their touch, reviled in anger, cursed with deceit, and cursing in turn. Payment to atone the sins to the child. Payment to atone the sins *of* the child. And the tears of the rain shall wash away the pain but only with the destruction of the Wizard's tears, shall truth be born... Caitlin, you can't hide forever..."

So speaks the one who refuses to believe, to remember... The voice was bitter, railing against whatever she perceived as her fate. *Your memories are not clear, but mine have always been. At least your Savage loved, gave you the choice to fight. The Wizard stole my very mind and took the memories of all I knew, all I loved...*

She couldn't excuse him. Ariel knew, had known since first seeing Derek, that somehow he had betrayed, and he paid the price daily.

"We can't fight without you, Cait..." she murmured the words, flashes of memory slowly taking their place within her mind. "I'll make no excuses for him. I will only say that we need you. Just as you need us."

There was silence once again. A long, pain-filled silence that filled her with sadness.

I need no one... But she did, Ariel could feel it. *Give me peace, Ariel; I ask you one last time, turn them from me. Only you can do that.*

Ariel stared into the dimly lit stairwell, fighting to make Caitlin understand.

"I can't," she whispered then. "My life, Chantel's life, and the life of one that sleeps yet never rests depend on finding you. We fight together or we die..."

The Legacies her grandmother had told her were slowly becoming clearer within her mind.

"Cait, the Wizard's Tears will only be found by facing the Wizard. To gain what you so desperately need, you have no choice but to accept what destiny holds."

I will escape him, Ariel. Anger blended with a sigh of pain. A masculine, resigned sigh that Ariel knew could be none other's than that of the Wizard's.

She kept her knowledge to herself, feeling the added tendrils of power that shadowed her own, seeking the woman who had finally become desperate enough to reach out to her.

Then laughter echoed around her. Amused, yet tainted with a woman's fury.

Bastard! The very air sizzled with Caitlin's curse before she was gone.

"Well, that was interesting," Shane said from the landing above her, his voice dark with disapproval.

"You heard it?" She almost winced at the sound of hope in her voice.

Despite the fact that Shane was quick to assure her she wasn't crazy, episodes such as this one were always prone to make her doubt her own mind.

"I heard." He nodded shortly. "It would appear the legend lied in no way. Caitlin is well aware of her past life, and fully intent on seeing vengeance. Derek has much to pay for it would seem. But the Wizard is not alone in learning his lessons from the past."

Her eyes widened at his arrogant tone, staring back at him as he descended the final step, watching her. His hair flowed around his shoulders like a wild mane, the bare muscles of his chest and abdomen gleamed like well-oiled silk, flexing beneath the layer of flesh with a powerful effect.

Ariel's breath caught in her throat as past and present merged once again. She saw him, ages ago, centuries ago, staring at her from the castle steps, his eyes narrowed in lust and yet with gentleness as she stood defiantly before him.

Caitlin's voice no longer taunted her; it was now a memory, a past she sensed she had no desire to remember.

"We ride on them." She couldn't halt the words or the memories.

Fury washed through her, pain unlike anything she could have known as shock filled her, nearly incapacitated her.

"They killed her." Her voice lowered as she shook her head, fighting the memory, fighting the knowledge of what had been done to a sister, the sudden overriding suspicion of what had been done to her.

"Ariel?" She watched him approach slowly, a battle waging within his gaze, his expression filled with concern.

She was shaking. She could feel every muscle in her body shuddering as the memory overwhelmed her.

"He killed her," she repeated, her voice hoarse, her mind dazed with the sudden knowledge that began to fill her.

She didn't need this now. She didn't need the pain that filled her, couldn't deal with the struggle to hold herself up beneath the onslaught of memories.

Blood and death, a sister who had sacrificed herself and had paid the ultimate price. And another, misty memory, another death, and a sacrifice. She shuddered, remembering the dark-haired woman lying near death, the unnatural wound on her abdomen slowly draining her lifeblood as Ariel stared on in horror.

I can save her, for a price... The voice had been a deadly hiss of evil. *Will you pay the price?*

"Stop!" Shane stood before her, his hands gripping her shoulders as he gave her a rough, demanding shake.

"What did he do to me?" She stared up at him, so thankful that he had broken the hold the emerging memory had on her that she could almost forgive him for his earlier, callous attitude.

"What did he do to us?" she whispered then. "I remember so much and yet so little. Was I a terrible wife, Shane? Did I betray you?"

He glanced away from her briefly, his expression tightening convulsively before he shook his head.

"You never betrayed me. You were a most loving, gentle wife."

"Then why?" she whispered, tired, weary of the battle growing between them, the memories that made little sense. "Why are you so angry?"

He drew in a hard breath, his lips thinning, nostrils flaring as he turned back to her.

"You know the answer to that, you just won't face it," he growled roughly.

"I don't know." She hit out at him, fury surging through her. "What do you want from me? I'm giving you everything I have. Why isn't it enough?"

"Because there's more." His answer shocked her. Confused her.

She stared back at him, her eyes wide.

"What am I not remembering?" She met his gaze directly, her heart racing out of control, her breath tight in her chest.

"Only you can answer that, Ariel," he snapped then, one large hand lifting to frame her face. "Only you can answer the questions you have. Until you find the courage to do so, there is no more that I can do."

Chapter Twenty-Four

ဢ

She was breaking his heart and had no idea of the damage being wrought. As he led her back to the room, Shane fought himself, fought his heart and every need he had to reach out to her, to comfort her, to assure her that she needed do no more than she was already. But he knew it would be only false comfort. It could be a deadly mistake, one he didn't dare make.

He wouldn't allow her to hide, not from him, her past, or the emotions he knew bound them together. If it was her rage that was needed to thaw the ice that encased her heart, then by God, he would enrage her.

"Son of a bitch, you have no right to drag me around like this," she hissed behind him, digging in her heels as she pulled against his hold.

He glanced behind his shoulder, stilling the smile that wanted to cross his lips, instead holding onto the anger he knew he needed to do what must be done. She was stubborn as she had ever been and in as many ways, just as close-minded.

"I've a right to do whatever it takes to protect your ass, Ariel," he snapped in response. "Do you think Jonar takes breaks? That somehow you can flit from safety and remain unscathed?"

"I won the last battle, didn't I?" she sneered in response, and he could hear the triumph echoing in her voice.

"By luck alone." It enraged him, infuriated him that she would think she could defeat Jonar alone. That her confidence was so heady, so overwhelming that she would actually

178

believe that she could face such evil without his presence and be victorious.

He threw the door to their room open, pulling her inside as she kicked at him, struggling against his grip. When she was clear, he slammed the panel furiously, ignoring the shuddering of the doorframe as he swung her around to face him, releasing her and preparing for the battle to come.

He ducked the first blow, more from fear of her breaking her hand against his jaw than any fear of damage she could wring. Her hands were delicate, her fingers slender and easily damaged while the bones in his body were like steel, reinforced by the alien technology and nearly indestructible.

"Bastard, stand still!" She came at him again, swinging furiously as he extended his arm, pressing against her chest and holding back easily.

"You won't win this battle, Ariel," he informed her harshly as her eyes narrowed, her body tensing.

He knew that look well, though he had never seen it aimed at him. It was a look reserved for enemies, a glitter of retaliation, a gleam of hunger, a need for blood.

"And you think you will?" she snarled, moving back, obviously searching for a position that would afford her the ability to deliver the most damage.

"Do not ever doubt I won't." He smiled, knowing the arrogance would make her livid. "I am by far stronger than you, woman. As well as more experienced. I won't allow you to win."

Her jaw tightened, rage glittering in her eyes. The veil of cool defiance was being stripped away; the woman she had been and the woman she was now began to merge in perfect balance, in harmony. And despite the pain that ripped through him for what he was forced to do, he had to admit that this new Ariel aroused him as she never had before.

He knew her. He had helped train her for months after their marriage, teaching her what she hadn't already known, learning the knowledge she had already gathered in fighting. That knowledge had survived rebirth, instinct guided her movements, making her a lethal fighting machine.

He sidestepped quickly as she went into a crouch, one leg sweeping out to trip him, instantly she countermoved, coming to her feet in a blinding rush as one little foot kicked out toward a most vulnerable area. A hard, swollen area that would have been highly displeased had she managed to follow through with the blow.

"Do you not cease this instant, then I'll paddle your rear," he snarled, deliberately pushing back his need to play with her, to turn the battle into a love match.

His heart clenched, a raw wound ripping into it as he countered her next blow as well before gripping her wrists, twisting her around and anchoring them behind her back.

She stilled immediately.

"Let me go!" The harsh order was filled with rage. "Now!"

"Not in this lifetime, wife." He wanted to shake her, wanted to rage at her for her stubbornness, for her inability to see past her own fears. "You will not battle me. Not now, not ever. And I'll be damned if I'll allow you to endanger yourself alone."

"Allow me?" She struggled against his grip then, a fierce snarl of fury escaping her lips as she attempted to kick back at his spread legs. "You allow me nothing, Savage. I don't need your permission for a damned thing."

"Wrong." He lowered his voice, allowing the harsh, gravelly tone to deepen into a sneer. "Until you can defeat me, wench, then you will obey me. And we both know you have no hope of defeating me." At least not until she realized the full potential of her power and her heart.

His soul bled as he heard the pain in her fierce growls, the tears she refused to shed as she cursed him.

"You're mine, Ariel." His teeth gripped the lobe of her ear, tugging at it gently as she strained away from him. "And I will prove it now."

He felt her still, tensing against him as she felt his erection pressing against her lower back, hard and demanding, forceful.

"Don't even think about it." She bucked in his hold, more determined to be free than ever before.

"I will do more than think about it, wife," he assured her coolly. "You'll learn how easily your body can control you. How much you belong to me. There is a very, very old custom, a practice of complete submission that has conquered more than one unwilling maiden through the centuries. One you will learn this night."

He punctuated his words by hooking his fingers into the neckline of her T-shirt and ripping it from her body. He heard her gasp, a sound of part excitement, and yet, part fear. That fear pierced his soul like the sharpest dagger.

He hid his face against her hair, grimacing, holding back his own pain as he gripped her wrists in one hand, allowing the other to smooth up her abdomen to the thrusting curves of her breasts.

"Shane..." her voice quivered as he gripped a hardened nipple between his thumb and forefinger. "Are you going to hurt me?"

A silent scream echoed through his mind. It was her scream, a remnant of nightmares she had once endured in the past. The memories of Jonar raping her, taking her innocence, her very will.

"Such trust you show me," he forced the sneer past his lips.

"You aren't doing much to gain my trust." She was breathing roughly, her body responding to his touch, though he felt her mind fighting to distance itself, to examine this new situation before she allowed herself to give into it.

"I do not ask for your response, Ariel. I demand it. I will not plead for your submission, I will enforce it."

"That doesn't answer my question." Her voice was rough now, her nipples hard, proud little points as his fingers tormented each in turn.

"There is a pain so sharp, so intense, it is the greatest pleasure," he whispered at her neck then. "A submission that comes only when forced to endure the pleasure and the pain. You will realize this night, wife, that I alone hold the power to bring you that pleasure and that pain. And you will remember it. I will ensure it."

He lifted her easily then, carrying her to the bed despite her fierce struggles. Her cursing, her rage was a tangible thing, yet so was her arousal. The very air itself was tinged with her heightened lust, her tension, her fear of the unknown. Yet, it was also scented with her pain. No amount of pleasure would still the fact that in this, he was forcing her response, taking her despite her fury, bringing her slowly closer to the demonic nightmares of the past.

He threw her to the bed, facing her with his own surging emotions and the anger growing inside him.

"Coward," he bit out, his voice a rough growl as she moved to jump from the bed.

Just as he anticipated, she paused, staring back at him with narrowed eyes, her hands braced behind her on the mattress as she held herself up.

"I have never been a coward," she snapped back.

"You were always a coward," he accused her then. "In one way or another, you were never courageous enough to awaken to who and what you were. That has not changed."

It wasn't entirely fair. He knew the reasons why she had been unable to awaken in that first life and he didn't blame her. No one could have blamed her. But he would not accept it in this life. Her life meant too much to him.

"And you think fucking you now, letting you dominate me will make me courageous?" she sneered as he placed his knee on the bed.

"There is no letting me do anything, Ariel," he informed her with mocking amusement. "I will fuck you. I will dominate you. Better yet, I will do it in a way that will prove to us both, once and for all, that you belong to me. Completely."

Heart and soul. There was only one act that would prove her unconscious trust of him and the bond he knew existed between them. One that would demand her complete willingness and sow the seeds within her own mind, of the emotions they shared.

"What are you going to do?" Her eyes were wide, suspicion shadowing them.

"Why, my Lady." He smiled. "I'm going to fuck that sweet, tight little ass of yours. I'm going to take the last of your resistance, the last of your denials and impale them with every inch of my dick until you know, heart and soul, Ariel, exactly who you belong to, and why. When this night is finished, you will beg me for more. Scream for me to fuck your ass deeper, harder, to spill myself inside you and brand you forever." Anger seared each word, his own desperation roughening his voice further. "By God, you will admit you are mine."

Chapter Twenty-Five

இ

Ariel stared back at him in shock, at first, unaware of the fact that his hands had moved to the clasp of her jeans until they snapped free.

"You're crazy." She tried to jerk away from him, to smack his hands, to force him to stop just long enough for her to think, to consider the underlying emotion she heard echoing in his voice.

He was relentless though. Before she could do more than attempt to claw at his face, his shoulders, he was jerking her pants down her legs before pausing only long enough to unlace her moccasin boots and jerk them free of her as well.

Within seconds, she was completely naked before him, staring back at him in surprise an instant before her own rage boiled over. She launched herself at him, fists flying, the dark emotions that whipped between them refusing to allow her to submit so easily.

Though she knew she would submit. Her blood pumped, rich and hot with arousal, the juices spilling from her cunt at the thought of Shane taking her in such a primitive, dominant fashion. Would she open for him? Would she scream in pain, or in pleasure?

His cock was like living steel, thick and long, a sword proportioned to the massive frame of his body. As she fought him, pushing, shoving, her nails raking the tough skin of his shoulders and chest, she knew the battle would end only one way. Exactly as he predicted.

"Wildcat!" he snarled as she managed to slam her knee into his thigh as he took her down to the bed.

He kicked her legs apart, her struggles useless as he came between her thighs, the wide, flared head of his cock nudging into the folds of her pussy as she stilled immediately.

His expression was forbidding, his gaze resigned; he finally shook his head wearily. Then slowly, as he watched her, she saw the flames of passion begin to burn brighter.

"I won't submit to you." She fought to smother her own arousal as she attempted to push away from him and the heat that beckoned to her.

"I know so, wife," he growled as her hands pressed against his chest. "I warned you, this night is mine. You will not defy me again in such a way, Ariel. I will make certain of it."

He meant it. She shivered at the threat, both sensual and physical. He meant to push her past her limits, and she wasn't certain she was ready to face them. Pride goes before a fall, she reminded herself as she stared into his implacable expression.

"I'll be good," she gasped as his head lowered, his lips smoothing over a nipple that became instantly hard at his touch. "I promise."

"Hmm. I can attest to the fact that you are good," he praised her then in a voice husky with desire. "Very, very good. Nice and tight and hot as you grip my cock. But you are a willful woman. Stubborn. That stubbornness will endanger you no longer."

The naughty words had her face flushing, her pussy heating. She could feel the moisture easing from her vagina, preparing her as ripples of remembered pleasure washed over her.

"Stop it, Shane," she gasped. "This won't prove anything. This isn't submission, it's a damned perverted game."

He chuckled at that. "It makes you hot. I see the heat building in your face, in your eyes. I bet it's making your cunt all soft and wet for me, your juices thick and sweet. I want to taste the delicacy your desire creates. I could make a meal of your sweet pussy."

Oh God. She was going to come just listening to him talk dirty to her. It was perverted. Depraved. She should hate it, should hate him for it, but it was burning her alive with hunger.

"Ask me to do it," he growled, the stark order rasping over her nerve endings, sending her mind spinning with the dark promise in his voice.

She blinked back at him in confusion. "Ask you to do what?"

"Ask me to eat your pussy," he whispered, his expression turning carnal, hungry. "Tell me what you want."

Shock had her eyes widening as she stared back at him for long, silent minutes. He didn't appear to be joking. Neither did he appear to be in the mood for a refusal. Would he force her? Would he have to force her? She could feel her cunt growing wetter, creamier, soaking her thighs with the sudden excitement building inside her.

"Are you crazy?" she gasped.

"You can ask me to fuck you in the heat of the moment, but you can't ask me to lick your pussy?" He snapped, his eyes darkening. "Wrong, baby. You will beg me to eat that little cunt of yours. To shove my tongue inside you and fuck you with it."

She stared up at him, aware of the long, thick strands of his hair that fell around them creating a curtain of sensual intimacy. She could feel the heat rising in both their bodies, the need to do just as he asked, to be carnal and wild and as free in her hunger as he was in his. To allow the darkness raging in his eyes freedom.

This was the Viking. Wild. Untamed. Unrelenting.

"It's different then," she gasped as his lips parted, the moist warmth caressing her nipple a second before he looked up at her.

His teeth rasped her nipple in retaliation, causing her breath to catch, her cunt to flame in eager anticipation. The dark vision of the gentle warrior she had first met was gone now, in his place was a warrior unwilling to give any quarter.

"You will say the words," he snarled. "Do it, Ariel. Ask me. Beg me to lick your pussy." His teeth scraped her neck, his need smothering her with an answering response that overwhelmed her senses.

She moaned hoarsely. She could feel the need growing inside her, the heat and the madness he built consuming her. How was she supposed to deny him? All he had to do was touch her and something inside her responded with a wildness, a craving she couldn't explain.

The bond between them confused her. It pulled at her, left her defenseless before him, unable, unwilling to fight his passion. Her soul ached when he looked at her as he was now, his eyes so dark, that almost imperceptible glimmer of pain in them wounding something deep within her spirit. What hold was this? How did he do this to her?

"Why are you doing this?" She watched him with an edge of desperation now, fighting herself as much as she fought him, as his mouth lingered only a breath from the hard tip of her breast.

"Because I want to." His breath was like a flame, lashing at the sensitive flesh of her neck, her chest, then the swollen peaks of her breasts.

Her nipples were so sensitive that the brush of his lips sent spasms of need convulsing in her womb.

"That's a horrible reason, Shane," she gasped, straining against him as she felt her pussy weeping against the head of his cock.

"Do as I say, Ariel. Whisper the words to me." Pure steel ran through his voice, determination that she would obey him, that in this, she would give him what he needed.

She swallowed tightly, bit her lip, then whimpered in growing hunger.

"Shane..." She shook beneath him. "Why?"

"Because they are your desires too. I would hear them from your lips the same as I taste them on your body. You will say them, or we will lie here with my lips merely teasing you, testing your limits. But in the end, you will do it."

She could see the hunger in him the same as she felt it in herself. But there was more there as well. A growing darkness, a determination she wasn't certain how to fight.

"Suck my breast." Surprise shot through her as the words whispered from her lips.

The effect on Shane was greater. He groaned, a low sound of tortured pleasure as he opened his lips and consumed her.

"Oh God. Yes. Like that." She arched closer to him, her hands gripping handfuls of his hair, holding him to her as his tongue lashed at the tender nipple that his mouth sucked at so desperately.

She was twisting beneath him, her hips rising to meet the hard, flat plane of his stomach where it pressed against her mound, grinding her clit against him, held suspended in an agony of pleasure as his mouth drew on her.

"What else?" He was breathing fast. Hard.

His face was flushed, his eyes almost black as his hands framed both full mounds, pressing them together to make it easier to suckle at first one, then the other.

"Tell me." He pressed harder against the wet flesh that pressed against his stomach. "Tell me what else you want, Ariel."

"Eat me," she snarled, so wet, so hot for him now that she could barely think, let alone deny him whatever he wanted. "Lick my pussy, Shane. I want to feel your tongue on me, inside me..." Her breath caught at such a thought. "Fuck me with your tongue, Shane. Fuck me with your tongue..."

The growl that broke from his lips was almost animalistic. Before she could draw breath, before she could whimper in anticipation he had moved. His hands gripped her knees, pushing them back, opening her wide for him before his head lowered and his tongue plunged deep inside her melting vagina.

Ariel heard her scream echo around her. The pleasure was agony. The feel of his tongue parting her tight muscles, licking inside her. He was licking her.

She bucked against his hold, her hands locked into the blankets at her side as he ate her with decadent hunger. His tongue thrust in and out in hard, driving strokes. His lips suckled at the juices that ran freely from her, his hand held her legs wide, making certain there was no touch he couldn't freely make.

She was so close to coming she could feel it, at the edge of awareness, building and building, but Shane refused to make that one touch, that one stroke that would send her over the edge. He kept her poised on the brink, his tongue working her sensually, sexually.

She was barely aware of what was going on as he used one arm to hold her knees back toward her stomach. His other hand then smoothed down the side of her thigh, his fingers caressing, warm and calloused.

She took only a distant note of the fact when his tongue left her rippling pussy to lick and caress her clit, because his finger was there, dipping into her, filling her before retreating. Her juices were rolling from her cunt, along the narrow crevice to her rear, making the area, slick, hot.

But when she felt his finger press inside her anus, sliding with one sure, firm thrust deep inside her, she bucked, crying out as she nearly reached her peak.

His finger retreated, and next two filled her, tighter this time, working inside her, building the pleasure/pain to an explosive peak and filling her mind with an image she didn't want to see, didn't want to know, yet it was there.

His thumb moved to her pulsing pussy, pressing inside her, filling her as his fingers continued to work her anal muscles. Pressing, stretching her, opening her with slow, patient thrusts until she was fighting to breathe through the pleasure as the third was inserted.

"Shane." Her head tossed on the bed now, depraved pleasure sweeping over her, making her mad for him.

This was insanity. Not the whispers on the wind or the craziness her father swore she had. This was madness. The words she fought valiantly to hold back and failed, would be her downfall.

"Fuck me," she groaned, panting as she felt his fingers work deeper, deeper inside her. "There, Shane, fuck me there."

"Where, Ariel?" His voice was strained at the effort to hold onto his control. "Where would you have me fuck you?"

"There." She pushed against the invading fingers driving inside her ass now.

"Tell me where, damn you," he snarled. "Give me the fucking words, Ariel."

"Fuck my ass!" She wanted to scream, but could barely gasp as the three fingers plunged inside her with forceful dominance. "Damn you, shove your cock up my ass."

He jerked from her. Her eyes rounded in surprise when he jerked a small tube from one of the duffel bags in the chair and moved quickly back to her. One hand lifted her legs again, a second later, she felt the cool rush of a lubricant sliding deep inside her anus from the small opening of the tube.

She moaned in rising lust. The forbidden act was washing over her with such carnal hunger that she was lost within it.

"There is a line between pleasure and pain," he told her as he placed her feet at his shoulders, lifting her hips in his hands until the head of his cock lodged at her anal entrance.

"A line filled with sensation and ecstasy beyond anything you know."

As he pressed against the relaxed little hole, one hand moved between her thighs, his thumb exerting a heated pressure against her clit. Ariel gasped, her muscles convulsing a second before she felt the entrance flare open around the tip of his cock.

"There you go, baby," he crooned roughly, his thumb feathering her clit again, producing the same reaction along with an involuntary cry from her lips. "Milk me in, Ariel. All the way in, baby…"

Her head thrashed on the bed as perspiration coated her skin. She couldn't believe it. Fire was racing through her anus, her cunt, striking her clit with deadly blows as his thumb continued to massage the flesh along the side of it.

She could feel her muscles flexing, convulsing around the flared head of his cock, doing just as he said, milking his cock up the narrow, sensitive channel of her ass. Inch by fiery, destructive inch, she began to fill with him. Untried muscles clenched and throbbed before spreading wide for the impalement.

It hurt. She clenched her teeth, her groan rushing through her throat as her neck arched against the sensations. He was filling her slowly, stretching her impossibly, the pain blending so deeply with the pleasure that there was no fighting it. Hell, she wanted more of it.

She relaxed further, a short scream tearing from her as the head of his cock pushed past the tight anal ring, locking him inside her, making it impossible for her go back, to change her mind about it.

She could have never imagined there was such pleasure in pain. That her cries would ever echo around her as she begged for more of the agonizing rapture. But she was doing just that. Her heels braced at his shoulder, she allowed her hips to arch against him, working him deeper, deeper, until finally, with a ragged groan she felt him slide in to the hilt.

His erection throbbed inside her, the heavy pulse of blood through the thick veins echoing through her body as her muscles rippled around him. Slashing fire streaked through her nerve endings, sensitized her further, pushing her higher, leaving her craving more.

"God. Ariel. Dammit..." His cock flexed within her, causing her to whimper at the exquisite pleasure that echoed through her. "Son of a bitch. You're fucking tight. So fucking tight you're killing me."

Hot steel filled her ass. Thick, and so hard. She could feel every inch, every thick vein pounding with blood, stretching her wide, filling her with fire.

"Fuck me, Shane." Her voice was a thread of sound as his hands spread her legs once again, his eyes going to where he had lodged inside her.

"Stroke your clit," he ordered harshly then. "Touch yourself first."

Desperate lust, incredible pleasure. Her world narrowed down to his voice, whatever he commanded, whatever he needed, if he would just push her over the edge she was teetering on.

Her hand lifted from the bed, her fingers stroking over her engorged clit as the fingers of the other hand began to pinch and pull at the nipple of one breast as well.

"Oh yeah, baby," he growled, his gaze darkening further as he watched her and began to move.

It was the most intense sensation she could have imagined. Burning, streaking strokes of pleasure that defied description. His cock stroked the nerve endings in her anus like velvet fire, rasping and caressing, sending electric shards of sensation ripping into her pussy, pulsing through her clit.

Her fingers stroked her clit but it was her cunt making her insane. The building heat was throbbing there, streaking from her ass to her vagina, tormenting her with the escalating need.

Then his fingers were there. As though he knew she needed more, two pushed forcibly past the tightened opening of her pussy, pressing inside her as his hips began to move faster, stronger, driving his cock inside her ass as his fingers fucked her pussy with a deep driving rhythm.

The explosion that ripped through her tore something apart in her soul. She felt it rip, shred, felt something pour free of her, even as she fought to understand what it was amid the violent tremors that shook her helpless body.

Her wail was quickly followed by his harsh cry as he thrust one last time, burying deep inside her ass before she felt the hot spurts of his semen jetting into the gripping, rippling tissue there.

Her legs spasmed as she tightened. Her womb shuddered. Taut as a bow her body arched as the final, climactic surge burned along her nerves and flung her past any preconceived notions she may have had of true pleasure.

It could have been minutes later, it could have been hours later when she felt him pull slowly from her and collapse on the bed beside her. His arms pulled her close to him, sheltering her against his chest, where she could hear the ragged thump of his heart.

And that something, that unexplained emotion, that had torn loose inside her rose once again, causing her to flinch, to attempt to escape his hold.

"You fear me?" he asked her then, his voice quiet, reflective.

"I don't fear you," she whispered. "Maybe it's myself I fear."

Chapter Twenty-Six

ဢ

There were so many unanswered questions. Too many. As the rush of adrenaline from the fight and their passion slowly faded away, Ariel was able to feel the shift in the air that hadn't been there before.

Shane's anger was like an echo around her. She could feel it vibrating on the air, despite the fact that he was now in the shower. But it wasn't just anger. It was pain. Emotion. A hunger she couldn't define, yet one she was beginning to feel herself. As though the sex, despite the pleasure and the power of it, was still missing something. Something deep, something overwhelming.

But there was more than that moving around her now. She could feel it slowly wrapping around her consciousness, making her wary, on guard.

Her skin prickled with a strange sort of awareness, her mind felt energized, on guard, the power rushing inside her warning her of danger. At her breast, the crystal throbbed with an increased awareness that had her nerves on edge.

The shower she had taken earlier hadn't eased the nervous tension and now, as Shane made use of the bathroom, she paced the suite slowly, her arms clasped across her chest as she tried to make sense of it.

She walked to the tall, wide windows, lifting the curtain aside to stare into the darkness with a frown. In the distance, she could see the lightning. There wasn't a cloud in the sky, but jagged, furious streaks of lightning lit up the sky like bursts of fireworks toward the mountain in the distance.

They were only a day's ride from their destination, she knew. Did that have something to do with it? It couldn't.

Caitlin controlled the water, not the lightning. Was Caitlin somehow in danger? Had Jonar found her?

Swallowing tightly, Ariel slid the lock on the window free, opening it the mere six to eight inches before the steel lock stopped its progression. The wind blew into the room then, twisting around her, a cool breeze filled with scents and sounds that seemed to whip around her in a chaotic jumble.

There were no screams of pain, though. No pleas for help. The wind didn't call out to her to go, to run, to aid.

Closing her eyes, she took a deep hard breath and in that second made a decision she prayed she wouldn't live to regret. She had the power, she controlled the winds. It would do her bidding, she knew, stream through time and space to bring her what she needed.

"Find her," she whispered to the breeze as it grew in strength. "Find her. Let me know if she's safe."

She felt it whip through the opening in the window, crying out in joy at her command as she waited, silent, listening to it to carry the order until all she heard was the echo of her own voice coming back to her.

Ariel... There was surprise in the voice, a vague drowsiness as though Caitlin had only just awakened. *Do you need me?*

Ariel breathed in roughly in relief.

"Are you well?" she murmured. "Do you need me?"

Ariel sensed a flurry of movement from the other woman before the connection increased, became stronger. The smell of rain in the distance reached her sensitive nose.

There's no danger here, Ariel. There was an edge of confusion in the voice. *Is there danger there?*

Was there?

"I don't know," she kept her voice soft, trusting the winds to carry even the softest breath of sound. "Tell me where you are, Cait. I don't like this feeling. It frightens me."

She sensed the winds wrapping about her in comfort, in protection, even as her words were carried to some distant point.

There was silence then. She could feel Caitlin's indecision, her need to reach out to the crystals connecting to her. And Ariel was well aware that in the space of seconds, Chantel had added the power of the Earth Crystal to that of the Wind. There were no commands from Chantel for the wind to seek more than Ariel wished, even though she sensed the sister crystal could have done so. She merely waited, loaned the power needed and drew on a patience Ariel found herself lacking.

As she stood in the window, slowly, gently, she felt the moisture that began to join with the breeze outside. Rain. A light, gentle shower that washed over the land, seeking, searching.

She tilted her head to the side, searching silently for more information, before a smile tugged at her lips. The rain had come from all directions. Her sister wasn't a fool.

Ariel, you've been followed. Caitlin's wind-soft words had her eyes opening in surprise, staring into the darkness outside her window. *The danger is to you, but it seeks me as well.*

"Cait, please," she whispered again. "Stop running."

Light laughter filled the silence.

I'm not running little sister, she whispered then. *I'm merely waiting.*

A soft caress of mist touched Ariel's face, a gentle kiss of consolation to her cheek as the rains receded as quickly as they had come.

You've been followed.

The words echoed around her.

"Who follows me?" she whispered to the winds.

They swirled around her, whipping outside then back, whispering to her, but none of the sounds that met her ears carried her name or a hint of danger. As though whoever or whatever tracked her, knew her power. Knew that once whispered, sound never ceases and was then at the mercy of the winds.

She could feel the oppressive sense of danger thickening around her. The air itself was attempting to place a shield around her, one that would be impossible to penetrate.

Leaving the window open, she paced to the far corner of the room, hearing the water in the shower turn off as Shane finished. She needed him to hold her, but she felt like a baby. Only a baby needed to be held when confused or frightened.

She curled up in a chair instead, biting her lip as she stared around the dim room. It was too dark. Even the low lamp beside the bed wasn't casting enough light. It was dimming, growing darker.

"Shane!" She moved to jump to her feet, her feet tangling in her gown when she felt the first streak of pain.

Blinding light shot through the room, white-hot and destructive as it caught her across her shoulders. It seared her flesh and sent her tumbling to the floor as a scream of rage and pain tore from her chest.

Another bolt shattered the coffee table at her side as she scrambled past it, hearing the roar of rage that echoed from the bathroom.

Everything happened so fast. Too fast. The bathroom door flew open as Shane rushed into the room, only to take the next strike to his chest.

Ariel watched in horror as a bloody slash streaked across his flesh, the blow bringing him to his knees as he threw himself at her.

"No!" She knew what he would do.

"Protect him!" She screamed out to the winds as they roared around her now. "Protect him!"

She couldn't lose him. Oh God, she couldn't let this happen, she had to stop it. She screamed as he was struck again, the bolt so powerful it flung him across the floor, charring his flesh.

"I command you to him," she screamed desperately, fighting, struggling against the restraining winds that held her in place. "Leave me now, damn you! Protect him as I command you!"

Her voice grew hoarse as her screams went unanswered and each sizzling strike at Shane's undefended body ripped further into her soul. She was going to lose him. God help her, she couldn't survive it. How could she go on if she lost him? If she lost the only warmth she had ever known in her life?

Another lit up the room, this time, striking him across the shoulder and throwing him backwards.

"Chantel, where are you?" she screamed out, staring around wildly as she fought to find a way past the winds that pinned her securely in place, keeping her from reaching him, keeping him from her as bolt after bolt of white-hot heat slammed into his flesh.

He was enraged. His eyes were black with it, his furious bellows echoing with it as he jerked his sword from his sheath, rolling to his side and countered the next blow with the steel he placed in front of it.

"Get out of here," she screamed desperately.

"Use the winds, Ariel," he ordered savagely. "Command them."

"They won't," she cried, nearly suffocated by the thick shield of the winds swirling around her.

"They will. Command them damn you!" He blocked the next strike at his defenseless body, but jerked in pain with the next as it seared his calf.

"Find them. Make it stop..." she screamed out to the winds, tears pouring down her cheeks as they refused to leave her, refused to heed her commands, they only swirled harder, faster around her.

Another slash of destructive light whipped into the room, barely missing Shane as he rolled to the other side of the room, his sword blocking it in the nick of time.

"It's Jonar, Ariel," he yelled desperately. "He can kill with these bolts, dammit. He'll kill both of us. Command those fucking winds."

She saw the next one coming. Larger, thicker, if it hit him, it would destroy him.

The winds allowed her to move, but swirled thicker, furiously around her rather than Shane as she had commanded.

The crystal was burning hot, impressions, memories, scattered phrases singing around her as she watched, as though in slow motion as the bolt zipped from the stars above and headed for them.

Her hands lifted, power raged inside her as she heard the bedroom door behind her splinter. Lightning crashed outside, rain fell in thick, blinding sheets that did nothing to slow the powerful energy missile as it came toward them.

"You will turn it back." She forced the power from her, her hands rising sharply. "You *will* turn it back now! Obey me, I am the Mistress of your existence, I command you, turn it back now!"

Her voice rose, she turned into herself directing the energy pouring through her to the winds that screamed both outside and in. Instantly, pure violet light shot from her crystal, shooting to the weapon aimed for her. The winds followed, shrieking and moaning, screaming in fury as they rushed toward the destructive surge of energy, meeting it only feet outside the window, dissolving it, disintegrating it before the violet ray shot further into the night.

Ariel stood in shock, in horror, watching as a kaleidoscope of color filled the night sky, high above the mountains, like a dozen super fireworks setting off at once.

"The bastards!" Rage filled Chantel's voice as she rushed to Ariel's side. "Damn them to their own hells," she screamed as Ariel turned to her in shock, seeing her white features, the emerald glow of her sister's eyes. "Fucking Guardians!" She turned to Devlin, shaking, shuddering with fury. "The murdering bastards would destroy us all."

Devlin's face was dark with rage as he bent to Shanar, checking the wounds that slashed across his upper body.

"Prepare to ride. Joshua, call the Primes. Now! If I don't see them in thirty minutes flat, I call all the warriors together and it becomes open season on Guardians." Devlin's voice was cold, calm, his black eyes blazing within his expressionless face as he moved to Chantel.

"Shane." Ariel rushed to him as he staggered to his feet, grimacing at the rapid healing of the wounds across his body.

"It's okay, Ariel." He wrapped one arm tight around her, breathing in deeply as he tucked her securely against his chest. "I'm fine, baby. I knew you could do it. I knew you would do it."

She raised her head, staring back at him in shock.

"I didn't do it," she whispered. "I don't know where that bolt came from out of my crystal, Shane, but I didn't do it. All I called were the winds. They wouldn't leave me until that bolt of violet light did. They couldn't fight it."

All eyes turned to Chantel then as the other woman stared back at Ariel, her own shock darkening her eyes further.

"Neither did I," she whispered. "I don't know where it came from. I felt my crystal reaching toward it, felt it aiding it, but I don't know the origin of it."

Just what they needed. Ariel laid her head on Shane's healing chest and closed her eyes tiredly.

"Let's at least hope it was a friendly interference," she sighed. "Another problem and I just might lose what little mind my father left me."

Chapter Twenty-Seven

ை

The three Primes arrived in less than fifteen minutes. Alyx, along with his wife Lynn, the psychic bodyguard who had once protected Ariel. Gryphon, the tall, blond warrior whose exceptional good looks did nothing to hide the dangerous glint in his eyes. And Phoenix. Flame-red hair flowed around his shoulders as he watched everyone with silent, emotionless eyes as Devlin faced them, his voice cold, murder glittering in his eyes.

"At last count, there were over two hundred bloody warriors that you bastards created and left to fend for themselves here." Devlin stood before them, his tall, well-muscled body tense and on guard. "If I don't get an explanation immediately, it becomes open season on aliens."

Alyx stared back, one brow arching mockingly before he glanced at the other two Primes.

"You command only three of the warriors, Shadow." It was Phoenix who spoke, his silky, dark voice sending shivers up Ariel's spine. "Many of those warriors were once your enemies."

"Times have changed." Devlin smiled coldly. "We banded together centuries ago, Phoenix, and pledged ourselves where needed. I can and will command them all should it be necessary."

Alyx grimaced. "We should have expected such a move, you bloody bastard." Despite his words, there was a vein of amused admiration in his voice. "But it changes nothing. The Guardians would not have struck against you."

"I can have Barik's group here within twenty-four hours, Devlin," Joshua said softly. "He's on standby with over a dozen other groups awaiting word. The others will only be hours behind him."

Alyx frowned at this, glancing at each warrior before his gaze came to Ariel.

"The wind brings you truth or lie, Mistress," he said gently. "Do we lie?"

Ariel started in surprise. She paused a moment, tipped her head and listened closely as she sent out the silent call. It was becoming easier, calling the winds to her, hearing the information she needed.

"There is no answer," she finally said softly. "Which means nothing. The wind only knows those words spoken within its hearing."

"Had the Guardians struck against you, they would have had to drop into the atmosphere of this planet," Alyx reminded them all. "They would have then been within the air itself."

"No words were spoken," she said again. "I can't say who it was."

Alyx's lips tightened irritably as he glanced at Gryphon.

"Return to the mothership. See what you can learn."

"They are out of contact," Gryphon said then, watching Ariel thoughtfully. "We've been out of contact for nearly twelve hours."

The tension that filled the room was palpable.

"If it wasn't the Guardians, then who else has such technology?" Devlin questioned harshly. "What the hell is going on here, Alyx?"

The Prime sighed wearily as his arm curved around the smaller frame of his new wife.

"I have only suspicions, Devlin. I have no answers," he finally said. "There is much going on within the upper echelon of the Guardians. At the moment, there is a struggle for a power that may or may not play out in all our best interests, which is why I do not believe they would have struck out at you or your warriors. At this moment, your group alone has the power to defeat Jonar. Undefeated, the potential of his threat is too severe."

The air swirled around her then.

The air cannot live…

The keys must be found first, they will lead us…

Alyx has failed us…

The fourth key has been stolen. Who holds the key…

The whisper of voices around her was accompanied by a misty march of memories. Lynn Carstairs, dressed in leathers, her expression closed, her eyes cold as she stood at Ariel's side. Another warrioress, wounded by Jonar and determined to gain her vengeance.

"Ariel." Shane pulled her closer to his side, his warmth enveloping her as the battles flashed through her mind.

"There are too many threads," she whispered as all eyes trained on her.

Her gaze locked with Alyx's.

"What are the keys?"

He flinched just enough for her to detect the movement. His nostrils flared as he inhaled deeply then, his gaze sharpening.

"The winds truly do speak to you." He inclined his head in respect. "What else have you heard?"

"That the air cannot live… That you have failed someone… And that the fourth key is missing."

Phoenix cursed just below his breath as Alyx and Gryphon grimaced with similar expressions of concern.

"Have you found the Water Mistress?" Alyx asked then. "Until you do, there is little we can do to help you. She holds more information and more power than you could imagine."

"We'll worry about Caitlin, Dragon." Derek stepped forward, facing Alyx with an edge of violence now. "You stay the hell away from her."

When Alyx would have spoken, Lynn laid her hand on his broad arm, shaking her head slightly when Alyx glanced down at her.

"Ariel, we were friends once," she said softly, moving to step around Derek as Ariel watched her silently. "Am I different now, than I was then? Would I lie to you, Mistress?"

Ariel sighed wearily. She could feel the honesty, the integrity that was so much a part of her, just as it had always been.

Ariel moved slowly from Shanar's grip, facing the other woman silently, seeing so much, and remembering so much more. She smiled softly as those memories, gentler than most, eased through her.

"You were a sister in battle, a friend of the heart," she said, her voice misty with those memories. "But you can still be tricked, especially by those they trust." She nodded toward the Primes. "And I have a feeling, Lynn, that they know it..."

* * * * *

Traveling through space and time sucked. Lynn stumbled as they arrived back in the mountain chateau the Primes had been calling home for the past months.

"Son of a bitch," Alyx cursed roughly, his hand sweeping out before him as energy flew through the room.

Thankfully, there was no longer anything breakable, except the windows, which had been shattered before they left. Alyx hadn't been pleased by Joshau's summons.

"That arrogant, pissant upstart!" he raged, furious at Derek. "The bastard steals his wife's mind then dares stand in front of me, as though protecting her. I should have reminded him why I'm a Prime and he's no more than an experiment in the fucking making."

Energy slammed through the room again, brilliant shards of light that clashed and bounced against the walls, spraying plaster and leaving charred, broken holes.

"Dammit it, Alyx, you destroy another room and you'll be on your hands and knees cleaning it up," Lynn yelled then, aware that the rage was capable of bringing the room down around them.

It wasn't often she got to see her sexy, powerful husband ripping something up. Normally, it turned her on. Now, it just worried her. Alyx was pissed, and that was a bad thing.

A sizzling growl snarled from his lips a second before the room vibrated violently. An unsettled hush slowly evolved as Lynn watched Alyx warily. The room wasn't in a shambles, thank God. It was damned hard to explain the damage when repairs were needed. The Primes could destroy anything. Making them fix it was close to impossible.

"She holds the second key," he snapped. "It's obvious someone wants Joshau dead, because we both know Arriane is protected even from us."

"Jonar is moving too close. But how could he have found a ship to strike at them with?" Gryphon asked quietly. "That would have been impossible."

Lynn watched as Alyx's eyes narrowed broodingly.

"They would not strike at the only group capable of defeating their enemy," Alyx snapped. "It makes no sense."

"Just as the splintering factions within the Guardian Directive make no sense," Gryphon shrugged negligently. "Personally, they can all go to hell for all I care, but Jonar doesn't have a ship. We all know that."

Lynn could hear the belief that the Guardians, or at least a Guardian, was behind the attack.

"Our heir must awaken," Alyx snarled then. "As dangerous as he may be, we must find a way to awaken him."

"The time is not yet right." Phoenix spoke. That was a scary thing, Lynn thought, shuddering at the sound of his hollow, dark voice. "At this moment, our best course is to find and protect the Water Mistress until the Wizard finds her. We can do nothing until that Legacy is fulfilled."

"Be damned," Alyx cursed. "They could all be dead by then."

He swiped his fingers through the long strands of black hair and regarded the other Prime angrily.

"We are already under suspicion," Gryphon reminded the red-haired warrior. "The Directive has cut off our access to many of our weapons, and is now questioning our missions more closely. It is only a matter of time before we are hunted as well."

"Awaken him now, and the balance will be tipped in Jonar's favor," Phoenix said softly, or as softly as such a guttural tone could manage. "We can do nothing but wait and aid them as best we can. We need to stay closer to the Water Mistress. Ensure they do not find her before Derek can."

"And our Prince?" Gryphon snapped. "What of him?"

Phoenix stared directly at him now, a flash of red burning in his eyes for a long, endless moment.

"We protect him, as we have always done, Gryphon. He will awaken when the time is right. When it is prophesied that he would. We do not tamper with his destiny, or he will pay the highest price of all. We can do no more than protect him now, as we were born to."

Lynn now regarded the warrior thoughtfully for long moments. The secret of the heir was never spoken, even to her. It was one secret Alyx would not reveal to her. But if her suspicions were proving correct, then life was going to get very scary, very fast. She wasn't looking forward to it.

"Fine. We go to the Water Mistress then," Alyx sighed. "Gear up with what weapons we now have. I'll see if I can contact Mayan for more. It's the only way I can think of to bypass the Directive and attain the weapons we need. We leave in an hour."

The other two left the room quickly to follow his orders as Lynn watched him worriedly.

"Alyx?"

"No." He shook his head quickly. "I can answer none of your questions, Lynn. From here on out, each word spoken must be monitored. The Wind has ears, and trust me when I say that can be more than dangerous."

Chapter Twenty-Eight

 හ

They arrived in Newhalem just after dark in the pouring rain. A rain so heavy that they were all drenched when they pulled into the graveled drive behind the cabins Devlin had rented.

Lightning raced across the sky as clouds thickened and rolled together ominously. On the winds a familiar voice had whispered to her.

Not yet... Caitlin had called to her more than once. *I'm not ready yet...*

And she would have heeded her sister's plea if it hadn't been for the air of danger that thickened around her as well. The unvoiced threats, the smell of death. She could smell Jonar's warriors on the winds, and that terrified her more than anything else.

"Let's get inside," Devlin called out as the engines cut off and Shane helped her from the seat. "We'll meet in our cabin in an hour. No later."

Just enough time to shower and dress in dry clothes, Ariel thought tiredly as she glimpsed Kanna's van in the central parking lot.

"Come on." Shane caught her hand, pulling her quickly to the cabin on the right, toward the beckoning light that shone through the windows. It looked peaceful, warm, a haven amid a chaotic storm of emotions whipping around her. Not just inside her, but around her, whispering to her, a lone, eerie cry following the distant voices.

They burst into the warmth of the house and Ariel could do nothing but slump against the wall as Shane closed the door and began stripping her sodden clothes from her body.

She closed her eyes, weariness washing over her, weakening her.

"I loved you then," she whispered, feeling him still, feeling the air pulse with tension. "All this time I've fought to define the joy, the happiness I've felt in each memory of you, your touch, your voice..." Her own voice broke as tears clogged her throat.

"Don't, baby." He touched her face then, his fingers calloused but so gentle as they smoothed over her cheek. "You need to rest. Soon, I'll tuck you into our bed, warm you with my body and you will sleep."

Ariel opened her eyes and her chest ached with pain at the look in his eyes. He still looked at her the same as he did in that life before. With equal parts adoration and pain.

"I don't know what love is, Shane." She forced the words past her lips, feeling a chill race over her skin as he stared back at her, his expression heavy with heartache, her heart heavy with a pain she couldn't define. "I just don't know. I feel like I used to. I feel like I should know..." She shuddered with the sobs that would have released had she given them voice, but she couldn't. She held them back, the knowledge that tears were weakness too ingrained to release so easily.

"God, Ariel," he whispered her name as though it were a benediction.

His hands framed her face, his cheeks raking over the warm dampness that lingered there from the stubborn tears that fell despite her best efforts.

She was shuddering now, her body tightening as she tried to hold back the emotions tearing through her. She didn't want to feel this, she didn't want feelings she had fought to hold back, to keep at bay for so many years, breaking free of her, now, when she needed to be strong.

"They almost killed you." She stared up at him, her hands lifting, gripping his wrists, only barely aware of her nails pressing into his flesh. "I saw them. I saw those bolts hit you, saw you draw them away from me. You can't do that..." she wailed the words, staring back at him desperately. "You can't sacrifice yourself for me, Shane. Not ever."

She had to convince him. She had to make him understand that he couldn't ever risk himself in such a way again, that he couldn't die for her. The hollow, bleak pain that had filled her since the moment she realized he would indeed do just such a thing tore through her soul again. It ripped at her heart, sliced through her soul and left her spirit bleeding from a wound she feared would never heal. He had dedicated himself to her through all these centuries, waited for her, dreamed of her, remained faithful to her memory.

In his body, in his heart, there was such strength that it amazed her. To think of him dying before her eyes because of her weakness was more than she could bear. She would prefer death herself.

"Ariel, beloved." He leaned down, his lips feathering over the tears that continued to fall from her eyes. "Don't you know yet, I'd walk through the fires of hell itself to save you from the smallest scratch? I will never see you harmed and not do all I can to protect you."

And he meant it. She could see it in his eyes, in the heavy pain that lined his face.

"The pain of those bolts were nothing compared to the pain I knew as I watched you die in that first life." His voice was rough, tortured. "It is nothing compared to my pain when I remember the blows that were dealt to you, even before that final battle. I would give my soul itself to the Guardians, if it meant saving you. What small price then, is my life?"

"Listen to yourself." She jerked away from him, barely restraining her screams as her hands came to her head, her fingers clenching in her own hair as she fought the energy and the pain building inside her. "Are you crazy? Why can't you listen to reason? See sense?"

She turned back to him, staring at him as he stood before her, watching her with a curious blend of gentleness and irritation.

He sighed heavily. "Not many years ago, I lay in my bed, staring into the night, my mind searching for you, as it always does. Slowly, before my astounded gaze, a faint thread of light pierced the darkness, a violet aura so weak, so small I was certain I was seeing only that which I wanted to see. And through this aura whispered a child's voice, one filled with such fear, thick with her tears. And I knew it was the child that would grow to be my woman." He grimaced tightly. "As quickly as it was there, it was gone. The rage I knew in that year was like nothing I have ever felt, Ariel. All I could hear was your pain. Your fear. And in those days I prayed as I have never prayed in all these centuries. For you."

She flinched. There was no mistaking the truth in his declaration. She could read it in his eyes, the dark, swirling grays clashing together. She could see it in the pain in his expression.

"I love you, Ariel." And now she heard it in his voice. "And you can deny it until hell freezes over, but I know you. I know your heart and I know your spirit, and I know you love me."

She stilled, staring back at him shock.

"Love doesn't exist." She heard the ragged sound of the words, felt the effort it took to force them from her lips. "You don't realize that. That's all. When you do, you'll understand…"

His lips tilted in a bittersweet smile. "A thousand years I've loved you, wife," he said then, no regret, no second thoughts. "I will love you until eternity. Of that I am certain."

He moved to her slowly, staring down at her in a way that had her heart clenching with that strange joy again. She could feel it spreading through her, warming places in her that had been cold, healing wounds that were ages old.

She blinked back at him, confusion filling her as she saw the steadfast resolve in his expression.

"But…why?" she whispered, unable to understand that devotion, that certainty that such an emotion existed. "Why, Shane?"

"Such questions you have," he sighed then, a small smile quirking his lips. "Once, you easily accepted and returned my love. You questioned only the power that was so unfamiliar to you. Now, you accept your power, and question that love that was so much a part of you. I failed to aid you in gaining your power then, but I will not fail in showing you love now."

He caught her wrist, pulling her to him, placing her palm against the damp, broad chest before her.

"Feel my heart, Ariel. It beats for you. It aches for you. For a thousand years it has cried for you. That will not change overnight, beloved. It will always be, for as long as time carries on and there is breath in my body. Always, Ariel."

She wanted to feel that. She wanted to know that certainty, that dedication within herself and each time she searched within herself for it, darkness overwhelmed her. She could feel the warning, the sharp-clawed demon crouched and waiting, ready to attack.

She leaned against his chest, her lips pressed to his heart, feeling the pulse of life beating through him, feeling life, heat, as his arms wrapped around her, holding her close against him.

"I'm scared, Shane," she whispered the words then that had tormented her for months. For years. "What if I'm not strong enough? What if I fail?"

His fingers slid into her hair, gripping the sodden strands until he could pull her head back and stare into her eyes somberly.

"I have your back," he whispered, his fingers leaving her hair to move to the crystal where it lay between her breasts.

The touch of his hand against it had her breathing in roughly from the sensations suddenly singing through her body. Warmth, gentleness, joy and passion. And strength. She could feel his strength filling her, flooding the very center of her being.

"He's coming, Shane." She knew Jonar wasn't far behind them.

She was terrified that he would stand in front of her again, that he would protect her with his last breath, and leave her alone again.

"And we will face him," he told her calmly, his expression assured, confident. Almost confident enough to give her hope. "And we will win, Ariel. I trust you, baby. You are growing daily in your power, more than I ever dared dream. We will win."

Before she could protest his belief in her, or argue her own fears, his lips took hers in a kiss of pure passion and emotion. Her breath hitched in her chest as his tongue licked at her lips, parted them slowly before sliding inside in a smooth, heated thrust.

She whimpered beneath the kiss, she could do nothing else. It was a benediction, a fiery vow and one that had a sensual, heated ache whipping from her chest to her thighs, swelling her clit and leaving her pussy drenched with need.

Whether anger or hunger drove him, she had no defenses against him. One touch, that was all it took. One kiss, and her knees weakened, her flesh sensitized and she found her mind dazing with a matching hunger that left her with memories of similar events, a remembered passion and joy in his touch that made him more familiar to her than anyone she had known in her life. At least, in this life.

"We need to get you out of these wet clothes." He was breathing as roughly as she was when his head raised, his eyes darker, nearly black in passion.

Ariel gasped when he bent, one powerful arm sweeping her off her feet as the other cradled her back. He lifted her to his chest, while her arms circled his neck. Here, she felt at home. She felt safe, damn him, and if she believed in love, she would have felt loved.

But she did believe in need, in hunger, in a passion so all-consuming she could feel it burning through her soul as he carried her from the living room into the bathroom.

"Such beauty should be criminal," he whispered then as he lowered her to her feet, watching her closely as he pushed the hair back from her brow. "I look at you, and my soul whispers in joy, my body burns in hunger. You, Ariel, are the very breath that sustains me."

"Shane—" She tried to protest, tried once again to secure his promise that he would not stand before her, that he wouldn't die in her stead.

"No, Ariel." He shook his head. "I forced myself from you for days, hiding behind my anger, my male pride because your love was not as vocal as it had once been. It took this past night to show me, to prove to me, that time, no matter how vast and limitless, can still be finite for me, or for you. I will not live another day without whispering these words to you. Until one day, you will awaken, and they will pass from your lips as well as you realize what your heart already knows. You do love, Precious. Beautifully, passionately. And you do love me."

He gave her no time to protest his claim, even had she wanted to. But Ariel knew she was more prone to cry from the tender reverence in his voice, so at odds with the rough sensuality of his hands as he ripped her shirt from her.

"You're always tearing my clothes," she gasped as his lips zeroed in on her hard peaked nipples.

"Then don't wear any," he mumbled roughly, nipping at the delicate points as his hands fought with the wet clasp of her jeans. "And those boots have to go. I can't get you undressed fast enough."

He knelt at her feet, making very short work of the leather laces before jerking the moccasin boots from her feet. The jeans quickly followed, leaving her wet and naked before him as he ran his hands slowly up her thighs, spreading them as Ariel fought for air.

"This is perverted," she whispered as his thumbs slowly spread the swollen lips of her cunt apart, revealing the engorged bud of her clit.

"No." His voice was strained. "This isn't perverted. But I can show you perverted if you like."

A breathless little laugh escaped her. "I have no doubt. Oh God, Shane…" she cried out his name as his hot, moist tongue circled the hard little bud.

Her hands buried in his hair as she fought to keep her knees steady. It felt too good, too hot and filled with carnal delight to allow the weakness in her legs to halt it.

He licked at her, his tongue running around her clit before delving lower, tickling at the entrance to her vagina before dipping into it erotically. Ariel whimpered against the onslaught of pleasure, biting her lip to hold back her cries as she felt her heart expand with the dominance of his touch.

This was no easy lover, despite the obvious care he took in driving each sensation higher within her. He had been…once. So very long ago. The memories of his touch then washed over her, a contradiction to the demanding caresses he was bestowing on her now.

His tongue was like damp velvet, licking her, eating her decadently as she trembled beneath his touch. Hard hands gripped her thighs, opening her further as he growled against the sensitive flesh of her pussy, his tongue thrusting inside it, sending her to her tiptoes as the pleasure of it slammed through her body.

"Oh God, it's too good," she whispered as he came up again, his lips covering the throbbing point of her clit, suckling at it as his tongue circled it heatedly. "I can't stand it, Shane."

He murmured something, she wasn't certain what, but the vibration of the sound against the sensitive nub of flesh nearly sent her over the edge. Her fingers tightened in his hair, her head falling back against the wall as she fought for breath, for sanity amid the chaotic sensations whipping through her now.

"Your taste is like nectar," he whispered then, sipping at her again, drawing her juices into his mouth as she trembled on a peak of pleasure unlike any she had yet known. "I could drown myself in you. Your taste, your heat."

As he caressed the fiery button of her clit, one hand slid up her damp thigh until Ariel felt him parting her further, his finger sliding through the dampness that eased from her body. She gasped in pleasure as it slid slowly, diabolically inside her, rasping the sensitive tissue of her pussy, sending her spiraling higher.

She shook her head, fighting to hold onto her last remnants of her control, but he was stripping it from her as surely as he was losing his own. She could feel his breathing, hard and rough as the muscles of her pussy clenched around the invading finger. Heard his groan of male hunger, like a hungry beast held back too long.

"So tight..." he growled. "Do you know what it does to me, Ariel, to be held in such a grip, gloved and caressed with ripples of this sweet flesh?"

She convulsed with pleasure, fighting to breathe as his finger slid in deeper, crooked and began a slow, destructive caress against a spot more sensitive than any other. She shuddered as she fought for release, tilting her hips toward him, her legs spreading further.

He teased and taunted her with the promise of her completion. Pushed her to the edge, only to pull her back. Her moans filled the room, husky pleas filling them as his touch became just rough enough to tempt the edge of pain, making her hunger, beg for more. She needed more, needed him, all of him.

"Burn for me, Ariel," he snarled as he drew back a second before her release could rush over her. "Make me burn."

She gasped as his hands gripped her hips, pulling her to him as he sat on the closed lid of the commode and lifted her to him. Her legs spread, gripping his as she stood poised over the hard flesh of his cock.

"Take me," he demanded roughly, his hands easing her hips down until the flared head was easing between the plump lips, nudging at the entrance to her vagina. "Take all of me, Ariel."

Slowly, and not so easily, he slid inside her, stretching her, making her burn as sensitive nerve endings flared to life, sending vibrant, heated pulses of pleasure tearing through her.

"Look at me, Ariel." His voice was strained, so rough the sound was nearly animalistic as her eyes opened with drowsy sensuality.

She needed to breathe, but the look on his face, coupled with the extreme pleasure torturing her sensitive body locked the breath in her throat. Could it truly exist? Was it really love shining in the dark depths of his eyes? What else could it be?

Joy, pleasure and pain swirled in the gray depths, tightened his expression and in that second, opened something inside her that she never knew existed.

"Yes. Fuck. Yes." He grimaced tightly as her eyes widened and a small cry escaped her throat. "Feel me, baby. Feel all of me."

His hands tightened on her hips a second before he drove his cock deep inside her, filling her, stretching her, sending her careening on a journey she couldn't have imagined.

Her hands tightened on his shoulders, her head shaking desperately as she fought against the response. Not the physical pleasure, that she could take, eagerly looked forward to. But the scarred wound in her soul was slowly tearing apart, emotions, dreams, a lifetime of fears were hidden there. Would she survive if they escaped?

His hips were moving furiously, his cock plunging inside her, retreating, returning in hard, driving strokes as his gaze held hers, refusing to let her retreat, to repair the crumbling walls of her inner sanctum.

"Please…" she cried out hoarsely, feeling perspiration drip from her hair, run down her face, mingling with the tears that began to fall from her eyes. "Don't…"

He was stripping her, leaving her bare. She didn't know if she could survive it.

"See me, damn you," he snarled, his lips pulling back from his teeth as the sounds of each driving stroke inside her pussy pulsed around them. "See me, Ariel. See my love for you. Feel it. By God, you will feel it."

One hand slid from her hips to the curve of her buttocks, tracing the small crease there until he found the tightly puckered entrance to her ass. There was no resistance to his invasion there. Her body had no will left to fight him. One demanding stroke of his finger sent him deep inside the tight little channel as his cock buried itself deep inside her pussy. She was moving against him, desperate to hold onto the pleasure, to focus there, rather than his eyes, his face, her own inner fears.

"Keeper of the wind…Mistress of my heart…bride of my soul. Take to your body my strength, to your heart my warmth, and forever warm yourself in the fires of my love."

"No…" She could feel the crystal pulsing at her breast in time to the thrusts of his cock deep inside her pussy. A pulse of life, rebirth, filling her as surely as he was filling her cunt.

"Yes," he snarled. "Give to me, Ariel. You are mine. Only mine and you know this. Damn you, give to me…"

She screamed his name as the white-hot heat of pleasure consumed her. It wasn't just her body convulsing in release, but her soul. Her release spilled from her as she felt her heart fracture.

Vows, spoken so long ago came to her lips. In jerky, broken whispers, memories pouring over her, she returned the words to him.

"Into my heart...part of my soul. The winds will whisper, scream of my joy. Take to you my soul, my fears, my pleasures. Know my passions, my heart..." she screamed as power infused her, whipping on the white-hot bolts of pleasure tearing through her body. "...know my love..."

A savage male cry of pleasure echoed around her then as he drove into her hard, deep, releasing not just his seed into her, but pouring through her, over her, memories and emotions she had hid from so effectively, that she was convinced they could never exist.

Racking shudders tore through each of them as she fell forward against his chest, the crystal pressed between them, fiery hot, yet soothing. She could feel the power of it binding them together, reaffirming what she already knew. There was love, and she felt it. Deep, all-consuming, destructive, renewing. An emotion that defied description or denial.

Tears fell from her eyes as he tried to soothe the cries that tore from her chest. He lifted her from him, cradling her to his chest as he rose and stood her in the shower. He cleaned her beneath the spray of the water, washing away the perspiration that coated her body as he whispered soothingly, trying to ease her tears as well.

"I'll always protect you, Ariel," he swore when he finished, wrapping a towel around her as he dried her tenderly. "I swear I will not let them take you from me again."

Her breath hitched in her throat.

"They won't try to take me this time," she whispered, staring up at him miserably, knowing that Jonar's punishment would be even more demonic. "This time, he'll take you..."

Chapter Twenty-Nine

ॐ

What had he done? Shane stood in the living room, staring beyond the window at the steadily falling rain as the others sat behind him. They had arrived minutes after Shane had carried Ariel to bed, tucking her beneath the blankets as exhaustion overcame her. She was sleeping there now, a light breeze playing over her hair as the winds she commanded comforted her.

What would she remember when she awakened? he wondered. The love they had shared? Surely she would, it had been the strongest part of what they had known together, that love. Would she remember the child she had been, the one Jonar had raped and stolen so much power from? And what would that memory do to her?

So many questions and there were no answers. He had spent the better part of the past two hours as Devlin and the others discussed the upcoming battle, trying to figure out where he and Ariel could possibly go from there.

He remembered his last glimpse of her, as the Guardians stole him from her side. He had been but seconds from death himself, his wounds so severe he had known that only they could heal him. He had tried to hold onto her, to take her with him. She had been dying before his eyes, whispering his name on a sigh of regret as he slowly disappeared.

She had died alone.

How many centuries had it taken him not to awaken in a rage so fierce that he would attempt to tear down the very castle that protected him and the others? More than he cared to count. That nightmare had ripped at his soul, often tearing away any peace he could have found in his life.

They had taken him away, forcing her to die alone, without his love to carry her into death. Now, he feared she would blame him for the pain she must have endured. She would remember it now; there would be no way she couldn't. The power of that damned crystal was more far-reaching than any power love could hold.

"We need to awaken her soon," Devlin commented from behind him, his voice compassionate, but firm.

He alone could understand how Shane felt now. The fear of losing what had been taken so long ago would torment Devlin now, perhaps nearly as much as Shane felt himself tormented.

But Devlin hadn't spent the centuries regretting, awakening in a sweat of fear and pain at his wife's death, or feeling her touch in his deepest dreams. He had been given the tender mercy of forgetting the bride he had so adored. Until her return to his life, Devlin had not known what he had lost so long before. But Shane had known. Known and ached and regretted until at times, death would have surely been easier.

"She's been pushed too hard," he finally said roughly. "She needs to rest."

To be honest, he didn't know if he could face the anger or recriminations she might feel when she awakened. He had forced her to endure the memories she had wanted only to hide from. Had it destroyed the love she felt for him, then he would prefer not to know.

"I disagree, Shanar." Had it been anyone other than Chantel who spoke, he would have ripped their heads off. Instead, he was forced to turn slowly, to restrain his rage and face the petite woman rising from her chair to confront him. "Ariel isn't a delicate person. She's a fighter. You can't coddle her."

He grimaced tightly. Ariel was more than just a fighter. She was so damned willful and headstrong that there had never been a chance of protecting her, let alone actually putting it in effect. She had waded into the thick of danger with a smile on her lips and her laughter echoing around her.

He wasn't so certain she would feel the same now, though. After so many years of peace from the nightmares, she wouldn't thank him for bringing them back.

"I pushed her too far." And it ate at him, how hard he had been pushing at her. He could have protected her until she came into her powers on her own. He could have, no matter what it took, held onto his own control until she was ready for the life he was throwing her into.

Instead, he had pushed, prodded, distanced himself from her and forced her to unlock the memories and the love she had for him. In doing so, he had unlocked so many things that he would have let her hide from, if it were possible.

He had seen it in her eyes just before they closed in sleep. The sudden awareness, the flash of pain it had brought her.

"Shane, there's no time to allow them to come to terms with who and what they are, on their own," Chantel said gently, her hands pushing into the pockets of her jeans as her shoulders hunched defensively. "Ariel had to remember, and she had to do so quickly. Jonar isn't far behind us, and Caitlin is still hiding. We have to get to her before he does."

"Do you think I don't know this?" His lip curled furiously. "Do you think I'm unaware of what the stakes are in this game between the Guardians and Jonar, Mistress? I know well. Perhaps better even than you for I have lived it, every fucking century, waiting, watching, knowing what was coming. But she cannot continue in this manner. I will not allow it."

He faced off with her, aware of the tension that suddenly filled the room as the three men with her watched him warily. He had fought to contain his rages for so long, knowing that the very blood that ran through his veins would make him a risk when combined with the strength the Guardians had given him. He was a Viking. Berserker rages were a part of who and what they were. The adrenaline coursing through his blood was even more volatile when combined with the strength those fucking aliens had cursed him with.

He growled. A low, dark sound as he pushed his fingers through his hair and turned from them again.

"She believes Jonar will strike at me, rather than her." He pushed back the anger, barely, concentrating instead on protecting the one person that meant more than life to him. Above all else, he must protect her. "She will seek to place herself in front of me should that happen. We can't let her do that."

She might be angry with him. She might very well hate him. But he had seen her commitment to that when the memories washed over her. She wouldn't be able to hide from what they had shared in that past life; adding that to the woman she was now, would only make her more determined than ever to be certain that no one, ever, died in her stead.

Whoever had struck at them the night before had made a mistake. The power that poured from that crystal had begun unlocking the remainder of the power trapped inside Ariel's soul. Something had broken free within her during that attack. Shane had sensed it, felt it during the remaining ride to Newhalem.

"I agree," Chantel said then. "You must fight side by side, not one before the other."

She was deliberately misinterpreting his words. He wouldn't allow it.

"No." He gritted his teeth, wondering what it was they weren't understanding.

Turning back, he stared at her furiously. A look he knew others had trembled before over the centuries.

"She must be kept away from me, Chantel. I will fight; you and Ariel will battle with the crystals alone."

Surprising, a small laugh came from her throat as a sad smile shaped her lips.

"And do you think Ariel will allow that?" she asked him patiently. "Shane, she refused that route in her first life, she will object even harder now. You are dealing with a woman only now learning all that she is. If you try to protect her, you will make her foolhardy rather than wise, as she attempts to aid you. Don't make that mistake."

It was a bitter truth that he fought hard to swallow.

"So what do you suggest I do, Mistress?" he snapped. "Place her in the thick of battle where Jonar can strike at her, not just physically, but through her memories as well? He will kill her."

"He might try," she sighed then. "But we'll all be there, Shane, to protect each other and to fight against him. You can't baby Ariel. You can't place her out of danger. If you try, then Caitlin will pay the price, and in turn, all of us will die. This is our last chance. We have no choice but to accept the risk."

And when Jonar faced Ariel and she remembered the raping of the child she had been, what then? God help him, Shane didn't think he could stand to see it.

"I cannot bear her pain, Chantel," he whispered then. "It's like the sharpest sword cutting into my soul. She doesn't deserve this. Not like this. You know what he will do to her, how he will use her memories."

Compassion filled her gaze. "None of us deserved the pain," she said then. "But it's the price we must pay for whatever will come later, after Jonar's defeat. We were promised happiness, long lives and joy by Mother Earth herself, Shane. She would not have lied to me. And she would not have broken the vow she made. The pain will be but a small price to pay for our rewards."

"Enough of this sappy stuff," Joshua moaned mockingly. "The heart of the matter is simple. She will fight, we will take Caitlin, she will tell us where Arriane is, and all of you will live happily ever after. Now awaken the woman and let's get on with it. We don't have all year to finish it."

Cold, brutal, the Mystic faced them all as he rose from his chair as well.

"Aren't you the eager one?" Shane grunted. "Of course, why would you care? You intend to destroy us all when you finally find Arriane again anyway."

It didn't sit well with Shane, the suspicion that Joshua held no love for his tiny wife, no caring of any sort. Only a man of little honor could be so cruel to such a fragile creature as Arriane had been. The problem was, Shane knew Joshua's honor, and knew it was as strong, as abiding as any of the other warriors. The contradiction of the man continually surprised Shane.

Joshua smiled coolly. "I don't have to love the bitch. I just have to get her to fuck me, I believe were the terms of the legend. And remembering what a hot little piece she was, I doubt it will be too difficult."

Chantel sighed as a clash of lightning struck outside the cabin.

"Arriane will fry your ass before it's over with," she warned him.

His smile was more a sneer. "She is welcome to try. Until then, we need to get this little show on the road and stop bitching and moaning over the price we may or may not pay. I grow tired of the debate."

Shane clenched his fists, wondering how he had managed not to kill the other man through the years. Someone needed to knock a bit of that arrogance out of him before his gentle little wife was found and forced to pay for whatever sins he laid at her feet. To be honest, Shane didn't blame her for that blade she sank in the other man's chest. He had deserved it more than most.

Chapter Thirty

80

"I can see Joshau is being his normally polite self." Ariel's mocking voice had them all turning to the doorway that led into the bedroom.

She was a vision. Dressed in the soft, supple leathers Kanna had packed for her. Leather boots were laced to her knees, the silver wristbands that had been locked to her sword now encircled her wrists. On her upper arm, a twisting dragon wrapped around the muscle, its snarling mouth pointed to the outside of her arm.

Defense. The armband had been given to her by her father, the sorcerer Galen, before she fought in her first battle. Each adornment had been decoratively locked to the hilt of her sword, until the day she could release them.

The weapon was now strapped to her back on the open-faced sheath that would allow her to free it quickly. A quick twist of her wrist would whip the sword from its protective covering through the simple means of dislodging it through the open front.

She had strapped her dagger to her thigh, and looked like a warrior princess with her violet eyes glowing with strength and with purpose. She was an angel of vengeance now on a mission, and Shane wondered if anything could be more arousing than the sight that stood before him now.

"You should be resting." Shane frowned at the lines of weariness beneath her eyes.

She glanced at him, and for a moment, he was lost in her gaze, and in her memories. He flinched at the pain he saw there and for the first time since finding her, feared that he would lose her from his own machinations, rather than Jonar's.

"We need to leave soon." She didn't break the look, but neither did he see a hint of her feelings either. "I know where she is."

That declaration spurred everyone into action. Swords were jerked from their resting places, guns strapped on, daggers prepared and placed in easy reach.

Shane was thankful that he had already armed himself and was now ready to go. It gave him time to watch Ariel, to let the full effect of who his woman was seep into his soul.

"Where?" Derek's voice was rough, filled with longing as he waited close to the door.

So many centuries of waiting, Shane thought. To have been given such bright, glorious love, for such a very short time, only to have it snatched away so brutally that the memories could draw blood from the soul. A thousand years had been too long to wait to set aright the wrongs done then.

"Not far from here." She paced into the living room, and in her movements he saw the confidence of the warrior she had been. She held her body loosely, relaxed, prepared for whatever was coming. "Jonar's already moving in, which is the reason for the storm. But there seems to be another threat. One she can't detect."

"I've felt it as well, thought I can't locate the cause." Chantel nodded as she checked the loaded clips of the compact machine gun she carried. The Mistress of the Earth couldn't handle a sword if her life depended it. And Shane was afraid it might.

"Jonar is only a minor threat." Ariel glanced at her sister then, pausing. "When this is over, Chantel, we need to talk. I do not approve of the decision you made in your past death. I'm really quite pissed over it."

Chantel had the nerve to smile. A true, joyous smile that spread from her lips to her eyes.

"I look forward to it, sister." She inclined her head a bit mockingly. "Though if I remember correctly, you could never stay angry with any of us for long."

Ariel snorted rudely. "We'll see."

Shane stood back, not approaching her, giving her the space he was certain she needed. He had forced her into this, and though he knew beyond any shadow of doubt that he had no choice, he vowed he would push her no further now.

He was ready for battle. Had been since she had dropped off to sleep. Dressed in the lightweight black mission pants and sleeveless shirt. His sword was strapped on his back, dagger on his lower leg. He refused to carry a gun. The powerful little gun could wound and delay Jonar's warriors, but only the swords could truly kill them.

"Don't try to stand in front of me." Ariel's furious voice, directed at him, had him stilling before her.

He lifted his brow mockingly. "Would I do such a thing?"

Her eyes narrowed warningly. "I'm not pleased with you, Savage, and you know it," she snapped. "You could have told me what was coming. You could have warned me. And yes, you would do such a thing. Try it this time, and I'll cut your heart out myself."

He winced. At the moment, he wouldn't put it past her. He had a feeling that his battle with Ariel was only beginning.

"Where is she, Ariel?" Derek waited by the door, his expression dark, forbidding.

She flashed the other man a cold look. There was little mercy in her gaze for the Wizard or the memories she had of him.

"And you think I'm just going to tell you, and allow you to jump right in and snatch her away?" she snapped. "Caitlin is holding her own for now. We'll arrive in time."

Shane watched as she tilted her head, then he felt it himself. The air was speaking to her, bringing to her whispers, secrets. He could stand and watch her like this for hours, that peculiar expression of excitement, of satisfaction that flitted across her face. The pride and confidence that filled her body. Finally, she was who and what she was meant to be.

"The Primes are in position to protect her should Jonar arrive before we do. But we can't expect much help from them. They're here to hold back whoever or whatever attacked last night, because it wasn't Jonar."

Surprise, surprise, Shane thought, a rough snarl building in his chest.

"Ariel, we can't hear what the winds tell you," Chantel said then. "You'll have to help us."

Ariel gave her a surprised look. "You can hear everything I do, Chantel," she said carefully. "You're just not listening to it. But you will. We need to move out."

"Ariel." Devlin stepped in front of her then, tall, dark, a power more fierce than any of the warriors controlled, building around him. "Where is she?"

A smile tilted her lips.

"Ask your wife," she said softly, moving around him and heading for the door. "She knows."

Chapter Thirty-One

ဢ

The storm was brutal in its intensity. The winds, following her commands, whipped through the mountains, surrounding the cabin Caitlin had been living in for the past year. Rain fell in sheets, tinged with either the salt off the ocean, or her tears, Ariel wasn't certain which. The other woman was fighting well, using nature and the strength of her sisters to hold back the dark evil moving steadily closer as she fought to complete the mission she had set for herself here.

It was impossible not to know what she was doing. The winds were screaming in warning, violently protesting the coming attack, as well as Caitlin's own stubbornness. She wouldn't be taken easily, not by Jonar, and most especially not by Derek. Ariel could feel the power charging within the Water Crystal, feel it whipping through the air around them.

Caitlin was reaching the fullest potential possible without Derek's powers to back her. She was also hedging her own bets though. Caitlin had no intention of relying on Derek for anything, especially her own power.

"Ariel, we can't allow her to do this," Chantel snapped through the comm link as they moved along the protective barrier fence that ran around the stately mansion.

"The dogs are sleeping." Derek's voice was a self-satisfied murmur through the receiver at her ear. "Rottweillers are just too easy."

"Remind me to buy a Shepherd," Ariel grunted, sensing Derek's mocking amusement as they found the breech Caitlin had used to enter the house.

"Does she even know who the fuck she's stealing from?" Shane cursed as he wedged himself through the small opening of the iron fence.

Caitlin had somehow managed to loosen the iron bars, removing several entirely, to allow for a wide door of escape when she managed to sneak away.

She was a thief.

It was just too damned ironic that the woman who reviled her husband for his stealing, was now stealing herself. A different kind of stealing, Ariel admitted, but it was stealing all the same.

"What the hell is she after anyway?" Shane asked as they maneuvered through the darkened landscape, heading for the hulking three-story mansion in the center of the mini compound.

"The Sapphire Dagger," Chantel murmured softly. "It carries a ward of protection from Mother Earth herself, and will not just protect its wearer, but strengthen her as well. It was given to Caitlin at her wedding, though rather than wearing it, she had hid it in her chest for safekeeping. She wasn't a fighter, she was a Lady. She didn't believe in carrying weapons."

"Will it protect her from Jonar?" Devlin's voice was cold as they drew closer to the house.

Ariel could feel him using his own gifts, whatever the hell they were, to shield them all from the roving red eyes of the cameras mounted along the upper story of the house. Derek was controlling the animals and the guards that moved along the perimeters, while Joshua brought up the rear, providing reinforcement to the other two men.

"I don't know how protective it is," Chantel answered, her voice transmitting to everyone in the group. "It was a gift from the Mother. She never truly explained its powers to me."

"So why don't you have a dagger?" Joshua suddenly asked. "If the other three possessed one, surely you did as well?"

"Devlin is my dagger." Ariel could hear the shrug in her voice. "The Mother brought three daggers the night before the four of you arrived at the castle. Wedding gifts for the others. My gift was less material, but just as special all the same."

Ariel remembered it then. The power she had felt in the dagger that was now strapped to her thigh had nearly had her tossing it out the castle window when it was first given to her.

"There's more here than just the dagger," she told them softly as she and Shane made their way to the back entrance of the house. "What else could she be searching for, Chantel?"

"I'm also scared to guess," Chantel said softly then. "There were many items that were stolen from the castle during that time. Many of them items that Galen had gifted us with."

There was something just as powerful, just as deadly as that dagger, Ariel thought, tilting her head as she sent the winds searching for the secret. Caitlin would of course be more than aware of the fact that Ariel was searching; she wouldn't dare voice whatever else she was after.

"This house belongs to Walter Mooresite," Joshua said then. "He collects ancient weapons and scrolls. He's especially enamored of ancient Irish relics."

There wasn't a whisper from Derek.

"We're in," Shane said softly. Ariel moved behind him, entering the darkness of the house.

"Let me in front of you, Shane," Ariel hissed as he continued to block her attempts to move into the lead. "It's too hard to sense where she is from behind you."

"Then try harder," he grunted.

She would have fought him for the position, but the wind that followed them inside brought a message she knew would leave them stretched for time.

"Jonar is almost to the grounds," she whispered, pushing at his back. "We have to hurry."

"She's right," Joshua reported from his position, still outside. "Looks like we have quite a crew moving through the forest, boys and girls. Do your job and get your asses out of there."

Ariel inhaled harshly before she feigned a move to Shane's side, let him counter it then quickly slipped around the other side. She ignored his curse, concentrating instead on slipping quickly along the deserted halls and heading for the basement.

The air led her in her search, whispering of Caitlin's movements, her steady search through an opened safe, her frustration mounting as the final object she had come searching for eluded her.

Devlin, Chantel and Derek met them on the landing that led into the darkened bowels of the house and before she could stop him, Derek was leading the way, rushing down the stairs silently, intent on reaching Caitlin before she could slip away from him.

Nothing else was said. They were too close now, though Ariel could have warned them that Caitlin was already aware of their presence.

As they neared the landing, Ariel stumbled, aware that Chantel had paused behind her. They could both feel the renewed surge of power through their crystals, the satisfaction, the sense of triumph.

"No." She heard Chantel whisper as the air thickened, sending a subtle warning whizzing through her mind as they rounded the stairwell and started down a long stretch of hallway.

Toward the end of the hall, a faint, soft blue aura emanated from beneath the doorway a second before it opened and Caitlin stepped free.

She was a small, delicate woman with elfin features and light, sea green eyes. Her long red-gold hair was braided down her back, her bow-shaped lips curved into a soft smile. Dressed in black knit pants and a long-sleeve top, she presented a most unlikely picture of a burglar.

"You're fast; I have to give you that." There was a thread of affection in her voice as she glanced from Ariel to Chantel.

The small sapphires in the dagger's hilt gleamed from her waist, an unearthly glow that almost mesmerized when combined with the protective aura wrapped around her. A small, velvet pouch hung heavy at her waist, sending fragile whispers of power throughout the room.

"Caitlin, come with us." Derek stood still, his expression intense in the glow of light that surrounded her. "Jonar's moving in on us now."

A smile tipped her bow-shaped lips, as her eerie eyes watched him with cold amusement.

"As though I would trust you to protect me, Wizard," she said mockingly. "Wouldn't that be like trusting the lamb to the wolf? I think not."

The faint Irish accent gave her voice soft, musical quality that filled Ariel with memories. They whipped through her mind, one after the other, unlocking yet another portion of that first life. A time that she had spent in safety with her sisters, each holding onto the other to still the pain in their hearts.

"You can't run forever, Cait," Derek warned her, his voice calm, though Ariel could sense that he was anything but calm.

"Of course I can, Wizard," she rebutted patiently. "All I have to do is find your tears. Tell me, lover, where have you hidden them?"

Ariel glanced at Derek, watching him tense; his eyes narrowed a second before a cold, brutal smile twisted his lips.

"The same place you left them," he told her then. "And I think you know the only way to retrieve them is through me."

Caitlin's lips thinned.

A second later the house vibrated, a violent clash of pure energy striking it from outside, shaking it on its foundations.

Ariel stumbled against Shane as she felt the winds rushing through the house, wrapping around her and Shane, binding them together with a power she hadn't felt before then.

She could feel the crystal reaching out to him, drawing on his strength.

"Who attacks us?" she called out the command as Caitlin sprinted away from them.

They must die… The voice was familiar, chillingly evil and filled with determination.

For a moment, an image flashed before her eyes. A face of such perfect male beauty it defied reality. Until you looked into his terrifying, soulless black eyes.

Who would dare attack… Jonar. She knew that voice. Knew him.

Pain struck at her as she fought back the memories of the young girl she had been, held beneath him, screaming in pain as her mother died beside her. Now was not the time to allow this memory to invade her soul.

She holds the third key…why would they strike at her… From another direction came Gryphon's voice, a snarl of fury as he moved to help ensure their escape.

A starfighter is above the house… Phoenix, his hollow, emotionless voice reported whatever he had seen.

*Hear me, Wind Mistress. Leave. Only death awaits you there…*the Dragon Prime was screaming out her name. *Get the hell out of there before the place is flattened…*

"Move out," Devlin shouted the command as the winds howled in a deadly chorus of warnings around Ariel and Chantel.

She heard Derek yell Caitlin's name as they all moved to follow her, following the direction the winds pushed at them now, urging them out.

"Brace the walls, secure the ceilings," Ariel screamed to the winds as they began a desperate flight up another stairwell, stumbling against the blasts that repeatedly hit the house, bringing down plaster in chunks and cracking the steps beneath their feet.

Shane gripped her waist, nearly carrying her himself as he raced up the steps behind Devlin and Chantel. They were thrown against the walls, fighting to find their feet before they were moving again, clearing the doorway with only seconds to spare.

Behind them, the crash of walls echoed with a hollow eerie sound as the floor they raced across now began to buckle beneath them.

The front door was just ahead, opening into the pitch-black of night and the storm raging beyond it. Brilliant flashes of lightning lit up the night sky, joining the bolts of energy between the craft aiming at the house and the Prime Warriors fighting from the ground.

The stench of evil swirled around them as Jonar's men began to converge on them from the forest, swords held aloft and evil glittering in their demonic red eyes.

There was no time to scream out the commands. Ariel locked onto the power of the crystal as she and Shane met four of the dark creatures. His war cry echoed around her as sparks flew from his sword.

Her mental commands to the winds became second nature then. More feeling than thought as she began to fight. One particularly strong gust of air tore the sword from her enemy's hand as he raised it above his head, giving her the opportunity to sink her blade deep into his chest.

With one foot she kicked the body free as she jerked the sword back, ignoring the mournful howl from his throat as his body began to decompose.

Turning, she glimpsed Chantel firing on half a dozen of the creatures as Devlin struggled with two others. She sent winds there, wrapping them around the couple to deflect the attacks until Devlin could dispose of them.

Joshua was like the wind itself, weaving through the mass of warriors that converged on him, laughing in glee as their swords began to weave and dance in the air before being propelled by an unseen hand, deep through their chests.

Derek stood at the entrance to the wall that Caitlin had escaped through. There, he fought off the maniacal warriors Jonar had sent, giving the other woman precious time to escape. Though she still aided them.

Water opened up from the heavens, literally drowning many of the enemy, giving the rest of them precious time to pierce their hearts with their swords as they made their own way to escape.

There was no lingering around to destroy the full force, there were just too many of them. And with the blasts of white-hot energy slamming into the earth around them, the risk was too great.

They cleared the break in the fence a moment before the bolts slammed into the ground where they had stood, rocking the ground with enough force that Ariel cursed as she fought to stay on her feet.

The Prime Warriors met the renewed attack by slamming yet more energy toward the craft hovering over the house, though they did little to dent the threat it posed. As Shane pulled her into the tree line, the sudden searing heat of the crystal had her pausing, jerking around to gaze into the sky.

Around her, the winds whispered of what would come. What could come. The death of the Primes, of Lynn, the woman who had once been her second-in-command.

"Chantel," she screamed out her sister's name. "They can't die. They're needed."

The winds were screaming in her ear, bringing information she couldn't process, couldn't understand, except for the compulsion that they must live.

"What do we do?" Chantel screamed back.

Ariel stood still, feeling Shane's arms around her, his strength enfolding her, and she knew the secret. The force she had used before hadn't been unnatural. It had been a part of her, a product of Shane's strength and her own power as she drew on the crystals reaching out to aid her.

She closed her eyes, envisioned the strike and threw her spirit toward the man holding her close.

It was like drowning and then rebirth. Like death and hope and life all rolled into one as she felt his soul meet hers. It was a merging more sensual, more heated than even that of the sexual acts they had shared. It was intimacy, knowledge and it was love.

A second later she felt the crystal open, spilling from it the brief, hard surge of power needed. Her eyes flew open as she heard the chaotic screams from above and watched in fascination as the sky lit up with a colorful explosion. Simultaneously, dozens of bolts of lightning had slammed into the small craft, aiding the power striking from below.

It wasn't destroyed, but neither was it a threat. In a spray of light it banked and then whipped out of sight.

"Let's go," Devlin screamed then. "We have to lose Jonar's men. Derek, where's Caitlin?"

"Safe," he yelled back, though there was no explanation how.

Ariel could feel her safety though, her flight away from the fight now that the worst of the danger had ended. She would run, just as she had been running for years now.

Chapter Thirty-Two

ॐ

They reached the cabins at daybreak, though they hadn't been that far from the now demolished mansion, the roundabout course they had used to lose Jonar and his men had taken much longer.

Chantel and Devlin were leaning into each other as they entered their own cabin. Joshua headed for his, his head bent down, his shoulders oddly slumped as the door slammed behind him. Derek was still following Caitlin, but Ariel was certain they would be safe, at least for a while.

As Shane led her into their cabin, Ariel frowned at the continued discordance with the crystal. It hadn't cooled since the battle, though the battle was long finished. There was no sign of his men in the area, even Joshua and Devlin had agreed that there was no way they could have been followed. Still, the crystal was filled with warning, causing the air to thicken around her and Shane as they entered the cabin.

Ariel hesitated just inside, her eyes probing at the dim room as she sent the silent call to the air, once again, to find the reason for the crystal's warning.

There was no answer. Not a ripple, a footstep, or a breath came to her.

"Something's wrong," she whispered as Shane closed the door behind them, sliding the deadbolt home before turning to wrap his arms around her waist.

"The battle was a hard one, Ariel," he whispered at her ear. "Perhaps you just need to rest."

She listened again, her frown deepening. There was no sound. Not a single sound coming to her. That was too odd. When she sent out such a call, the winds brought her any sound, every sound that could mean danger to her, even if was spoken ages before.

Her hands lifted to the strong arms wrapped around her waist, her fingers curling over Shane's strong, leather enclosed wrists. The air was trapped, the winds were silenced.

"We have to get out of here," she kept her voice low, but the desperation rising inside her was smothering her.

Shane didn't take time to ask questions, he turned quickly, drawing her to his side as his hand rose to the deadbolt to unlock it and throw open the door. A second later Ariel gasped as she felt the blinding force that rushed past her face, slamming into Shane's shoulders and throwing him across the room.

She turned, her breath locking in her throat as she tried to run to him, only to be picked up from her feet by an invisible hand and tossed to the opposite corner.

The impact with the wall jarred every bone she possessed and sent waves of agony through her vulnerable head as it cracked against the rough wood logs. Dazed, shaken by the fury and hatred that thickened in the air around her, she fought to get her bearings.

Pain radiated through her body, stealing her breath and her strength as she tried to regain her feet.

From the other corner, she heard Shane's enraged war cry and turned her head, eyes widening as she watched him crash into the wall again. The building shook from the force of his crash, windowpanes rattling as dust exploded into the air around him, forced free of the logs from the heavy impact.

She called out to the winds, heard them screaming outside the cabin, felt the vibrations of them slamming into the outside of the house. But they weren't entering, they weren't heeding her commands.

Groaning at the pain each movement caused, Ariel turned to her side, leaning heavily against the wall as she watched Shane. His gaze met hers, narrowed in warning and black with fury as a movement at the other side of the room drew her attention.

"Strangely, Mother Earth has forgotten that even for her powers and her safeguards, there is an alternate power, a force strong enough to counter or to balance her insipid sweetness."

Ariel's breath caught in her throat as her father stepped from the bedroom, watching her with sadistic mockery.

She hadn't expected this. She would have expected Jonar, or even Oberon, but not Markham St. James. Lean and tall, with an expression of arrogant superiority, he stepped slowly into the room, staring back at them through cold hazel eyes, a sneer twisting his lips.

"While you ignored the power you held, I studied and perfected every defense against it." He smiled, a cold turn of his thin lips that sent fear striking her heart. "Even as a child you were so easy to frighten. All it took was the threat of that closet to make you obey. Until that devil's bitch of a grandmother of yours left you her inheritance. I should have known better than to trust her."

Ariel breathed in roughly, allowing him to talk as she sent her crystal searching for an opening, a break in whatever force he had placed around the cabin. It wasn't natural, she could feel that, sensing the enveloping power that surrounded them. Natural Earth power wasn't tainted with such unnatural strength.

"Who the hell are you?" Shane's rough voice darker, more dangerous than she had ever heard it as he turned to face the other man.

"Why, Ariel, you haven't mentioned me?" Markham questioned her with polite mockery. "If you're going to lie beneath such filth, you should at least warn him of your father. Traitorous bitch. I can't believe you'd screw anything so undeserving as a Viking. And a Guardian lapdog to boot. Your taste is atrocious, daughter."

"I'm not your daughter." She knew she wasn't. She had known it those hours before the past battle. Held in Shane's arms, her eyes locked with his, memories overwhelming her. She was no blood of his.

His gaze sliced back to her, narrowed and filled with retribution.

"I raised you. My money bought your clothes, fed your sorry ass. That makes you mine," he snarled.

"Money you stole from my mother and grandmother before you had them committed," she cried out harshly.

He smiled cruelly, his laughter almost maniacal as he watched her.

"And when you're committed, your funds will revert to me as well, daughter," he sneered. "If it hadn't been for that hidden inheritance Laken managed to cheat me of, then you would already be inhabiting your own little padded cell. That's where they died, you know. In a padded room, screaming out to a wind that couldn't find them. How sad."

Ariel fought back the pain, the sudden image of the mother she had never known, the grandmother she had wanted to know. Fragile, delicate women whose hearts had been too soft, too gentle to understand the man who had destroyed them. They had been the protectors of the crystal, just as generations of women belonging to Ariel's line had been. Women sworn to guard the power, to pass it down, mother to daughter, until the true Mistress was born again.

But she understood him. He was evil. Evil had no heart, it had no soul. It survived only to feed on the pain and terror it could create.

"What goes around, comes around, Markham," she told him then, keeping her voice cool, confident. Any sign of weakness would be exploited by him, used to weaken her. "Whatever power you're using isn't natural. It's not Earth power. You can't sustain it forever."

"I won't need to," he assured her, his voice all the more evil for the very gentleness of the assurance. "I will only need it long enough to remove that cursed crystal you wear. After that, you'll be powerless. Won't you, Ariel?"

He stepped toward her.

Ariel didn't bother to fight. She could feel the power building inside her, drawing on the others. Even if the winds couldn't reach her, the other crystals could. She could feel that power moving through her, in her, as disjoined bits of information flashed through her mind.

Could she do it? she wondered painfully. She could feel the demand rising inside her, the power reaching out of her, but not to strike against her father. Rather to aid Shane. There was no wind, no air to draw on, and she didn't have the strength to fight against the force her father was controlling. But Shane could, with her help. With her power.

Shane was her strength. His arm was her protection. She reached out to him, drawing on that strength to hold the link with her sisters, concentrating on the power slipping through the shield Jonar had placed around the cabin.

She smiled herself then. A brutal, cold smile that had him pausing before he reached her.

"Jonar is helping you," she said then. "It's his power you're using. Isn't it?"

"It will be mine soon." He shrugged, though she saw the rage burning in his eyes, the knowledge that he could never possess such power.

She laughed at him. Mocking, cold, a slap in the face of his arrogance.

"Jonar doesn't share, Markham, didn't you know that? You were no more than a sacrificial lamb. A final desperate attempt to weaken the warriors. Nothing more."

"That's a lie," he snarled furiously. "Had it not been for me he would have never found you to begin with. He failed to kill you as he was paid to do. But I, daughter, I will destroy you forever."

He raised his hand and Ariel saw the power he used to throw them across the room. The small metallic disc began charging in the air around them, she could feel it because it weakened the shield around the cabin, needing more force than the small room could afford.

She didn't waste time trying to strike at him herself. While he was focused on her, on thoughts of her death, she opened herself to the forces that had gathered within the crystal. The winds couldn't reach her, but her sisters had.

As the force Markham was drawing on began to reach its full limits, Ariel leaned back, closed her eyes, and directed the energy filling her now, to her Viking. He was her strength. He was her protection. His sword would smite her enemies, his dagger would sever the heart of the evil stalking her.

She couldn't see what happened. As the energy flowed out of her, weakness and exhaustion overcame her as she slumped against the wall. But she felt Shane. She heard his war cry, louder, stronger than ever as she felt the weapon Markham was using begin to discharge.

Had she been too late? Had she trusted Shane too late? Turning the power over to him had been one of the hardest decisions she had made in her life. It had been that power, unfocused and dormant inside her that had helped her keep her sanity through her father's cruelties. It had been that power that had saved her from Jonar, that had kept her alive until Shane could find her. It had been that power that had saved her sanity.

Finally, she forced her eyes open, staring in shock at the warrior who stood before her, deflecting the power that would have killed her. His arms were outspread, a violet glow surrounding his body, his sword held ready in his hand as waves of power shimmered on the air around him.

His head was thrown back, his mane of hair rippling down his back a second before it jerked up again and he was ready to battle.

The sword arm came forward as he went into a battle crouch, an almost inhuman growl of savage triumph echoing in the air around them as Markham slammed another blast his way.

Shane tilted the sword, catching the force and sending it back toward the other man. Markham jumped to the side, his face twisted into a grimace of rage as chunks of wood flew from the logs where it struck.

As Shane paced to face him once again, Ariel saw his face, a gleam of bloodlust glittered in his eyes as he twirled the sword before him, a snarl pulling his lips back from his teeth as his other hand motioned Markham to try again.

"I'll kill you both," Markham growled demonically as he sent another wave of energy slamming toward Shane.

Shane's laughter mocked him as he ducked and rolled beneath the strike, using his long legs to kick out at the other man and send him flying against the wall.

"Does it feel good, you little nit?" Shane snarled. "Being slammed into the wall, your weaker body absorbing a blow it was never meant to know. I imagine it's much the same as Ariel felt when you threw her to the wall. Come little man, let me pay you back in kind once again."

The sword deflected yet another strike, this time, sending the force slamming into Markham's midsection. His body heaved and lifted against the wall as his eyes widened in shock and fear, choking gasps emitting from his mouth as he fought to breathe.

Shane didn't waste time playing with him. In an instant, before Ariel could protest or voice her shock, he sent the sword deep into Markham's chest, piercing the black heart as blood sprayed in the thickened air around him, falling slowly, almost like molasses, to the floor below.

Shock held her rooted in place as she stared at the other man's expression. Shock and horror rounded his eyes a second before life left them. That expression would live with her for the rest of her life, Ariel thought. That look of complete surprise, the shock that he had been defeated.

A second later, Shane jerked the blade back, turning away in unconcern as the body dropped bonelessly to the floor, crumpling like a forgotten doll tossed in a corner after a child's tantrum.

The winds rushed into the house then as the front door shattered, and once again the warriors stood en masse. Swords drawn, Devlin, Chantel, Derek and Joshua rushed into the cabin, staring at the destruction in shock.

At the same time, the power she had sent surging into Shane, began to ease back into her body. Not the same, energizing force she had sent, and it was different than it had been. As though in sharing her power with him, it had met and merged with his own, changing its structure forever.

"Get him out of here," Shane snapped as Joshua and Derek moved to the body.

"Boy, this one is going to be easy to explain to the authorities," Derek grumbled as he checked the body. "Do you have any idea how much power it takes to make those suspicious bastards overlook things like sword wounds to the chest? Not to mention how hard it is to mess with a coroner's mind."

"You'll manage," Shane snapped.

A tremulous smile crossed Ariel's lips as he bent to her then, his fingers reaching out to touch her cheek.

"Welcome back, wife," he whispered then.

She shook her head slowly. "There has been no love as strong as I feel now," she whispered tiredly. "Thank you, husband, for believing in me."

A smile crossed his bloodstained features. "Always, Ariel. I always knew you could do it."

Trust. Love. The foundations of power surged within her. She hadn't believed in them, she had never sought either out. But now, they bloomed inside her like a newly formed rose, opening its petals to the world and embracing the warmth awaiting it. Awaiting her. She was free. Who she was and who she had been was no longer separate, no longer a mystery. There was pain to face, and many things that she and Shane had to discuss. But for the first time in two lives, Ariel felt free. Free to laugh, to trust and to love. As free as the very winds...

Epilogue
ॐ

The castle was just as she had seen it in her dreams. Ariel stepped into the huge great hall and stared around her in wonder. Within these walls, the modern coexisted perfectly with the past. Centuries-old artifacts gleamed on tables, as ancient tapestries filled the walls, and paintings from a bygone era stared down at them with an eerie sense of familiarity.

There were several areas of comfort laid out in the room. Couches and chairs arranged for discussion, or private areas enclosed by ornamental, potted trees. At the far end, a long table gleamed beneath a crystal chandelier, filled with an arrangement of light foods, sandwiches and salads.

The castle itself was huge. As they had flown over the fortress, Ariel's eyes had widened in disbelief. She had visited many ancient castles while searching out unique little buys for her store over the years, but never one so large. It was two stories high, with two excessively wide wings coming off the central stone building. A wide moat, bridged and running with beautifully clear water surrounded the entire castle and its gardens, with many small houses and buildings scattered surrounding the grounds around it.

It was the size of a village, or larger. And it was one of the most beautiful sights she had ever seen in her life.

"Welcome home, Ariel." The voice that greeted her wasn't that of the warriors, but of a tall, older man who had stepped from the left hallway and walked slowly toward her.

He wasn't as tall as the warriors, but he was muscular, strong-boned and held himself proudly. His nut-brown hair was flecked with gray, his blue eyes quiet and sad despite the gleam of pleasure within them.

She stilled, feeling Shane's hand at her back, his comforting presence surrounding her as always. For a moment, she truly was back in time and she saw this man, perhaps a bit younger, tears wetting his face as he held the nearly broken form of the child she had been...

If I had known where she had taken you, he had whispered tearfully, *I would have come for you before. Dear God, Ariel, if my life would have prevented this, I would have gladly made the trade...*

Ariel stilled the pain that the memory brought. She knew Jonar had raped her in that first life. Little more than a child, terrified and desperate to save her mother, she had lain beneath him, little knowing what he had in store for her.

The memory wasn't as brutal as she would have expected, though. It was misted, an event that happened in another place and time, and dimmed by Shane's love. But she remembered this man, her father then. Her father now.

"Mother kept your picture," she said as he stopped just in front of her. "When she died, it was placed with her only belongings until I was old enough to collect them."

His expression twisted in pain as his eyes closed briefly.

"I couldn't find her, after she left," he told her then. "I met her while she vacationed in Paris. She never told me where she lived, or much about herself..."

"Because she was married," Ariel said tightly, though she felt no resentment toward him, or her mother. "She would have tried to protect you."

"As she couldn't protect you," Galen sighed wearily. "If she had told me, I would have come for you, Ariel. I would not have left you with such a monster."

Ariel could feel the others behind her, watching this reunion with curious eyes. They were her family now, but she still hadn't grown used to having so many people around her.

"I'm not sure how to be a daughter," she said then.

"That's okay, child." He smiled gently. "I know well how to be a father. I will guide you, if you will allow me."

She didn't fight the tears that welled in her eyes, instead, she walked to the arms that opened wide for her and then enclosed her in a circle of warmth and protectiveness. She had known Shane's security, his strength and determination to keep her from harm. But this was different, innocent, and renewing. It was a father's embrace. A true father.

"I missed you, Father," she whispered, thinking of that first life, when he had often held her just like this, against his heart, chasing away the demons that haunted her dreams and filling her life with a measure of joy.

"As I missed you, daughter. As I have missed all my daughters..."

* * * * *

Ariel was home. Caitlin sighed in relief as she felt the emotions that surrounded her in the early morning mist, called to her by the crystal she commanded. She reached into the stone, immersing herself in the soul of it, and letting her sister's joy wash over her. Did they know how adept she had become at connecting with them, she wondered? If they did, they never spoke of it.

Ariel had sent the breeze to her several times, enfolding her with the love she and Chantel sent her. Sisters. They were indeed sisters, not just in the past life, but in the present as well. Sisters that would always be separated.

As she stood within the damp comfort of Ireland's mists once again, a new sensation came to her. A touch to her cheek, her neck, the feel of lips feathering against her breast.

"Bastard!" she muttered fiercely, immediately attempting to break the connection the Wizard was invading.

Damn him, he was giving her no rest, no respite from his determination to find her. She broke the connection quickly with the crystal as she pulled the mists in further, thickening them to hide her from him as she hurried back to her stepfather's home.

Unlike Chantel and Ariel, Caitlin enjoyed a very loving relationship with the man who had adopted her at her birth. Sean O'Reilly had loved her mother with a passion and tenacity that survived her death and enabled him to love and raise her daughter as well. His sons, one from a former marriage, the other younger than she, but from his marriage to her mother. Both were devoted, caring brothers. They had followed her for years, ensuring her safety where she allowed it, though they often raged in anger at her stubbornness each time she trained for the steal of a lifetime.

She was a cat burglar. And a damned fine one too, she assured herself as she reentered her father's home and headed for her bedroom. She had been training since her sixteenth year, and had excelled in ways she never imagined she could. She wasn't Robin Hood, yet neither was she criminal. She stole things back and returned them where they belonged, for the most part. But she also stole those objects that would add to the power she already held, such as the Sapphire Dagger.

As she entered her room, she paced to the small chest that contained the priceless object. It was over a thousand years old, perfectly preserved and once again with its rightful owner. Beside it lay the sapphire, emerald, amethyst and ruby bracelets that had once belonged to the daughters of Galen. She had finally managed to locate all four, but hadn't yet been able to part with the three that were not her own.

Above the dagger was a gold ring, the Celtic inscriptions more of a curse than the promise others saw them as. *...until time is no more, my love follows you...*

Fury burned in her heart at the thought of the words. His love. The bastard Wizard had never known love; he had known only deceit and treachery. But his hold would be broken on her soon, she promised herself. There were three pieces left to steal. A slave bracelet of gold and Connemara marble, a headband of gold, dripping with marble tears, and a gold and marble armband, inscribed with the words to break the hold the Wizard had on her.

Each piece was said to be fashioned of the purest gold and silver, dripping with tiny, beautifully carved tears. The Wizard's Tears, created to hold the heart of the bride he had deceived, enchanted with the magic that reinforced his commands when he stole her mind.

They would be next.

She closed the chest, smoothing her hand over the gleaming wood as she closed her eyes and allowed a smile to touch her lips.

They were where she had left them. She touched the crystal, seeing in her mind's eye where they lay. They lay in a box identical to her own, the velvet that cushioned the jewelry after they were removed from her dead body. The chest was then set beside the bed she had shared with the demon who had taken her. Derek.

She pushed back the instinctive protest that coiled within her mind at that thought. God, what pleasure she had known in that bed, even before he had stolen her mind. She had come to him, lured by the dreams he had invaded before she met him, believing him to be the man her soul had been born for. Instead, he was the demon her family had reviled for centuries.

He had brought plagues to their land, had cursed their people, and had seen her as little more than the whore upon whom he spilled his vengeance. *Your daughters will lie as whores beneath my body...*

The curse he had laid on the family had come to pass. For she had lain beneath him as a whore, accepting his touch, begging for it.

Her hand fisted as she pushed herself violently from the desk that held her stolen treasures.

"I curse you," she whispered painfully. "As I have cursed you since the day these memories returned to me. I curse your touch, the very breath you take..." But she could go no further.

Her lips thinned as she inhaled through her nose, forcing control, forcing back her rage. She had sworn to her mother as she lay dying that she would never, ever curse the man who had begun to invade her dreams.

At that time, the dreams had been soft, filled with love, with pleasure. There had been no darkness, no hint of the fury she would feel later. But somehow, her mother had known what would come.

Swear to me, Cait, she had whispered, weak with the illness that stole her from her family. *Upon my life, swear you will never curse this man you dream of. That you will never whisper aloud a need for his pain, or his destruction. Swear it to me, daughter, or I will never rest when death takes me from this life.*

I swear. Her words haunted her to this day.

"I may not be able to curse you, Derek," she whispered. "But I can destroy you on my own. Beware, *husband*," she sneered the title. "I'll own your tears, and when I do, I'll own your soul…"

Derek lay on the bed he had shared with Caitlin, her words echoing in his mind.

I'll own your tears, and when I do, I'll own your soul…

A mirthless smile twisted his lips. How easily she remembered only that which she wanted to remember.

He looked at the table that held the wooden box. Inside it rested the tears he had shed when he had wiped her mind of the memories of her family. Destructive, brutal memories laid in place by his own blood, a descendant of his brother. Weak, ineffectual, Duncan had been more than willing to see his older brother cast out, branded a demon and cursed to never know peace or true love should he survive the death his parents had ordered for him.

Damn them all! He moved quickly from the bed to stand at the opened window, staring into dawn's awakening as he pushed the fury back, pushed back everything but the connection he felt to his wife.

He snorted at that thought. His wife. Perhaps, for a few blissful days, he had known the joy of her acceptance, her false love. Aye, he had stolen her memories, had unintentionally dimmed the power she possessed and through his own pain, had stolen her will. He would have made it easy for her then. He would have lessened the pain and the fight he knew he would have from her if he hadn't done so. Because she was his wife. And what belonged to the Wizard, by God stayed the Wizard's. And this, she would soon realize.

"Come on, Caitlin." He sent the words into the early morning mists, knowing it would not take long for them to reach her. "Take my tears if you can..."

Why an electronic book?

We live in the Information Age—an exciting time in the history of human civilization, in which technology rules supreme and continues to progress in leaps and bounds every minute of every day. For a multitude of reasons, more and more avid literary fans are opting to purchase e-books instead of paper books. The question from those not yet initiated into the world of electronic reading is simply: *Why?*

1. *Price.* An electronic title at Ellora's Cave Publishing and Cerridwen Press runs anywhere from 40% to 75% less than the cover price of the exact same title in paperback format. Why? Basic mathematics and cost. It is less expensive to publish an e-book (no paper and printing, no warehousing and shipping) than it is to publish a paperback, so the savings are passed along to the consumer.

2. *Space.* Running out of room in your house for your books? That is one worry you will never have with electronic books. For a low one-time cost, you can purchase a handheld device specifically designed for e-reading. Many e-readers have large, convenient screens for viewing. Better yet, hundreds of titles can be stored within your new library—on a single microchip. There are a variety of e-readers from different manufacturers. You can also read e-books on your PC or laptop computer. (Please note that Ellora's Cave does not endorse any specific brands.

You can check our websites at www.ellorascave.com or www.cerridwenpress.com for information we make available to new consumers.)

3. *Mobility.* Because your new e-library consists of only a microchip within a small, easily transportable e-reader, your entire cache of books can be taken with you wherever you go.

4. *Personal Viewing Preferences.* Are the words you are currently reading too small? Too large? Too... ANNOYING? Paperback books cannot be modified according to personal preferences, but e-books can.

5. *Instant Gratification.* Is it the middle of the night and all the bookstores near you are closed? Are you tired of waiting days, sometimes weeks, for bookstores to ship the novels you bought? Ellora's Cave Publishing sells instantaneous downloads twenty-four hours a day, seven days a week, every day of the year. Our webstore is never closed. Our e-book delivery system is 100% automated, meaning your order is filled as soon as you pay for it.

Those are a few of the top reasons why electronic books are replacing paperbacks for many avid readers.

As always, Ellora's Cave and Cerridwen Press welcome your questions and comments. We invite you to email us at Comments@ellorascave.com or write to us directly at Ellora's Cave Publishing Inc., 1056 Home Avenue, Akron, OH 44310-3502.

erridwen, the Celtic Goddess of wisdom, was the muse who brought inspiration to storytellers and those in the creative arts. Cerridwen Press encompasses the best and most innovative stories in all genres of today's fiction. Visit our site and discover the newest titles by talented authors who still get inspired - much like the ancient storytellers did, once upon a time.

Cerridwen Press

www.cerridwenpress.com

Discover for yourself why readers can't get enough
of the multiple award-winning publisher
Ellora's Cave.

Whether you prefer e-books or paperbacks,
be sure to visit EC on the web at
www.ellorascave.com

for an erotic reading experience that will leave you
breathless.